We stood there, staring at each other.

"Good God," she said, a massive grin illuminating her face. "You're going to make me do it."

I didn't ask her what she meant. I knew just what she was talking about, and she was dead right.

She steepled her fingers by her mouth, her eyes seeking confirmation. The woman read body language like a pro. The next thing I knew she had me pressed against the rose trellis. If there were thorns, I didn't know it. Her palms pinned my shoulders back and her mouth started a slow, torturous path down the side of my neck. I groaned.

She whispered, "Honey, this ain't nothing yet." Her body moved closer. "I'm not going to make love to you, Robin Miller. No. What we're going to have is sex." I could feel the moisture of her lips on my earlobe. "Hot, raw, heaven help me, I'm going to die, sex. Do you understand?"

Books by Jaye Maiman

I Left My Heart

Crazy For Loving

Under My Skin

Someone To Watch

The 4th Robin Miller Mystery

BY JAYE MAIMAN

Printed in the United States of America on acid-free paper
First Edition

Edited by Christine Cassidy
Cover design by Bonnie Liss (Phoenix Graphics)
Typeset by Sandi Stancil

Library of Congress Cataloging-in-Publication Data

Maiman, Jaye, 1957 –
Someone to watch : a Robin Miller mystery / by Jaye Maiman.
p. cm.
ISBN 1-56280-095-7
I. Title.
PS3563.A38266S66 1995
813′.54—dc20 94-43988
CIP

Dedicated to my basheert Rhea,
to the children,
Isaac, Lina, & Olivia,
and to the miracles yet to come . . .

Acknowledgments

Magic happens in Provincetown. People fall in love. Wounds heal. Dreams unfold. And books are born. Few places on earth have touched me, and the lives of the ones I love, as deeply as P-town. The inspiration for this book came during a bike ride through the dunes near Herring Cove Beach. But as any creative person knows, inspiration is never enough. If it weren't for the special people in my life, who indulge my neuroses and obsessions with humor and love, this book would not have made it past the dream stage.

Special thanks to —

The Naiad team, for soothing my ego and tweaking my writing conscience . . .
The fans, who have written and cajoled me into writing faster and better . . .
Shalom, for his insights and enthusiasm . . .
My family of origin, who consistently amaze me with their unwavering support . . .
Elaine and Ann-Marie, whither thou goest . . .
Pauline and Risa, for the amazing expanse and strength of their friendship . . .
Jill and Joan, sugar poop and love chicken, for the laughs, comfort and long weekends . . .
Scott and Mark, for becoming part of our dreams . . .
Maureen and Victoria, for paving the way with courage, resilience, and love . . .

And the most humble, robust, and loving thanks to my partner in life, Rhea Stadtmauer, who works harder than anyone I've ever known to make life and love the best they can possibly be. The fact that she succeeds is only one of a million reasons why my love for her continues to grow at an astounding pace.

About the Author

In addition to *Someone to Watch,* Jaye Maiman has written three romantic mysteries featuring the private investigator Robin Miller: *I Left My Heart,* the award-winning *Crazy for Loving,* and *Under My Skin.* She is currently working on the fifth book in the series, *Baby, It's Cold.* A Halloween baby, she was born in Brooklyn, New York, and raised in a Coney Island housing project where she spent Tuesday nights consuming blueberry cheese knishes and watching fireworks from a beachside boardwalk. She resides in Brooklyn with her two puppy cats and her partner, playmate, editor, co-neurotic, and magic-maker Rhea.

Chapter 1

The sun caught on the rear reflector of her bicycle and made my eyes blink. We were on a fast, rough downhill that made my teeth clack together like castanets. I leaned over the handlebars and fixated on her calf muscles. The lady was in damn good shape. At least physically.

I had spent the better part of the previous three weeks tracking down this golden-haired siren. Julie Reed, a.k.a. Judith Ryan, had bilked one of my clients out of a quarter-million dollars and then disappeared with the skill of a sand crab. So there I was, zipping through the dunes of Provincetown with my prey in clear sight, my skin steaming in the noon heat and my lungs starting a nasty protest. The path rose again and I shifted gears with a half-muttered curse.

I'm in pretty good shape, mostly from running from store to store in search of my elixir of choice: bottled Yoo-Hoo (never cans) poured over exactly three ice cubes. I've tried the "Bond, James Bond" martini, but frankly it doesn't come close. In any case, I can run five level miles without succumbing to paroxysmal tachycardia, which is to say, the exercise doesn't kill me. In contrast, the twenty-six-year-old whose butt I was intent on following had ranked tenth in one of those torturous Iron Women triathalons. I pumped the pedals as hard as I could, but my body was giggling with pain. Little spasms flitted up from my calves. We had almost reached the crest when I gave in. Julie flashed a smile at me as she disappeared over the hill.

Damn it. She had known I was behind her all the time. In my business, that's called "getting burned." Except I wasn't so sure Julie hadn't assumed I was just one of her fans. And the woman had plenty. To be honest, I might have been at the head of the line if I hadn't known about her last gig in New York.

I walked my rental bike up to the top of the hill and paused. At this point I was less than a mile from Herring Cove Beach. The air was still and smelled of nothing but hot sand and damp armpits. Mine. I pivoted sharply from the hip, snapping my spine like bubble wrap, and wondered about Julie's taunting grin. She had enjoyed the chase, I was sure of it.

Given the rolled grass mat slung over her shoulder I had a strong hunch I'd find her at the beach, which was fine with me. I had a hankering for the ice-cold water of Cape Cod Bay, the smell of cocoa butter rising from the glistening arms, thighs and backs of half-naked women. I hopped on the bike and coasted down the slope, smiling at the way the wind pressed against my limbs.

A few minutes later I located Julie's eighteen speeder locked onto the bike rack in the beach parking lot. With a shudder of excitement, I chained my bike next to hers, then plodded through the thick sand path that connects the lot to the gay stretch of Herring Cove. As always, I stopped short at the first sight of the bay. The sunlight sliced around cumulus clouds, infusing the landscape so that every salt spray rose, beach plum and wind-carved dune seemed illuminated from within.

I stood at the end of the trail and scanned the crowd. It was June 21, the second official day of summer, and women were already sunning themselves in earnest. Elsewhere people were celebrating Father's Day, but here the event of note was the official commencement of what my friend Carly calls "Breast Season." For a moment I forgot that I was looking for Julie and slipped into a high cruise mode I hadn't known in years. With a twinge of guilt, I realized it felt good. Real good.

When I finally spotted Julie, she was at the shore's edge, sans shorts, T-shirt and bikini top. She stared directly at me, then dove into the rippling water. I shook my head and smiled. I was a sucker for this type of woman. In some inexplicable way, she was as irresistible to me as a frayed rope bridge swaying precariously over a violent stream. The danger didn't matter. All I wanted was to run out there and make that damn bridge swing.

I slogged through the sand, all the while watching Julie's progress. She was a strong swimmer. Her sure strokes had already carried her past an anchored sailboat. I kicked off my sneakers and stepped gingerly into the water. The shock was painful. I stood there until my feet went numb and Julie swam close enough for us to once again size each other up. She had long blonde hair tied in a ponytail, and her skin was lovingly bronzed. Her smile was broad; on another woman I'd call it horse-like. But Julie Reed was knee-buckling beautiful. She stood up, shook her head to shed water with all the enthusiasm of a pup, then winked at me as she ambled back toward her grass mat.

I had a new appreciation for the plight of my client, a fifty-two-year-old woman who calibrated the number of her gold baubles to match each gray hair that dared to appear on her head. Abigail Whitman had come out of the closet back when opening the door meant getting a combat boot in your mouth. By the time she was forty, she had inherited her mother's wealth and her father's alcoholism. Abandoned by the first woman she truly loved, Abigail soon decided the best way to beat life was by drowning it out. She spent the next decade drinking dry martinis and tequila shots. Then, last year, she developed diabetes. Abigail dried herself out and bought herself a ticket to Hawaii. That's when she encountered Julie.

The two women met while biking down the slope of Haleakala, a dormant volcano on the island of

Maui. I've done the same ride so I know first-hand what kind of high that trip can infuse in a romantic. Combine the setting with Julie's seductive skills and poor Abigail never had a chance. They made love that very afternoon, under the moist cover of clouds clinging to the mountainside. From what I gathered, Abigail's sightseeing had ceased at approximately the same time. They spent the remainder of the trip with limbs locked.

Back in New York City, Julie locked onto Abigail's sizable assets with a similar tenacity. Her scam was classic. Julie claimed to have been rendered nearly penniless as a result of a recent divorce. Worse, she had blown her last $5,000 on the Hawaii vacation. On their final night in Maui, the carefully devised confession came out: Julie had intended to end her vacation with a bottle of sleeping pills. But that was before meeting Abigail. All she had to offer Abigail in return was her love and devoted companionship. Ah, sweet, insipid romance! Abigail spent the rest of the night begging Julie to move into her New York condo.

Within the first month, Julie "borrowed" and supposedly lost several pieces of antique jewelry Abigail had inherited from her grandmother. Later she conned Abigail into purchasing a sexy red BMW for her. The garage fees alone cost Abigail a mint. In six months' time, Julie owned a fifty percent interest in Aphrodite's Retreat, Abigail's chic lesbian bar. Then she disappeared. When the damages were totalled, Abigail's six months of sexual bliss had cost her more than $250,000. In the process of suing, she discovered that the woman she knew as Judy Ryan was really Julie Reed, a con artist extraordinaire.

Abigail won the judgment, but that's like buying cotton candy in a hard rain. Collecting on a civil suit is difficult enough, but try collecting from someone who's more or less evaporated into thin air. That's where my organization, the Serra Investigative Agency, came in.

Now here the rascal was, so close I could smell the Bain de Soleil she was slathering over her wiry limbs, and all I could do was gape. Suddenly she turned those high beams on me, pointed the tube of lotion and said, "Might as well make yourself useful."

I scooted over and seized the tube. For a fleeting moment, I remembered the incredible woman I had left behind in New York, the one who had kissed me good-bye with a half-amused warning: "You'll have to be strong, darling. Provincetown can do funny things to the libido." No kidding. I squeezed a red jelly ribbon around Julie's naked shoulder blades and pondered the sacrifices this case might demand from me.

"I have a confession to make," she said, shifting suddenly so that my left hand almost skidded into a boob. "I know who you are."

Uh-oh. I dropped back.

She turned to face me. "I'm a dyke specialist," she said playfully. I wondered why she seemed so calm. No. Not calm. Elated. "Maybe one of these days I'll publish the Dyke Encyclopedia," she continued.

I could feel my eyebrows squish together in puzzlement.

"You're Laurel Carter, aren't you?" she asked, with the slightest hesitation. "The rich and famous romance writer whose career took a nosedive when some politico in San Francisco decided to out you, though I can't remember why."

I did. In investigating an ex-lover's death, I had unearthed some unsavory information about a high-profile politician. Icing my career was his revenge. Not that I minded much. Romance writing had been a means to an end: financial independence. Now that I had a hefty nest egg I was free to indulge in my career of choice. It was a choice most people didn't understand, including me.

Julie wiped a sweat bead off my chin with the familiarity of a long-term lover and the provocativeness of a grade-A temptress. Her next question came as a relief. "So what have you been doing since?"

"Resting on my laurels, so to speak," I retorted, feeling the balance of power shift in my favor.

She sidled closer, so that her perky breasts were a breath away. "So tell me, Laurel, are you a fan of mine?"

Julie was performing in town under the stage name Rush. The poster for her show read, "If you want excitement . . . Rush!" The accompanying picture was a killer — Julie clad in nothing but a tuxedo suit jacket, black underwear, and stiletto heels. Last night I followed "Rush" home from her midnight performance at Annabelle's. A young woman in skin-tight leather pants and a haircut fit for a Marine had accompanied her. I planted myself across the street with a thermos of coffee and a quart container of clam chowder from the Lobster Pot. Neither woman had emerged until ten this morning. The lack of sleep wasn't new to me; I suffer from insomnia. Still, my defenses were too low for me to limbo under them without a snag or two. I swallowed hard and said, "My real name's Robin Miller. And believe it or not, I haven't caught your act yet."

Her surprise seemed genuine. "So your, uh, interest, is purely physical?"

Ouch. Her words shook a response from my netherlands. The attraction was powerful and very, very inconvenient. "You could say that," I answered after too long a pause.

"Okay," she purred. "I'll say that. Now why don't we get down to business." She offered me her back with the air of a cat offering up her belly. The gesture said, "Take me, if you dare."

I was a brave woman. I proceeded to massage the suntan lotion onto her back with proper appreciation. From the corner of one eye, I noticed that the three baby dykes on the neighboring blanket had begun to ogle us. They all sported shoulder-length shags, imitation Ray Bans, biking shorts, and athletic breasts the size and firmness of tennis balls popped straight from the can. Clutching bottles of Bud Light, they were so intent on the action I turned and smiled at them. Two of the three blushed and turned away. The third one grinned broadly and gave me a thumbs up. The act brought me to my senses.

Abigail Whitman was paying my agency $250 a day, plus expenses, to locate not just Julie Reed but also her assets. If she was as wily as most cons, my job had barely begun. So far I had an address and her stage moniker. I gave Julie the massage of a lifetime, then planted my butt next to hers, and asked in a Brenda Vaccaro growl, "Was it good for you?"

She laughed, but I noticed with distinct satisfaction that goose bumps had erupted over her arms. The old girl still had some fire in her.

"So, Rush," I asked, letting my knee bounce against hers, "where are you staying?"

"With a friend," she said coyly. "And you can call me Julie. Rush is my last name. Great name for a singer, don't you think? Julie Rush?"

For an instant, she seemed engagingly transparent. It was an effort to keep myself from being sucked in by her charm. "Who's the friend?" I asked with sincere interest.

She placed a hand on my thigh reassuringly. Despite my best intentions, I shuddered. Our eyes met with surprise. We both had our acts in full gear, but the physical connection was no simulation. She seemed truly unsettled. And as much as I hated to admit it, she wasn't alone.

I placed my hand over hers and thought again of K.T. Bellflower, the woman I had been dating exclusively for the past eight months. "You didn't answer my question," I said, my voice breaking in two and making me sound like a boy on the verge of an ugly puberty.

"Refresh my memory," she replied, her hand still planted on my thigh. "What's the question? If it's your place or mine, I say yours."

I felt myself being rapidly reduced to a Lou Costello stammer. But that wasn't what worried me most. I was having one hell of a time. Truth is, I liked Julie. If there were no client and no K.T. back in old N.Y.C. I probably would have damned the torpedoes and proceeded full speed ahead. But instead of tackling Julie to the toasty grass mat, I said, "Sorry, I'm an old-fashioned gal. I kinda like to know a woman before I lock limbs."

A glint of amusement played in her eyes. "Sounds like foreplay to me," she said, then turned and bumped her back against the side of my raised leg. "Besides, there's nothing wrong with delayed gratification. Nothing at all."

Right then and there, I determined to summon K.T. to P-town *pronto*. She wasn't due until a week from Wednesday, the day before her thirty-seventh birthday. We planned to celebrate with a hot and salty reunion, but now I wasn't sure I could wait. After all, a shackled libido could be a mighty dangerous thing, especially in this part of the world.

Just then the beeper clipped to the inside of my short's waistband started vibrating. For a multitude of reasons, the teasing pulse came at the absolute worst time. There was no way I could ignore it.

I cupped my palms over Julie's shoulders, wondering briefly why the beeper's vibration seemed so unusually potent, and asked her if we could get together later on. My mouth was so close to that cute smooth-lobed ear it was a shame not to nibble it just a bit. The impulse convinced me I was sinking fast into some deep doo-doo. Before Julie could answer, I hightailed it out of there.

I found a public telephone out by the concession stand, dialed in, then listened to the number in surprise. I flipped through my address book. Sure enough, it belonged to Lurlene Hayes, a childhood friend of K.T.'s. Lurlene and I get along like hyper-hormonal Akitas tussling over a plump rodent. An eyebrow twitched nervously as I punched in the digits.

The busy signal wailed into my ear.

I moved the receiver away and redialed, my focus now locked on the horizon. The sun had edged to the right, beginning its languorous descent into a bank of wispy cirrus clouds. Sunset would be exquisite. For a guilty instant I envisioned myself tunneled inside a beach blanket with Julie Reed's greased limbs tight against me, the sun sinking with a delirious orange splash.

My beeper quivered again. Ignoring it, I tried Lurlene's number for the third time. This time K.T. picked up on the first ring.

"Hi," I said lightly, "it's your dyke in shining armor. I don't know if you need rescuing, honey, but I sure as hell do."

There was no answer on the other end.

"Hey, are you there?"

"Hold on," she said at last.

I didn't appreciate the curtness. Or the fact that she had obviously switched the phone to mute. Besides, I thought, glancing at my wristwatch and working myself up to a good frothy indignation, what was she doing at Lurlene's when she was supposed to be taping the last few segments of her PBS cooking show?

"Hello," I yodeled into the phone impatiently. "I got a life here that needs some tending, so if you're too busy —"

A flood of sound. Someone crying hysterically, K.T.'s familiar voice murmuring little cooing sounds. "Robin," she finally said breathlessly, "you have to come back home. Right away." Again the phone went dead.

By then my temples were throbbing and I was starting to get mighty pissed. "K.T., will you please —"

"Christ, honey, I'm sorry, but Lurlene's a mess." The background howls finally crystallized into words. Lurlene yelled at K.T. to hang up, leave Robin out of it.

"Leave me out of what?"

"She had a date with Brian . . . okay, not a date." Now she was talking to Lurlene again. "I don't care what you call it, for Christ's sake. Robin *has* to know!" I was two seconds away from hanging up when K.T. blurted, "Brian Fritzl's dead. What? She *thinks* he's dead. Lurlene discovered his body at the studio about an hour ago."

I rested my forehead against the warm metal of the pay phone casing. Knowing Lurlene's tendency to exaggerate, Brian was probably just napping a little too soundly. "So what do you need from me?" I asked wearily.

"Brian was shot in the back," K.T. retorted sharply. She has the annoying habit of decoding the subtlest changes in my tone. Lowering her voice, she added, "I still can't get the story straight, but it sounds like her fingerprints are on the gun. She called me right away, but . . ." Her voice downshifted another notch. "Not the police."

I stood up straight. "*Not* the police?" I repeated in amazement. "Oh, Lurlene's real smart, isn't she?" A group of noisy teenage boys with bad skin walked by juggling greenish hot dogs and flat, syrupy looking Cokes. I wanted to join them. Instead I rifled through my address book again. I found what I was looking for and interrupted K.T.'s heated defense of her best friend's prudence. "You need to contact the police right away, K.T. Any delay could look bad for Lurlene. Have you talked to your brother yet?" K.T.'s brother T.B. is one of the city's medical examiners.

"I left a message for him."

"How about Larry?" A brother-in-law in the N.Y.P.D. could go far.

"He and Ginny are on a camping trip."

"Great," I muttered sarcastically. "Okay, baby, get a pen. I want you to call Mel Olson right away."

"Isn't she —"

"She's a damn good lawyer." I wasn't about to argue with K.T. about the niceties of hiring an ex-lover of mine. I read off Mel's number.

"Got it," K.T. said, then added in a voice designed to melt my kneecaps, "You *are* coming home, right?"

I pictured Julie Reed, the way she looked on the posters, tuxedo and stiletto heels. Even if Brian's death ended up being one of Lurlene's contrived tragedies, going home wasn't such a bad idea. I checked my watch again. "I won't make it before ten. I need to stop at the cottage first. If you need me before then, call the beeper."

She sighed heavily. "I love you, Robin."

I answered in kind, then ruined the moment with my next question. "What do you think, K.T.? Did she do it? Did she kill Brian?"

I can't say I was real surprised when the dial tone hissed in my ear.

* * * * *

It had been raining all day in New York City and some of the streets had flooded. My car dove into an undetected pothole, then jumped back to level ground. I cranked up the air conditioning and growled. Seven hours earlier my rear view mirror had held a glacier-blue sky and sun-washed sand dunes, a vista as refreshing to the eye as dollops of orange sherbet are to the tongue. Now I looked up at the rear view mirror and watched a begrimed man of indeterminate age and race straggle toward me with a spray bottle and rag. His bulging eyes trapped the red glare from my tail lights. In a drunken slur, he demanded a quarter in exchange for smearing my windows with a special grade of New York muck. I flipped the windshield wipers on high and cursed. The damn traffic signal wouldn't change.

"Open the window, motherfucker!"

I eased my foot off the brake, but apparently not fast enough. Before I could roll out of reach, he had ripped off my left windshield wiper. Now the bastard had a weapon. He began slashing the door like a skilled fencer, all the while conjugating the word "fuck" with a fair amount of creativity. Hubba, the name I've lovingly given my cornflower blue Subaru, is barely a year old and has already had her share of close calls, so it didn't take long for me to decide to run the red light and screech across Second Avenue like any other crazed New Yorker.

Hate to break it to you, Dot, but home ain't necessarily sweet. Given the choice, I would have opted for Oz.

By the time I pulled up to Lurlene Hayes's apartment building on the corner of East Fourth and Avenue C, it was just after eleven and my spirits had swished down the clogged sewers along with the day's rain. Being a pretty savvy P.I., I noticed right away that all her windows were dark. The good news scenario was that Lurlene had hallucinated the whole damn murder scene and was now fast asleep in her politically correct, albeit lumpy, futon-on-hard-wood-floor. The bad news scenario had her locked in some horrific holding cell with a gang of gun-toting psychopaths with bad teeth. And those were just the cops. But the worse scenario of all was that she had sacked out at K.T.'s place.

I had a few choices. I could leave my precious Hubba parked next to a rusted shell of a stripped, burnt-out, and rodent-infested Cabriolet and interrupt the drug deal commencing on Lurlene's doorstep, or I could head straight to K.T.'s. It was a close decision, but I'm known for taking the hard road. I pointed Hubba toward K.T.'s home, avoiding a near hit with a white Mazda whose front fender looked like it had recently scored some impressive road kill. For this I gave up sunset with Julie Rush. Sometimes life is unbelievably cruel. I shelved the resentment, checked my car at a nearby garage, and strolled over to the mews where K.T. lives.

If you think Manhattan can't surprise you anymore, you haven't been on K.T.'s block. Every time I pass through those wrought iron gates, it's as if I've walked into another era, a time when Greenwich Village was an artists' enclave and writers like Edna St. Vincent Millay glowed at its heart like a shot of brandy on fire. Washington Square Park is just a boom box's blare away, yet the cobblestoned street remains a sanguine haven.

I paused outside K.T.'s building, a slender carriage

house painted French-blue with shutters the color of pale pink tulips. The window boxes on both floors overflowed with brilliant impatiens and geraniums. I let myself in and immediately sensed the emptiness. For the first time all day, I started to really worry.

I better explain. If K.T. has one fault, it's a fixation on protecting Lurlene Hayes that dates back to 1963. I understand that part well enough. The two of them grew up together in Wizard Clip, West Virginia. The town's entire population wouldn't fill a single New York City subway car.

When K.T. was eight, her father died in a three-vehicle crash. He left behind a feisty widow and seven spirited children, ranging from age four to age eleven. Not surprisingly, when Lurlene's parents offered to take in K.T. for a spell, Emily Bellflower hastily accepted. But Potter Hayes's interest in K.T. wasn't exactly neighborly. I still don't know all the details — I'm not even sure that K.T. remembers — but apparently the bastard attacked her just a few days later. When he was done, Potter sent K.T. to the room she was staying in. She found Lurlene sitting on the bed they had been sharing, crying quietly. Right away K.T. knew that what she had just experienced wasn't atypical of the Hayes household. She dragged Lurlene back home with her the very same night. Days later, K.T.'s mother whisked Lurlene and the entire Bellflower clan off to a cousin's house in Charlottesville, Virginia. Lurlene's been one of the family ever since.

The problem is, Lurlene's never learned to stand on her own. The Bellflowers, K.T. especially, have made a career out of feeding, clothing, funding and, on at least one occasion, cheating for her. In her early twenties Lurlene took and failed the G.E.D. examination twice. When Lurlene consequently threatened suicide, K.T. masqueraded as her old friend and took the test in her stead. The dependency has never let up.

And then there are Lurlene's panic attacks. Nine weeks into my relationship with K.T., we received a frantic midnight call from Lurlene. A man was breaking into her apartment, threatening to kill her. She had already called the police, yet she insisted that we dash over to East Fourth Street and rescue her personally. The police wouldn't come, Lurlene argued, she couldn't trust anyone but K.T.; if the two of us came the man would be frightened away. K.T. didn't bat an eye. We caught a cab across town and found one of Lurlene's drunken neighbors arguing with a pizza delivery boy over a broken bottle of Pepsi. Noisy and stinking of sweat, tomato sauce and stale beer, they weren't half as frightening as our crosstown cab ride had been.

I know better than most people how devastating a childhood trauma can be, but I have to confess the relationship between my lover and Lurlene disturbs me. And that's on the good days. In the short time I've been with K.T., Lurlene's generated more headaches than the stray cat who's been howling in perpetual heat in my back yard. So I guess there was a part of me that half-expected to come home and discover the two of them munching popcorn in front of the telly, with Brian Fritzl's size twelves planted on the pine plank coffee table right beside them.

I trekked through both floors to search for a note, then tried my home phone to see if K.T. had left a message. Next I dialed my lawyer friend, Mel Olson.

Her service politely shooed me away. I knew I was really having an off day when I made the mistake of informing the police officer at the precinct house that I was a private detective. The thug practically snorted at me. Cooperate with a dick? I could almost hear him thinking. When roaches are extinct.

Frustrated, I resorted to a favorite pastime: raiding the fridge. K.T. recently told me in a pointedly dispassionate manner that since I'm now into my thirties, my metabolism's probably begun to ebb. All things considered, it was a pretty gentle way to inform me that my belly now has less in common with a pizza than it does with a ricotta-stuffed calzone. Didn't matter much to me, though. I still went for the Haagen-Dazs. Then I called K.T.'s brother T.B.

If you think the Bellflowers are initial crazy, you're wrong. They're just plain crazy. All seven kids are named after states: Virginia, Alabama, Montana, Georgia, Carolina, Kentucky (K.T.'s full name), and Tennessee — dubbed T.B. by his buddies at the medical examiner's office.

His girlfriend answered the phone. Apparently, T.B. had left the house three or four hours earlier. On a family emergency. Pumping more information out of Paulina was hardly worth the effort. Engrossed in a rerun of "Rocky" playing on cable, she barely managed to grunt when I asked her to tell T.B. I had called.

I was running out of options, a predicament of which I'm not particularly fond. Finally I retried Lurlene's home number. After seven rings, an answering machine picked up. The ice cream curdled on my tongue. Brian bought the machine for Lurlene's birthday back in February. A few weeks later, someone left a mildly obscene message on it. To tell you the truth, I thought the guy sounded an awful lot like Brian himself. In any case, Lurlene refused to turn on the machine after that incident. Strange that she had begun using it again.

I hung up, searched through the Partridge Family lunch box in which K.T. stores keys to assorted domiciles, including Lurlene's, then headed out. A few minutes later I stepped over the Dennis the Menace look-alike who lay zoned out on Lurlene's stoop and scooted up to the third floor, a frisson of apprehension tickling the back of my neck. I knocked first, then unlocked the door.

The kitchen light was on. As usual, I felt instantly depressed. A roach you could harness and ride side-saddle scampered out of the greenish tub located on the near side of the breakfast bar. The apartment had two rooms. The one in which I stood served as kitchen, bathroom and living room. The other room held a futon bed, an assortment of gray plastic milk crates, and a closet shielded by a yellowed bed sheet that once sported flowers of some kind. If Lurlene was home, she sure wasn't rushing to greet me.

I moved over to the pine toy chest. The PhoneMate answering machine light was still on. So was the message alert. I pressed the button and waited while the tape rewound. The first phone call came from someone named Jack who wanted to know when the photos would be ready for the gallery. I assumed this referred to the work Lurlene had been doing as Brian Fritzl's photography assistant. I waited for a time-date stamp, but was disappointed. The next call came from Brian himself.

"Look, this has got to stop. I know I hurt you, but I never promised you forever. It's over, babe. Kaput. The shit you're pulling, it's over the edge. Way over. It was bad enough when you scared that new girl off from working with me, but your last phone call was the limit." My head started to pound. "Listen closely, sweetheart, if my survival means your total demise, then don't be surprised, I'll do it."

I pocketed the tape. Wherever Lurlene was, I had better find her fast. The bullet in Brian's back had her name written all over it.

Chapter 2

"Make me go over this again," Lurlene warned me, "and I swear I'm gonna scream." We were sitting at K.T.'s kitchen table, six feet of pitted knotty pine separating us. Her boxy right hand flitted first to her eyes, then under the curtain of thick, black bangs that extended past her eyebrows.

If eyes are windows to the soul, then Lurlene keeps hers draped good and tight. Five-six, with black hair that stretches to her shoulders, Lurlene hardly ever looks at anyone straight on. Those cornflower blue eyes of hers settled on my Swatch, my kneecap, the mug of coffee K.T. placed in front of me, settled everywhere but on my face.

I turned to K.T.

"I'm sorry I didn't leave a message," she said right away. "There was so much to juggle."

Her skin was mottled, her lips pale, eyes bloodshot. The day's events had left a deeper mark on her features than on Lurlene's. She moved next to where I was sitting and rested her hand on my shoulder. I knew she wanted to hug me, but wouldn't. Not in front of poor Lurlene. I tried to cap my irritation as I asked for the second time, "What happened after we hung up?"

"I called Mel. She was really great, by the way," K.T. added, squeezing my shoulder in a subtitle that read, *I was almost able to forget she was your first serious lover*. "We met at a coffee house near the police station." She glanced nervously at Lurlene, then bit her bottom lip. Clearly she was waiting for a cue from her old friend. The message was obvious. Unless Lurlene consented, K.T. wasn't planning to tell me the whole story.

I scraped my chair away from the table, fully aware of how it drives her crazy, then asked, "When did you make the report?"

They exchanged glances, then Lurlene said, "Around seven."

I did a quick calculation. "Five hours after you found Brian?" She confirmed my estimate with a shrug. Sipping the coffee, I tried to imagine how New York's finest had reacted to a five-hour delay in reporting a homicide.

K.T. butted into my thoughts. "We decided to wait until we could talk to both Mel and T.B. His connections could help, you know."

The coffee tasted of chicory. I shivered a bit, then took another mouthful. Striving for nonchalance, I asked, "So they questioned you for three, four hours?"

Again they sought each other's eyes. Feeling like the proverbial third wheel, I continued jotting notes. The length of Lurlene's interrogation was in itself reason for concern.

"Take me through it." My tone was curt, impersonal. It was almost one in the morning and I wanted to spend a few dark hours wrapped tight around K.T.'s limbs.

"We broke up on Saturday. You should've heard him. He called me every kind of bad name he could lay tongue to," Lurlene whispered. "Like we'd never been in love." Staring past me, Lurlene looked strangely beautiful. Her high cheeks and coppery skin appeared to glow for an instant. More than once I've thought that one of her ancestors must have been Native American.

When she didn't continue, I asked, "What was his reason?"

She shrugged, then focused on K.T.'s back. K.T. was by the sink, peeling carrots furiously.

"I didn't tell the police about the break-up," Lurlene finally added.

I fingered the tape in my pocket and shook my head. "Did you tell Mel at least?"

A blank stare was my answer.

"Oh, for God's sake," I blurted. Almost immediately I forced myself to calm down. The fact that K.T. had the carrot peeler ominously pointed at me helped a great deal. "Fine, fine. Why don't you first tell me your *official* version so I know exactly what the boys in blue are working with."

The story boiled down to this: Brian called her around a little after one. He sounded agitated, ordered her to come right over to pick up her last paycheck and remove the items of clothing she had left in the upstairs bedroom. When she arrived, the front door was unlocked. Since the stereo system was blasting, she assumed he was in the middle of a photo shoot. Brian specialized in fashion photography with upcoming, nubile models with bulimic tendencies. Lately he had taken to blaring *Red, Hot + Blue* during his sessions. Jody Watley was singing "After You Who" when she entered the studio. The cameras and lights were set up, but she didn't see Brian anywhere. She called his name, but no one answered. When she stepped forward, her foot kicked an object across the hall and under a console table. What she retrieved was the pistol Brian usually kept locked in the equipment cabinet. That's when she noticed the door to his darkroom was open and the red light was on. She glanced in, saw him lying on his stomach, blood flowing from a hole in his back.

If I've made Lurlene's account sound lucid, believe me, it wasn't. Between her dazed pauses, frequent crying jags and repeated claims of forgetfulness, it took me almost two hours to obtain the basic facts. And I still hadn't penetrated the obvious omissions.

Like the tape in my pocket. Now I slapped it on the table as if it were a poker chip in a game for high fliers.

Both K.T. and Lurlene asked at the same time, "What's that?"

I gestured for them to follow me into the den. The room was a mini-museum of American memorabilia. A fire-engine-red flying horse from an old gasoline station sign presided over the fireplace. Posters for B-movies from the fifties and sixties hung over a jukebox and pastel ice cream parlor stools. Along a shelf running the length of the whole room K.T. had lined up a colorful collection of antique wind-up toys. The room was designed by K.T. to compensate for the childhood frivolity she had missed in Wizard Clip. Feeling a twinge of guilt, I contaminated the atmosphere by inserting the tape into the cassette deck and hitting the play button.

Lurlene's face went white. K.T. stamped a foot like an angry steed and snorted at me. "*Now*?" she shouted. "You have to play this *now*?"

For once Lurlene looked me in the eye. "Where'd you get that?"

As I told her, she began shaking her head. "No, no, no. Impossible." To K.T. she said, "You know I never use that damn thing. I haven't turned it on since, when, March? You've been at my apartment at least six, seven times since then. Have you ever seen me use it?"

K.T. crossed and hugged her friend, cooing assurances into her ear. For some reason, it pissed me off. I said, "The point is not how often you use the damn machine, Lurlene. It's why Brian left a message like that in the first place. Were you harassing him?"

Still embracing my lover, she wobbled her head in a negative, then mumbled something.

I sliced them apart and asked her to repeat what she had said.

"Never," was the unconvincing response. "Oh Lord, Lord . . ." she whined, collapsing into the dentist's chair. True confession: for an instant I wished I had a drill. A dull one.

Lurlene covered her face with both hands. "Why didn't I listen to Charon when I had the chance?" she asked no one in particular. It didn't matter. K.T. shot me a glance that was full of fire.

Great. Now the two of them were blaming me. Back in March, a fortune teller with the contrived moniker of Charon Centauri had warned Lurlene to end her relationship with Brian and get out of town at once, before tragedy struck. K.T. resolved to rescue Lurlene by shuttling her off to Hawaii. Since that meant a good month without my sweetheart, I had checked out the fortune teller myself. What the hell had Charon said to me? The new-age bombast came to me in a flash: "Lurlene's in grave danger. She flies like a finch into the brutal clutch of a hawk. This dark man she so foolishly loves will crush her spirit . . . Her life is in your hands."

As it turned out, the magical, mystical Charon was one of Brian's ex-lovers. I'm not saying she's a complete fraud. There were a few things she knew about my past I still can't explain. But the woman had bilked Lurlene out of hundreds of dollars, and I sure as hell wasn't going to feel guilty now for having exposed her con game.

I kicked the footrest of the dentist's chair so that it swung my way, knelt down and said in my best butch tone, "Cut the crap, Lurlene. The defenseless act may work with K.T., but it doesn't fly with me." I tried not to notice when K.T. stormed out of the room. "Why did Brian leave that message on your tape?"

Her gaze landed beyond my shoulder. I noticed with a grim satisfaction that her tears had stopped almost the instant K.T. left the room.

"You don't have to believe me," she began coldly. "I really could give a good goddamn. The fact is, there was no message on the machine. At least not when I left the apartment. So if you found it there, you've got another mystery on your hands, don't you?"

This was the side of Lurlene K.T. rarely saw, if ever. Beneath that quivering, rag doll persona lay a sliver of hard-edged steel.

I flopped back onto my butt and stared at her, waiting. The tick of a Howdy Doody wall clock rattled like distant artillery fire. Finally I asked, "Did you kill him?"

Our eyes locked briefly, then she cocked her head and glanced away, dark amusement flitting across her face. "Down in Wizard Clip," she began, her southern accent growing more marked, "my grandpa would take a slug of moonshine that set him all aquiver like a rabbit's whisker, then he'd wink at me and say, 'Honey, it kisses like a woman, but it kicks like a mule.' " She stood up with a bitter laugh. "Ain't nothing like being kicked in the ass by a friend. At least the cops *pretended* to believe me. Guess I should give you credit for honesty. 'Cept I'm not feeling too magnanimous tonight." With those words, she swept past me.

I couldn't help but notice that she hadn't answered my question.

I retraced my steps and found K.T. in the kitchen. Three in the morning, and she was sullenly pouring batter into a series of miniature loaf pans.

"Carrot bread," she said with importance, completely unaware of the inanity of her words. My vision blurred. For some inexplicable reason, my love for her at that moment was so acute, it stung.

"K.T., I'm sorry . . ."

She waved her free hand. "Don't. I'm too tired to talk about this any more." Her gaze never budged from the steady flow of the batter into the loaf tins.

I walked past her.

"Robin," she started. I glanced back. She extended a bowl in my direction. "Don't you want to at least taste the batter?"

With such a simple gesture peace was made. Still, when we lay down in bed an hour later, back to back, the chill in the room definitely did not derive from the air conditioner.

"I really appreciate this, T.B."

"Right," he said, nodding to the officer who had ripped the police tape off the door frame and now gestured for us to enter. "We won't be long, George," T.B. muttered. "Right, Robin?"

I waited till we were alone before I spoke. "What's with you? I thought you'd be eager to help Lurlene."

"Sure. Of course I am." He crossed his arms across his chest and pouted. On his best days, T.B. looks like a wiry version of Ron Howard, the director. At the moment, however, he looked more like Ron Howard in his Opie days, a lock of copper-red hair falling over his right eye. "It's just that I'm on pretty thin ice here . . . Lurlene . . . well, let's say this is a little too close to home."

He began playing with a button on his shirt and I felt my annoyance rise a peg. I changed the subject. "Have you heard anything about the autopsy?"

Suddenly all business, he shook his head. "It'll be a day or two. Maybe more. The department's pretty loaded down with that cement condo mess right now." T.B. was referring to the grisly discovery a wrecking crew had made in the basement of a condemned movie theater the week before. So far the medical examiner's office had identified limbs belonging to at least eleven different individuals. No one knew yet how many more bodies they'd find in the cement locker some still unknown psycho had constructed. "Anyway, Rob, I would appreciate it if you could make this quick. This isn't exactly kosher . . ."

I had moved past him onto the balcony. The duplex had entries on both floors. The upper floor consisted of a master bedroom suite, a small den, and a generous balcony that overlooked the basement-level studio. I leaned over the teak railing and surveyed the scene below. A sheet of background paper painted to resemble a cloud-swept sky lined the midsection of the left wall. Area lights, reflecting umbrellas, an oversized fan, and three cameras locked onto tripods sat ready for action. I took in the open dressing-room door, the garment rack, the pint-sized refrigerator, the drafting table where Brian sketched out his photo shoots. I had been here once before and the set-up appeared unaltered. Any minute Brian would enter, accompanied by some leggy brunette with a medically enhanced bottom lip, and begin clicking away.

I knew the murder had occurred in the studio, but I decided to take the classic investigative approach and circle in slowly. Ignoring T.B.'s high-strung chatter about some new Italian restaurant down the block, I headed into the bedroom. Right away I zeroed in on the photographs. In truth, there was no way to ignore them. Brian had designed the room so that it would be absent right angles. The ceiling and walls veered off along strange diagonals, creating a perspective fit for a Picasso. At first glance the effect was dizzying, then sheer instinct took over and my focus latched onto the photographs suspended from the ceiling on nearly invisible wires. Arranged in a strict symmetry, the photographs appeared to have been selected according to some mysterious mathematical formula, the size, shape, and hue of each one serving to stabilize the overall tableau.

Behind me T.B. exhaled loudly. "Wow. The babes must love this."

I spun around and raised my eyebrows at him. Instantly his bravado withered.

"C'mon," he said sheepishly. "You know what I mean. This is an artist's den. Look at that —" He wagged a finger over my shoulder. I looked up. The largest photograph was a black-and-white blow-up in which a woman's hip and belly hairline resembled a snow-capped mountain with a stand of bristly pines leading slowly south.

I half-heartedly punched T.B. in the arm, feeling a little uneasy because I found the photograph strangely provocative. Then my attention shifted to a different picture. The wall opposite the bed was about six feet high and contained a series of built-in drawers and shelves. On one of these sat an elaborately framed photograph. A younger-looking Brian squatted in front of a rickety wood fence. Balanced on his knees were two children with chocolate-smeared mouths. Next to them stood a slender woman holding four ice cream cones in serious stages of melt-down. I noticed that she had angled her leg so it pressed against Brian's flank.

T.B. read my mind. "That must be his wife."

Brian had separated from his wife over three years ago. Somehow the divorce had never materialized. Suddenly I wondered why. I glanced at the other family pictures, a few of the wife, a dozen or so of the children. In the latest shots, the boy looked around seventeen, the girl maybe fourteen.

T.B. nudged me and I moved on, opening and closing drawers and stirring up puffs of fingerprint powder. In the closet the hangers had been pushed to one side as if someone had been searching for something or had removed several items.

After a brief inspection of the bathroom and den, I headed downstairs. The back of one rollfilm camera was missing. I glanced at T.B., who said, "The film's being developed this morning." I nodded, then edged toward the stereo. As Lurlene had remembered, the jewel box for *Red, Hot + Blue* lay on top.

I clicked on the lights, then moved behind the center tripod and braced my eye against the camera's viewfinder. The backdrop loomed like a Kansas sky. Standing there, I remembered how focused Brian had been the time K.T. and I had dropped in to meet him and Lurlene. The fan had sent gentle ripples of wind through the model's over-permed locks while he cooed with pleasure. "Yes, yes, oh baby, that's the look. That's it. Give it to me. Oh, what a sweet shot."

What, or who, had interrupted Brian's photo session? I pivoted the camera, then halted abruptly. Stepping back I asked, "What's that?" T.B. followed my gaze.

He shook his head impatiently. "A stool, *cherie*."

I bit my bottom lip and crossed the room. Right behind the stool the background paper had torn. I leaned down and examined a smudged footprint and, next to it, a piece of fabric that apparently had been kicked under the edge. I tugged and a pair of pantyhose emerged. T.B. shrugged, as if to say "so what." The garment rack and dressing room were only a few feet away, so maybe T.B.'s nonchalance was warranted. Nevertheless I handed the stockings to him carefully. "Find a baggie in the kitchen and bring this to your boys. Just in case."

He started to protest, then thought better of it. I smiled, appreciating the increased leverage I enjoyed now that we were practically in-laws. "Thanks, T.B.," I said to his back. As soon as he entered the kitchen, I headed for the darkroom.

The room commingled the sick, musty smell of blood and the acrid odor of photographic chemicals. I examined the tray nearest the door and was surprised to find a piece of photographic paper disintegrating at the bottom. The faded image showed a green-eyed black woman, a knock-out with boyish good looks and incredibly sensual lips. The background looked the same as the one set up in the studio. I attempted to lift the photograph with tongs, but the paper melted away.

There was surprisingly very little blood in the room. I called for T.B. He entered the room and wriggled his nose. "Hate the smell of a darkroom," he muttered.

"Any guesses about what happened in here?" I asked.

He braced his hands on the sides of the door frame in a stance that would have suited Rocky Balboa. Knowing T.B.'s inexplicable fixation on all things Italian, I suspected the pose was intentional. I tried to ignore the incongruity of his West Virginia twang as he answered, "There's no spatter pattern on the walls, so if the victim was standing at the instant of impact the bullet probably didn't pass through the body." Using his nose as a pointer, he traced the stains on the floor and work counter. "Looks like he took the bullet over there, turned around, maybe to see who done it, then flopped forward onto the counter before sliding to the floor. See those stains there? Looks like he tipped one of the trays when he fell."

T.B. smiled at me now, a man pleased with his display of acumen. "Now, I'm only guessing, Rob, the guys in the C.S.U. are the experts here, but I'd bet money the gun was a twenty-two. Hardly better than a BB gun, but under the right circumstances a twenty-two's just as deadly as a three-fifty-seven magnum. You see," he said, aiming a pinkie at me. "A twenty-two doesn't have the velocity, the punch, to slam a bullet through muscle and bone." He poked me in the belly with his pinkie. "But if it starts bouncing around inside the body cavity, it doesn't matter much. The internal organs will suffer serious damage, and the victim's going to end up just as dead."

A heat flash swept through me and I planted my palm on the counter top to steady myself. Any second now memory would assault me like a marine in combat boots, kicking me back to the moment when I accidentally shot and killed my five-year-old sister with my father's .22 caliber pistol. When the nightmare didn't strike, I closed my eyes and trembled in relief.

"You all right, Rob?" T.B. asked.

I nodded and exited the room, whispering, "Give me a moment alone, okay?"

Outside, I began pacing. Something had changed and, amazingly, I wasn't sure I liked it. Ever since I was three years old, I've been haunted by my sister's death. The smoky emission of firecrackers, the scent of shoe polish or moth balls, the mere mention of a .22 caliber gun, all could plunge me into a fire pit of vivid recall in which I'd relive the instant I pulled the trigger and the gun discharged. But it didn't happen this time and a horrible guilt twisted my gut. Was I beginning to forget Carol? Or worse, had I begun to forgive myself?

"Rob, come on." T.B. gently boxed my shoulders with his open palms. "God, I knew this wasn't smart," he said more to himself than to me. "Crime scene investigation's a damned grisly business. I keep telling K.T. she should get you back into romance writing. Now let's get out of here. I don't know about you, but I sure could use a double espresso."

I nodded dumbly, afraid that the act of opening my mouth to speak would unleash the tears I did not want to shed in front of T.B.

It wasn't until we reached the restaurant that I remembered I had promised to call K.T. as soon as we were finished. I stood up and watched a good-looking waiter with a slight paunch make a beeline for our table. "Hi! I'm Mike," he announced meaningfully. I cocked an eyebrow, said, "Hi! I'm Robin" with equal enthusiasm, ordered a cafe mocha, extra whipped cream, then located the pay phone.

K.T. was at the television station where they were taping the final installment of her cooking show. As soon as I heard her voice, I knew the situation had gone from bad to worse.

"I don't know what to do, honey," she began. The metal phone cord was cold in my hands as I waited for her next words. "They've issued a warrant for Lurlene's arrest."

Trying to mask my lack of surprise, I said, "It's okay. They're just following procedure. The detectives probably think they can get this case ziplocked and shelved nice and quick. We'll get Mel —"

"Robin, stop. You haven't heard the worst yet. Lurlene's disappeared. She left me a note in my dressing room here. 'I'll kill myself before I spend thirty seconds in jail. I'll contact you when I can. But if you don't hear from me again know I've never loved anyone the way I love you.' Christ, Robin, I feel like someone's knifed me."

Outside the restaurant window a homeless man

who resembled David Crosby on a bad-hair day raised his grease-stained arm and shouted, "The world is too much to bear! The devil is on us, and time is fleeting!" For once, such rantings made too much sense.

Chapter 3

When I returned to the table, T.B. was talking with Mike-the-Happy-Waiter about a recent hit-and-run accident. I slipped into my seat and attempted to make eye contact with T.B., but when he's on a conversational roll the safest thing to do is duck. The guy would have made one hell of a lobbyist.

"Hit-and-runs are a bitch to solve," he was expounding, "unless you've got an eye witness. If you've got an eye witness, it's a different story. You wouldn't believe the stories I could tell you. Once I dissected three-quarters of a license plate from a victim's abdomen. We got the perp, too. Some lousy drunk. From Connecticut. Without the plate, who knows? He could've escaped. Tell you, I could make a T.V. movie with the things I've seen."

Mike nodded, as if he found T.B.'s diatribe fascinating. T.B. basked in the attention.

"So Mike," he said, ignoring the kick to his shin that I delivered under the table, "did you actually see the hit?"

The waiter looked like he was ready to sit down and join us. "Nah. But I did see the car." As Mike leaned toward T.B., the diamond stud in his ear winked at me. All at once it struck me that the waiter's interest might not be sheer civility. The realization gave me a way to cut the conversation short.

"Listen, Mike," I said, "T.B. and I have a few important matters to discuss right now. Maybe you boys could talk about this later. Perhaps over dinner?" I angled my head so T.B. wouldn't catch the mischief in my eye.

T.B. leapt on the idea. "Sure, that would be great." After they made plans, I gave T.B. the latest news about Lurlene. He slammed a hand against the counter top, his face suddenly streaked with red splotches. The same thing happens to his sister when she's upset. "Dammit!" he spurted. "Lurlene's always so, so . . ."

"Irrational?" I offered.

He glared at me. "You don't understand her. You never have. She's a good person. The best." Fishing for money in the back pocket of his slacks, he squirmed nervously. "She doesn't trust anyone. Not that I blame her much. Life's dealt her a pretty ugly hand. Now this." He stood abruptly, tossed bills onto the table, then wagged a finger at me. "You think this is her fault. Let me tell you something, Lurlene has only one problem. She doesn't believe in herself. Dammit. We have to find her fast."

He left without saying goodbye to me or Mike. Of the two of us, I think Mike took it harder.

It was only eleven in the morning, but I was dead on my feet. I finished T.B.'s leftover biscotti, collected my car and headed for Brooklyn and the brownstone I co-own with two friends. The house is in Park Slope, an enclave for lesbians, refugees from the sixties and other recalcitrant progressives. I took the Brooklyn Battery Tunnel, slammed into a few healthy potholes and raced down my block to steal the last remaining parking spot.

My key was in the front door of my apartment when I heard a familiar squeal. Despite my mood, I smiled. "Where is she?" I asked, swinging the door open.

Beth had the baby balanced on one hip as she poured dry food into the cat bowls. She didn't look pleased to see me. "K.T. called to let us know you were home," she said accusingly.

"You sound like a mother." I laughed and swept Carol out of her arms. She spat up on my shoulder. The emission had the consistency of curdled milk.

Beth grabbed some wet paper towels and dabbed us both. "I *am* a mother, and you're the worst damn housemate a family could have."

I knew she didn't mean it. Besides sharing a brownstone with me, Beth and her lover Dinah are two of my closest friends. In the past six years we've formed a steadfast, albeit peculiar, extended family. I kissed Beth's forehead, right on the worry lines I had helped to etch, and said, "And such a sweet mama you've become."

Her smile was reluctant, but it was there. She shrugged me off lightly and said, "I fed the cats because I wasn't sure if you'd make it here before traipsing off again to God knows where."

I handed Carol back to her and scooped up one of my cats in exchange. "You've been with Dinah so long, you're starting to whine alike."

She stepped around me and grabbed a pacifier from the kitchen counter. "By the way, I heard about Lurlene."

In between Carol's increasingly aggressive howls, I gave her the details. I wasn't sure how much Beth was absorbing, what with the baby's rapid descent into the cranky zone, but she surprised me. "If she was so distraught," she asked, "how'd she remember the exact song that was playing when she got to Brian's. Seems a strange detail to remember."

She had a few other insights, all of which seemed to indicate a lack of conviction in Lurlene's innocence. Hate to admit it, but her doubts comforted me. We chatted a few more minutes, discovered that Carol had learned how to pull hair and rip off shirt buttons, then agreed we had exceeded Beth's adult-conversation allotment. She returned downstairs and I zipped into the bedroom. After a short call to my office and an even shorter nap, Beth's questions began nagging at me.

I put on *Red, Hot + Blue*. The lyrics of "After You Who" reminded me of how I've felt after every break-up: an unshakable conviction that I could never replace the lover just lost. No wonder Lurlene had focused on the music. I started the disk from the first track, grabbed a Yoo-Hoo from the fridge, nestled into the couch with Geeja and Mallomar, my two quirky puppy cats, then dialed Mel Olsen.

Mel and I had been lovers while students at the University of Virginia in Charlottesville. The relationship lasted less than a year, but fire's fire no matter how short the wick. Like most break-ups, ours was not particularly pleasant. The indelible event occurred at an airport, and let me tell you, *Casablanca* it wasn't. Ten years passed before we had our first post-lover contact, and that was only because fate had tossed us the same sorry client. Mel's first words to me then were the same as she said now: "We have to stop meeting like this."

I wasn't up to banter. "How bad is it, Mel?"

"Let's see . . . they have an eye-witness who says she left Brian's studio around the approximate time of his death. They found Lurlene's fingerprints on the gun, the back of his belt, the upstairs and downstairs door knobs. Oh, did I mention that the eye-witness also overheard Lurlene and Brian fighting the previous day? Apparently, he wanted to end the relationship. Too bad Lurlene didn't fill me in on that tidbit. And then, of course, there's her disappearing act. All in all, you couldn't have sent me a more appealing client. Remind me to thank you."

I fingered the compact disk jewel case, idly reviewing the list of song titles. "They find other prints?"

"I couldn't get a straight answer, however my guess is there were plenty of unidentifiable prints. But Lurlene's were the only ones on the gun."

Suddenly I stood up, eliciting a squeak of protest from my moody black cat Geeja. "Hold on a second, Mel." I scrambled toward my office at the back of the apartment, found my calculator, and did a quick addition of the CD's running times. I picked up the extension and told Mel about the song that was playing when Lurlene arrived. "Assuming Brian was the one who turned on the CD player, he had to be alive at least seventy minutes before Lurlene entered the studio. That's pretty close timing." I retrieved my notes. "Lurlene got there a little after two, so —"

"You got your facts wrong, honey."

"What do you mean?"

I heard a car horn on the other end of the phone. "According to the eye witness, Lurlene *left* Brian's studio shortly after one."

"Is that what she told you?" I asked, planting my butt on the edge of my desk.

"No, and that's not what she told the police. But, Robbie, you have to admit the lady wasn't making much sense yesterday. And the fact that she's skipped town isn't helping her credibility."

For once I felt compelled to defend Lurlene. "You're not abandoning her, are you?"

She laughed. "Sure this is about her?"

I peeked through the venetian blinds at the deck garden K.T. and I had planted two weeks ago, pointedly ignoring her question. Mel and her lover broke up a few months ago. Since then her references to our previous relationship had become a little too frequent for my comfort.

"Sorry for the malapropos comment," she added quickly, acknowledging my silence. "It's just that sometimes I feel you and I have some unfinished business."

So nice of her to realize that more than a decade after she left me sobbing at the Charlottesville airport, road grit spitting at me from the wheels of her shiny MG. I shook the memory off. "Mel, a woman's life is on the line." I moved back to the desk, the blind clicking back into place.

"I know, honey, and I'm not about to abandon her." Her sigh was barely audible. "Still, we need to face facts. If Lurlene is innocent, she's doing a pretty lousy job of helping us prove it."

I turned the page of my notepad. "Well, let's try to work around that. Can you give me the name of the supposed eye witness?"

She spelled the name for me: Tzionah Stein.

"Do you have a work number?"

A buzzer sounded on Mel's end. "That's my two-thirty appointment . . . the woman works at home. She's a potter. Her studio abuts Brian's. Let me know if you learn anything."

I hung up, got Stein's number and made the call. The woman sounded sniffy and politely asked if my questions could wait a day. I jotted down our appointment, then reorganized my briefcase. I had the sinking feeling that Lurlene's case was going to absorb the bulk of my time for a while, yet I didn't want to shortchange Abigail Whitman, the client who had hired me to find Julie Reed. I decided to use the rest of the day to catch up on work. My brownstone is on Third Street near Eighth Avenue, just seven blocks away from the detective agency I run with an ex-cop named Tony Serra. I jogged most of the way.

The first thing I noticed when I entered was the silence, then a strange rattle. I took a deep breath and entered Tony's office. He was sprawled on the leather couch, his mouth agape, the walls practically rocking with his snores. I sighed and backed out quietly. Tony has AIDS. A lifetime ago, he walked into a Brooklyn bodega for a pack of Marlboros, interrupted a robbery, and took a .25 caliber bullet in his shoulder. The bullet shattered his clavicle. The subsequent operation left him HIV-positive. In the past year, Tony's health had begun deteriorating at an accelerated rate. If it weren't for the agency, he would have surrendered a long time ago.

The two of us clash more often than partners should, but I had begun to sense a reluctant affection lurking beneath our embittered exchanges. My therapist actually thinks we're two pit bulls who'd rather draw blood than admit we've grown to care about each other. As I tiptoed around the office, reading messages, updating files, I began to wonder if she was right.

"Goddamn it, Miller, you've got the stomp of a pregnant elephant." The one characteristic unaffected by Tony's illness was his voice. With a timbre like his, he should have been an opera singer.

"You're pissed 'cause I caught you napping, so get off my back," I snapped. At the same time I flipped the switch on the coffeemaker. French roast, high-test. Just the way Tony liked it.

"Jill told me you had an emergency in town. Does this mean she's taking over the Whitman case?"

From the corner of my eye, I saw him tighten his

belt strap another notch. When we first met he had weighed over two hundred pounds. Now he barely topped one-forty.

"Look, I can't talk until I rip into that Entenmann's chocolate chip pound cake someone hid at the back of the fridge. You want to discuss the case, fine. But first we eat."

I knew the ruse was transparent. Didn't matter as long as we both bought into it. And we did.

"You must take real pride in being such a royal pain in the ass," he said, washing out his coffee mug and brushing past me. A few minutes later we sat down at the fold-down table in the remodeled kitchen area and slurped coffee the color of mud. "Well, at least you're learning to make a real cup of joe," Tony muttered appreciatively.

I started to relate what I had learned about Julie Reed, but he interrupted me before I got too far. "We can deal with that later. First update me on what's happening with Lurlene."

I glanced up, surprised. Jill Zimmerman, our research and computer maven, had promised me she'd be circumspect about the reasons for my sudden return to New York. Tony grinned when he saw my expression. "You underestimate me, partner. I can still interrogate 'em like the devil himself."

I tried not to smile back. "And to think I gave up romance writing for this —"

"Can it and give me the details."

Half a pound cake later, I leaned back in my seat and waited for Tony's assessment of the case. When he stood up and poured himself a fourth cup of coffee, I knew he had an ace up his sleeve. He was too damn confident and too damn quiet. A cat ready to pounce.

"You've already made phone calls to your NYPD cronies," I said to his back.

A self-satisfied snicker was my answer. "Tell me, what will you do without me?"

An unexpected shudder rippled through me.

He turned suddenly, as if he could hear the thoughts I hadn't even allowed myself to form. Our eyes met in a moment of rare understanding. He broke contact first, rushing to erase the tension with words. "I still have a good buddy at the C.S.U. Alex Tesler. He told me something even your lawyer friend Mel doesn't know yet. Lurlene's fingerprints are the only ones they lifted from the weapon."

Tony didn't have to explain the significance of his statement. The gun had belonged to Brian. His fingerprints should have shown up somewhere on the pistol.

"So it's possible someone had wiped the gun clean before Lurlene picked it up?" I asked. He nodded.

The news was encouraging. Maybe Lurlene had told the truth after all.

He cut another slice of cake, picked it up with his still-fat fingers and said, "Before you get too excited, you better hear the rest. Alex said they found the guy with his fly unzipped."

The acidic coffee rebounded into my throat.

"There were traces of seminal fluid on the head of his penis." He paused. "Before he was taken out, the guy had himself a little good-bye party. And who do you think the cops think was on the other side of the merry *bon voyage*?"

Lurlene's boat was sinking fast.

K.T. and I spent most of the night not talking. We were at my house, an arrangement K.T. had protested vehemently, insisting that if Lurlene needed help she was far more likely to try her number first. I countered that the cops probably thought the same way and already staked out K.T.'s place. Besides, Lurlene was smart enough to try me sooner or later. K.T. capitulated, but not without a cost. Her kiss earlier had been perfunctory, and her body language now was loud and clear. It was after eleven, K.T. sat at the opposite end of the couch, clenching a throw pillow so tightly the side zipper had opened. Her eyes were glued to the television set. Dan Rather was talking about the upcoming Democratic convention and the new frontrunner, a chubby-faced Mid-westerner with eyes too small for his head and a bulbous nose that no doubt had had its share of Dristan. Right then I didn't care about how many points this guy Clinton had over Perot or Bush. I wanted my lover back in my arms.

I sidled over, paused, and when she didn't elbow me in the ribs, I licked her freckled earlobe. She shrugged me off, said, "Right, Robin. Great timing," and stormed toward the television set and stabbed the power button. I remained in the living room steaming while she noisily prepared for bed.

I finished some paperwork, ate cheese doodles, played fetch with the cats and joined her three hours later. She was on her back, so I knew she was still awake. Somehow that was enough.

I squatted between her legs, massaged her calves. She pretended to ignore me, but the change in her breathing gave her away. I worked my way up slowly. Once her knee flicked my hand off. I lowered myself to the bed and teased her with my tongue. She shifted to her stomach. I pinned her in that position, hunched over her on all fours and swept my breasts over her back. Her moan shook us both. I ran my lips over the back of her neck, down her spine, biting her buttocks, licking the inside of her thighs, craving her excitement with an intensity that ran through me like fire. She tried to turn over, but I wouldn't let her until she was writhing beneath me. We slid down toward the floor then, our limbs locked together, my tongue exploring her mouth with a voracious rhythm. More than anything, I wanted to drive K.T. wild with need.

At one point I draped my body over the length of her, my mouth just below her ear, and stroked her slowly and firmly with my wet fingertips, whispering over and over in a voice not my own, "Can you feel it?" Each time she moaned yes, I gritted my teeth and repeated the question, my stroke lengthening, my fingers closing in on what K.T. so obviously needed. I didn't enter her until she was screaming my name.

Afterward, I still wanted her. My appetite had not dissipated. She collapsed against me, her smooth skin wet, her limbs draped limply over mine. I remained famished, unable to sleep. Words rushed to my mouth like juice from an overripe fruit. But I couldn't open my lips.

When I woke up there was a note on the fridge from K.T. instructing me to call her at the studio. There was no "dear" and no "love," but at least I had last night. I ate a bowl of Cheerios, drew daggers on the box with a black magic marker, and headed into the office.

Jill and I initiated a financial check on Julie Reed using the information I had gathered, then I planted myself by the second computer and tried to locate the latest address for Charon Centauri, the crafty fortune teller who had warned Lurlene about the impending disaster she'd face if she stayed with Brian. By early afternoon I was ready to smash the monitor. If Charon Centauri was still in the tri-state area, she had probably changed her name to something like Haileys Comet. Whatever it was, I couldn't find it.

I transferred the computer search to Jill, left a message for K.T. about meeting her at the television station around six, then exited. An hour and two eggrolls later I picked up my car and aimed it for Manhattan. I made a quick stop at the storefront where Centauri used to operate, assured myself that she had not reopened for business at that location, then drove over to Brian's apartment building on Prince Street. By the time I parked in a nearby lot, it was half past four.

Tzionah Stein answered her buzzer so fast, she must have had it wired to her chin. I identified myself as detective Robin Miller, a slightly misleading characterization. Luckily, she didn't ask to see a badge.

She wore baggy jeans, a black T-shirt and a red bandanna. Her apartment was a mirror image of Brian's in both layout and mood. I entered on the upper level. All but one wall had been removed, creating a space that undulated naturally between den, living room and sleeping alcove. Every item of furniture appeared to have been rescued from abandoned farmhouses of another era, or constructed from material discovered decomposing on a beach or forest floor. The bannister leading to the basement studio was a slim birch trunk, the steps slate. Gray, weathered driftwood shelves stretched along the walls, bearing a stunning array of pottery: vases, plates, bowls, containers of every shape and size. In the filtered sunlight, the glazes flickered like embers in a dying campfire.

I complimented her on her talent, but rather than responding she returned to the potter's wheel, straddling the bench and centering the clay, all the while ignoring my presence. She was a striking woman, in no way traditionally pretty, yet she undoubtedly turned heads when she entered a room. A wild mane of chestnut curls had been forced into a twist that hung loosely along her nape. Her nose, a little too long and sharp-edged, carried my attention to her eyes, a dark blue, like a sky at dusk, topped by halos of thick, sun-bleached lashes. Her eyebrows were thick, her lips full and her skin radiant. Overweight by a good thirty pounds, her heft seemed to be the appropriate palette for her features.

Only when the lump of clay had risen into a smooth column between her palms did she glance up at me again and then only to say, "Excuse me," politely, like a school girl asking permission to speak.

I sat down on a stool and waited. A few minutes later she grabbed a wire from a nearby table, sliced the bowl from the wheel, shifted it to a clay disk, and covered it with plastic.

As she carried it to a pallet, she apologized again. "Once the clay's on the wheel, I'm committed to its form. I simply cannot allow distractions." She patted her hands with a wash towel, then faced me. "I appreciate your patience. The detectives yesterday were rather — how do I put this? Intrusive. Now, what can I tell you that you don't already know?"

Impersonating an officer is a pretty serious business, so I had to word my answer with care. "Well, I don't really work with the team who interviewed you. I'm afraid we'll have to start from scratch."

She glanced at the vat of clay positioned to her right and sighed. "Fine." She wiped her forehead with the back of her hand, apparently unbothered by the streak of clay she left there. I was surprised to realize that, somehow, Tzionah Stein's beauty was intensifying as we spoke. I looked away and asked, "You were home all day Sunday?"

"Well, I did escape my grotto for twenty minutes or so in the morning. To buy bagels and lox. Does that count?"

I turned back and noted the wry intelligence in her slight smile, a smile that heightened the color of her eyes. I stared at her until her features transformed from amusement into concern. How would a photographer react to a face like hers, I found myself wondering. The answer struck me like a kick to the shins. I veered onto a new track. "How close were you and Brian?"

She broke eye contact then, and I knew my instincts were right.

"We were friendly, friendlier than most New York neighbors. We had art in common. Our sensibilities had a similar rhythm, I suppose. Though you probably wouldn't guess that from our homes. Brian's decor is so cool and modeled. Like a Brancusi. It belies his soul, which is more like raku." She stood suddenly, lifted a vase from a nearby shelf, its glaze a thin skin of newly mined copper, streaked with lines of crackled turquoise. She held it out to me. "Glaze that's been subject to great heat, in an open-air fire." Her fingers gliding along the lip of the vase as she said quietly, "Brian's soul." When she raised her face, her eyes were moist. "This was his favorite piece. I was too selfish to give it to him." She shook her head sadly, then returned to her perch on the potter's wheel.

To be honest, her description of Brian didn't meld with my impressions of the man. She made him sound like a modern-day Gaugin, an artist of passion and brilliance. When I met him, he struck me as a slightly cocky but amusing fashion photographer who took himself, and his seductive abilities, a little too seriously. I had to proceed carefully with Tzionah, I warned myself. I crossed to the vat of clay and knelt. "Do you mind?" I asked.

Her smile was brief and speculative. She planted her palms on her thin-jeaned thighs and nodded. I dipped my fingers in. The clay was wet, cool and thick. When I pulled my hand out, it made a sucking noise.

"Wonderful, isn't it?" she said. "So primal."

She guided me to a table and instructed me on how to wedge the clay so that the air bubbles inside would be eliminated. There was something incredibly intimate about the way her hands cupped mine, pushing them forward then gently pressing my fingers and tugging them toward our bellies. After a few minutes, I asked quietly, "Were you lovers?"

Her hands clamped down on mine. She still held them as we turned to face each other. Instead of answering, she grinned with her eyes. "You're a lesbian, aren't you, Detective Miller?"

I couldn't mask my surprise.

She bit her bottom lip, obviously pleased. "I could sense it in the way you responded to me just then, while we were kneading. Most women wouldn't feel comfortable with that degree of closeness, but you practically leaned into me. And your breathing changed. Am I right?"

I slipped my hands out and walked quickly to the sink. Rubbing my hands vigorously under the too-cold water, I assessed her observations. Damn it if she wasn't right. She had turned my own game against me. "Ms. Stein," I said, snapping off a sheet of paper towel with unnecessary force, "my sexuality is not an issue here. Your relationship with Mr. Fritzl is, however."

We were a good ten feet away from each other, but I could feel her sizing me up. "Professional it is, then," she responded, the ironic note in her voice unmistakable. "Mr. Fritzl is married. I do not date married men."

Suddenly irritated I snapped, "Mr. Fritzl is *dead*. And I didn't ask you whether you were dating. I asked you if you were lovers."

Slowly she nodded. "Okay. On your terms. For now. But I don't want this written down."

After we took our places on a rough-hewn bench on the far side of the room, she resumed talking. Brian had moved into the building shortly after separating from his wife, Kathleen, who was also a photographer. "The split was her idea. He was pretty needy at first. She took the kids, and one of his best clients. Our physical relationship lasted a few months. The first time we slept together . . ." She smiled. "He wanted me to teach him the art of paddling." She waited to see if I needed clarification. I did. "Paddling," she repeated, as she swept over to an antique tool box and selected an object that resembled a small bat. "You beat objects with a stick or brush, or any object that can create texture and shape. The end result can be quite powerful."

I checked out the pieces she pointed to. Sporting sharp edges, jarring angles, and heavy masculine glazes, the pottery was arresting in a way that paralleled Brian's photography. I said, "The technique seems violent."

A grimace told me I had disappointed her. "Passion is a form of violence," she said. Then, as if she remembered the purpose of my visit, she amended, "I mean, the primal sexual impulse is not pretty. Not civilized. Romance is a fragile porcelain vase. But passion is this." She handed me a sculptured, open-ended obelisk.

"How did the relationship end?" I asked, returning the piece to the shelf.

She pinched the bridge of her nose and said, "By mutual agreement. When I realized that Kathleen was not about to let him go, I did."

"I thought the separation was her idea?"

"Oh, it was." She slapped the miniature bat against her palm. Clearly, Kathleen Fritzl was not one of her favorite people. "But she also didn't want to sever ties completely. She had some power over him, I'll never understand what, but whenever he seemed ready to break free she'd tug on the reins and haul him back in."

"Did you ever meet her?"

She shook her head. "Sure. She has a studio here in the city and a house in Truro." She gave me both addresses. From memory. "In the summertime," she continued easily, "if Brian wanted to see his kids he'd rent a car and drive up there. Those visits always made him nuts. Kathleen's not an easy woman, and the kids are, well, complex. The funny thing is so many of the women he dated looked just like her. Kathleen. Except for me, of course. I was the exception."

"You remained friends after —"

She waved the question away like an annoying fly. "Of course, we did. Our connection wasn't just physical. We understood each other in a special way."

"Even when he started sleeping with other women?"

"Even after I started sleeping with other men. Sometimes sex is just sex, you know? A physical reaction, like sneezing."

"But it wasn't like that with Brian?"

Her eyes clouded as she answered simply, "No."

"What happened yesterday?"

She moved back to the potter's wheel, kicked it on, licked the edge of her clay-stained flannel shirt and held it at the center of the disc. Slowly she eased it out to the edge and said, "Brian was in all morning. I knew because he always had some music on in the background. Sometimes opera, sometimes hard rock, but always something hot, forceful. Around eleven or so, he put on a strange piece. Fairly quiet. That's why I could hear him shouting. I didn't really think much about it. Sometimes he'd get like that with a vendor, you know, on the phone. Or with Kathleen. Sometimes he'd lose it with a model whose energy wasn't right. Then, at noon, I heard Brian's upstairs door slam and then footsteps on the stairs." She pointed her chin at the far wall that adjoined Brian's studio. "The only one who ever came in that way, besides Brian, was Lurlene. Maybe one of the kids. But Lurlene usually arrived around noon, so I assumed it was her. Now that did strike me as odd. I knew they had broken up the day before."

"How'd you know that?"

"As I told the other detectives, I heard the whole thing. It happened around midnight." Tzionah couldn't entirely conceal a tone of delight from sneaking into her voice.

I covered my mouth with my hand to cover a grimace that had sprung up and asked, "Are the walls here really that thin?"

She tilted her head at me coyly. "I shock you, don't I, with the honesty of my emotions. Most people play at propriety, they wear it like a new piece of clothing, afraid to sit down because the fabric might wrinkle. I won't apologize, Detective Miller. Yes, the walls are cheap plasterboard. And yes, I did feel a certain relief when I heard them quarreling. In fact, I put my ear to the wall so I could hear a little more clearly. I cared deeply for Brian, and Lurlene was not the right woman for him. She was too needy and too, well, undefined. Brian thought the affect charming at first. Apparently the charm wore off after some time had passed."

I stood now and said, "You don't seem particularly grief-stricken."

A sneer twisted her mouth and she seemed far less attractive to me. "*That*," she said sharply, "is one emotion I will not share. My grief for Brian is private. Right now, my focus is on one thing other than my work, and that's making sure justice is done. And that's what we have in common, am I correct?"

I agreed, then continued questioning her. She repeated what Tony had told me. Around one o'clock, she heard what sounded like a car back-firing. She finished throwing a piece and then went upstairs to call her father.

"He's eighty-two years old. Father's Day to him is second in importance only to his birthday." She pumped the pottery wheel pedal and clay spat onto my chinos. "I was on my way up when I happened to glance out a window and saw Lurlene getting into a white car."

The rest of the day was uneventful; she did notice the silence next door but she just assumed Brian had left the apartment. The first she knew of the shooting was when the police showed up later that evening. When she finished her story, she dug up a large handful of clay. "I suppose we're done now," she said rather dismissively.

I nodded, then checked my watch. The second hand was still. "Dammit. The clay must have clogged the works."

Tzionah had begun wedging. She shrugged. "You should never wear jewelry when you're working with clay."

I pocketed the watch and asked, "Do you mind if I make a quick phone call? I'm supposed to meet someone at six."

"The cordless one is over there." She had returned to her craftsman mode, her gaze fixed on the movement of the clay.

I called the television station and was told K.T. had left a half-hour ago. There was no message for me.

I hung up, concerned, glanced around for a clock. Finding none, I asked Tzionah for the time.

"There's a clock radio by my bed. You can check that if you need to, on your way out."

I headed upstairs, then stopped abruptly. "If you don't have a watch down here, how are you so damn sure of the times you gave me?"

She spiked the clay onto the tablet and looked up. "I'm an artist, Detective, I know light. I can tell time the way the ancients did." Her clay-smeared hand drew an arc over her head. "By the shadows, Detective, by the shadows."

I closed the door behind me quietly. The hallway was empty, the police tape that had earlier barred access to Brian's door now dangled loosely from one side of the frame, and a case of high-quality lock picks sat in the side pocket of my briefcase. In short, the opportunity was too good to pass up.

Nothing had changed since my earlier visit. Not that I had expected it to. New York City's Crime Scene Unit has fewer than a hundred investigators, and each one handles five or six homicides a day. If they manage to spend half a day at a site, they're lucky. In a case like this, where the evidence was pretty cut and dried, the investigation had probably taken less than an hour.

I entered Brian Fritzl's den. My earlier examination had been fairly cursory. Now I sat down at the black laminate desk and scanned the surface. In the rear were two slim hinges. I swept the papers and stapler to one side then lifted the desktop to uncover a thin storage compartment. I flipped through recent correspondence, noting names of vendors, modeling agencies, outstanding bills. Tucked under a stack of head shots for various models lay an open appointment book displaying today's date. I flipped back a page. A reminder to meet Lurlene, along with a street address, was scrawled next to the eight p.m. heading. Puzzled I checked the date at the top of the page. The listing was for Saturday, June 21. I thumbed forward with dread, then I bent the book so that I could see the binding more clearly. Sure enough, someone had torn out Sunday's listing.

I moved to the file cabinet. Some of the model's names sounded familiar. But one name in particular jumped at me. Lucille Lorelli. I pulled out the file and slapped it onto a nearby drafting table. Luce Lorelli was a local private investigator. Our paths had crossed briefly in the past. She had a reputation for being hard-working, dependable, and dangerous to cross. Our agency had referred a few cases to her, cases Tony and I had deemed below our standards. I remembered one client in particular. Mark Fisher, Inc., had a strict ban on office fraternization and wanted us to trail certain workers to determine if they were sleeping together. Photographs were required. The more explicit the better. Lorelli had pounced on the case.

Brian had clipped a glassine envelope of negatives to the inside cover. I started to remove the first strip when I heard a sound downstairs. I closed the file, dropped it into my briefcase, and padded to the top of the stairs. Slowly, I made my way down into the studio. Midway I again heard a muffled sound, like someone shuffling through a room in slippers. I crossed to where the kitchen abutted Tzionah's apartment and pressed my ear to an open stretch of wall. A hollow silence greeted me, then an indistinct whir. Probably the pottery wheel.

My pulse resumed its usual thump; still, I was taking more time than I should. I quickly checked the dressing room and equipment closet. In the bathroom I pocketed a silver embossed make-up case that apparently had not warranted the investigator's attention but instantly engaged mine.

I glanced at my bare wrist, then up at the wall clock. It was almost six. Maybe K.T. had gone directly home. I should call her again, I thought. A cordless phone hung on a nearby post, just outside the darkroom. I lifted it, tried to figure out how to turn the damn thing on, then hesitated. What if the cops had a trace on the phone? I hung up and headed directly for the darkroom.

T.B. had shut the door earlier, as if such a simple

act could seal off the reality of the murder. I pressed the flat of my hand against it and took a step inside. Instantly I realized the sound from earlier had not originated next door. The dim red bulb was lit and swaying. I heard the sharp intake of breath behind me a second too late, and jerked sideways as a piece of fabric wrapped around my neck. I dug my fingers underneath, kicking backward. No contact. Dammit.

A sour chemical smell burned my nostrils as I twisted in place. I reached backward, touched hair, someone shorter, but not by much. The lights were dimming and the air buzzed. *Go limp*, I heard someone say, realized it was Master Choi, my tae kwon do instructor. *Go limp*. As I did, the fabric loosened for a split second, long enough for me to take a quick breath, for the room to brighten, my muscles to react. I wheeled to one side, angled my elbow and shot it backward like a club. There was a distinct crunch, the fabric slipped, and I snapped forward, gasping for air. Before I could turn, something crashed into the back of my knee. I was down for less than thirty seconds, but my attacker was fast. I bounded up the stairs, out into the hallway, my throat sore, each breath like a kiss of fire. By the time I reached the street, it was too late.

I stood there, chest heaving, fists clenched. Cursing my own stupidity, I replayed the events. Then I slowly opened my right hand and grimaced. There, in the center of my palm, were three strands of hair. Dark brown. Straight. Just like Lurlene's.

Chapter 4

K.T. wasn't at home. And she wasn't at work or the restaurant she owned in Greenwich Village. I called T.B., who hadn't heard from her all day. I went to call their sister, Virginia, who lives near me in Brooklyn, then remembered she and Larry were still out of town. At my office, I dialed information. Scott Weschler worked as a cameraman at the studio where K.T. taped her cooking shows. His boyfriend answered first.

"Can you make it quick, Robin, we're on our way out," Mark asked.

Before I could reassure him, Scott's deejay baritone boomed over the wires. "Sure hope the emergency wasn't serious," he said.

A nerve above my eye jumped. I asked, "What emergency?"

I could practically hear him composing a response. "The phone call. Around five." He paused.

"Did she say anything about where she was going?" The pressure behind my sternum intensified.

A quick breath, then he said, "Shit, no, Rob. I'm sorry. I just assumed it was you. She said you were meeting her at the station. Then she got that call and bolted. Borrowed Otto's car. I knew it was serious if she was willing to drive the jalopy. Plus, the cake was still in the oven. Literally. The producer was mighty pissed. We're already a week over schedule. He had her assistant finish the show. The crew's pretty worried. Is there anything —"

Cutting him short, I said, "I'm sure everything's fine, Scott," in a voice that couldn't have sold water to a man dying of thirst, then hung up.

My hands were shaking.

"You okay in here, boss lady?"

Jill Zimmerman was standing at my door. One good look at my face, and her smile fell apart. She slid into a chair and leaned forward. I told her about the day's events. When I was done, she reached over and pulled the collar of my shirt away from my neck.

She tsked a bit and asked, "Have you contacted the authorities?" Then, apparently remembering how I had gained access to Brian's apartment, she changed the question. "Any guesses about who it might have been?"

I shook my head.

"Okay," she said, as if she had everything under control. "We need to get to K.T.'s apartment. See if she packed clothes . . ." The half-beat of uncertainty was enough. Our eyes met and she frowned. "Do you think Lurlene's the one who called her?"

I pushed back from my desk, suddenly angry. "Who the hell knows? It's possible, isn't it?"

She moved closer. "Let me handle this. For now." Her hands quickly enveloped my face, stopping me from signaling no. "I'll call in chits, Rob, put a trace on her credit cards, check bank withdrawals, call airlines . . . the works. I promise you." I shook myself loose from her grasp. She stood up impatiently and nodded at the clock. "At least do this — it's nearly eight o'clock. You've only missed a half-hour of your tae kwon do lesson. Why don't you work some of this out down there? By the time you're done, I may have some answers."

I felt like slamming my fist through the cement-block wall. Jill was right. In my current state of mind, I wouldn't be of much use. Without another word, I gathered myself and headed down to the Women's Awareness Center on Ninth Street. Master Janet Choi looked startled as I scampered into line. She knew I had planned to spend the next two weeks on the Cape. Instinctively she pointed to me in a gesture that demanded I stand front and center. Her dark, perceptive eyes focused on the bruise on my neck, then narrowed as she barked, "What is the secret to mastering tae kwon do?"

I held her gaze. "Mastering the physical and mental forces. Control." The last word echoed in my ears. With increased vigor, I repeated, "Control."

Her nod was almost imperceptible. "You're late," she said quietly.

The muscle in my jaw jumped.

Choi spun around. "Rita!" She pointed to a spot behind me. "Step up and secure Robin with an arm choke . . ." I noted the smallest hesitation. "From the left side," she added. Choi had obviously noticed that the bruise was worse on the right. I felt my eyes begin to burn and immediately dismissed the tears.

Rita's arm clamped around my neck.

"Directions?" I whispered.

Choi rewarded me with a rare smile. "You know. But I'll tell you. Execute a stamp kick, shift hip, execute a knifehand strike, then an elbow strike. Yes?"

I had Rita down on the mat so fast, the class gasped. And still the anger pounded in my temples.

Choi tapped my shoulder.

"Again. This time, remember control. The movements are not enough." She pressed her palm against my belly. "Your heart must be still, your mind focused, or you will not be able to see the attacker. You will see only fear. Or hate. And then, *you* will fall."

I stopped home to shower and check for phone calls. There were no messages. I exited quietly to avoid alarming Beth and Dinah, and walked back to the office. Jill was hunched over the computer. Guilt took over.

"Hey."

She turned around, eyes bloodshot. Her grim look told me she had not made much progress.

I forced a smile. "I'm sure K.T.'s fine. Now, it's way past your bedtime —"

"It's only . . . shit. Is this right?" She shook her wrist, moved the watch to her ear.

"Yes, darling. It's nearly eleven. Now go home before that husband of yours comes down here with a baseball bat."

She shook her head. "No, it's okay. I called him. He understands. Matter of fact, he wants to help. Remember, John knew Brian, at least professionally."

Of course. John Feyre occasionally freelances for us.

She continued. "You know how my hubby loves to gossip. He's probably been on the phone the whole night."

"Then you better get home before he sends your NYNEX bill sky high. As you keep reminding me, we don't pay you enough."

She shrugged. But I knew she was beat. After a few more minutes of lame banter she agreed to leave. The first thing I did was straighten my office. Papers were filed, books shelved, the pencils sharpened. Then I sat down and arranged my notes on index cards.

The facts: Brian had been shot in the back on Sunday, at approximately one o'clock, in his darkroom. Either he had just performed intercourse with the murderer, or the murderer had caught him copulating with someone else. I put my pencil down.

Could there have been another person present? Brian had obviously set up the studio for a photography session. Maybe the model had shown up and witnessed something. A phone call, or the arrival of an unanticipated visitor. Or maybe a model had been involved in the murder. That could explain why the appointment page for Sunday had been torn out.

I couldn't ignore the fact that Lurlene's fingerprints covered the murder weapon. But why were Brian's prints missing? Common sense said the murderer must have wiped the gun clean before Lurlene stumbled upon it. The person who killed Brian had been clear-headed, quick and methodical.

Whoever it was, it wasn't Lurlene.

K.T. was safe. She had to be.

I opened my briefcase and withdrew the file I had removed from Brian Fritzl's office. What was his connection to Luce Lorelli? I pivoted the head of my desk light and held up a strip of negatives. At first I couldn't make out the image. And then I couldn't figure out how anyone had been able to get such a close-up without being detected. I was staring at a man's butt, a tattoo of a cardinal smack on the right cheek. The other frames showed two men in various stages of love-making. I reached for the phone.

"John?"

"Hold on, Robin. Jill just walked in. Hey, love chicken, it's the slave driver."

Love chicken?

"It's you I want, John. How quickly can you turn around a photograph?"

He laughed. "Need a passport photo, do you?"

I explained the circumstances. He offered to pick up the negatives in a few minutes. In the meantime I searched through the remainder of the file. There were copies of notes to and from Lorelli, invoices, a list of numbers I couldn't decipher and a safe deposit key. Etched on top was the number forty-eight.

You may be able to find a private operative who doesn't own a gun. I'm one. But try to find a P.I. who doesn't own one or more cameras and you're bound to be disappointed. Most of us have a personal contact who can be trusted to develop sensitive photographs and keep his or her trap shut, no matter how explosive the subject matter. John was mine. And it looked like Brian Fritzl had been Lorelli's.

John picked up the negatives and left.

I tried K.T.'s again, hung up angry and worried, and made myself a fresh pot of coffee. Maybe Brian had used some of Lorelli's photographs for his own purpose. Blackmailing was a classic motive for murder. I ravaged the refrigerator for a container of half-and-half that didn't smell like old socks. Reluctantly I realized I'd probably have to search Brian's apartment again.

Around midnight, the phone rang. John was fast. "So when's the grand showing?" I asked.

"Hello? Is this Robin Miller?" The voice was young, unfamiliar, and belonged to someone who had been downing a fair share of booze.

"Who is this?"

"Do you know a place called the Alamo?"

I was half-tempted to give the kid a history lesson, instead I said, "It's a Tex-Mex restaurant on Ninth Street. Why?"

"You're supposed to be there in fifteen minutes," she slurred.

"Why?"

Now she sounded annoyed. "I don't know. Just be there."

She hung up and I cautiously headed outside. The

streets were quiet and the air humid. A shiver tickled the small of my back. I edged down the street, waiting for an attack. Someone could be setting me up. I moved into the road, walking briskly along the driver's side of parked cars, glad I was wearing dark clothes. In the shadows cast by street lights, head rests loomed like heads, steering wheels armed with Le Clubs tricked the eye into seeing rifles. I jumped twice for no reason at all. Finally, I broke into a run, hoping to outpace my fears if not my anticipated attackers.

On Seventh Avenue, I weaved my way between the twenty-four-hour Korean grocery stores, grateful for their lights, the flow of late-night shoppers searching for aspirins, a bottle of Maalox or a pint of Haagen-Dazs. I made it to the Alamo in one piece and only one minute late. I scanned the interior before entering.

The restaurant was getting ready to close. The bartender was wiping down the counter with a rag that looked like it had been run over by a few thousand cars on the BQE. He eyed with distaste the two men in baseball caps who were nursing Heinekens and leaning on the bar railing as if they intended to stay there a long time. They may not have been anxious to go home, but the bartender clearly was.

I entered just as a phone rang inside the kitchen; the bartender ignored it and glanced over at me. The room stank of stale beer. There was only one way to endure it. I ordered a Corona, caught him rolling his eyes in obvious irritation, and then surveyed the room. The only other person around was a waitress with knobby knees. An old Tarzan movie played on the television set clamped to the far side of the bar. Knobby Knees was clearly entranced.

I pressed a wedge of lime into the bottle's neck and waited. The phone rang again, and this time the bartender and waitress exchanged antagonistic glances. Knobby Knees gave in and huffed her way into the kitchen. A second later she exited with a cordless phone in her hand. "Anyone here named Robin?" she shouted as if there were more than three people in the bar. I stood up. She said, "Yeah," into the phone and then handed it to me with a look that said, "Get off fast, or your ass is grass." I love Brooklyn. We specialize in snide.

I grabbed the phone and tucked myself into the corner between the stairs and the jukebox. "Hello, this is Robin."

"Honey, it's me."

All the anger I had been suppressing exploded. I turned toward the stairs and growled, "Where the hell are you?"

I knew she was crying, but at the moment I didn't care.

"The Pied Piper."

I felt my jaw go slack. The bitch was in Provincetown. And suddenly I knew why.

"You took Lurlene to the cottage, didn't you? Goddamn it!"

"I didn't know where else to go. You have to —"

"Tell me I have to understand, and I'll sic the damn NYPD on you so fast, your pretty little head will spin." My voice had picked up a notch and without turning around, I could feel the eyes on my back. I took a deep breath and tried to focus. "Tell me what happened."

"Lurlene called me at the studio. From Newark. She was planning to leave the country. I told her the cops would probably grab her the second she bought a ticket. She went hysterical on me, Robin. What could I do? I had to make a decision fast. I knew the cops would be contacting me again soon. If I wanted to help her, it was then or never. And then I remembered the cottage. You rented it for three weeks under a phony name. Paid for it in cash. It was perfect."

"Perfect," I reiterated, biting down on the word with a sneer. "Do you realize what you're doing? You're getting deeper into this shit than you need to. What you're doing is called harboring a fugitive. And if Lurlene is guilty —"

"She's not, for Christ's sake. Say that one more time and I swear I'll never see you again."

My skin went cold. I said, "So glad to hear how committed you are to me."

There was a shushing sound on the other end. "I didn't mean it that way and you know it."

"Right. And by the way, have you considered the fact that you're jeopardizing my career?"

"What career? You mean this cops and robbers game you play for some reason you don't even understand? You're a writer, Robin. You could make a fortune writing romances. You *did* make a fortune. What I'm talking about is Lurlene's entire life."

I fought the temptation to hang up. "Put Lurlene on the phone."

Silence, then she said, "She won't talk to you."

Great. I went to hit the off button. "Robin!" K.T. was shouting over the phone lines.

"Thought I'd go home and go to bed. Any objections?"

"Not fair, Robin," K.T. said in that quiet tone of hers that makes my throat constrict. "I'm sorry for what I said, but these are unusual circumstances. None of us is acting rationally."

"Correction. I am, K.T. Now, I'm giving you and your good buddy a choice. Either she gets on the phone in the next five seconds or I turn her over. And, God help me, I mean it." I crossed my fingers and hoped she was scared enough to fall for my bluff.

For a moment I thought she had disconnected the line, then Lurlene came on. "Congratulations. I think you just put your lover over the line. She's in the bathroom sobbing her heart out."

If Lurlene had been standing in front of me, I would have decked her. I took a swig from the beer bottle still clenched in my fist and said, "You're welcome. Now how about helping me clear your ass?"

"What do you want, Robin?"

I quickly told her about my interview with Tzionah, the darkroom attack, and the file on Luce Lorelli.

"K.T. and I were on the road by six-thirty. Are you trying to accuse me of the attack on you?"

I squeezed the neck of the Corona. "You know, you're more of an asshole than I thought you were. I'm trying to help you, goddamn it." Behind me someone turned up the volume on the television. I waited until Tarzan had stopped yodeling. "Do you know if Brian had any appointments scheduled last Sunday?"

"Of course I do. I was his damn assistant. Hold on. I have my book with me. Brian loved to schedule appointments on Sunday. It was his way of thumbing a finger at religion. Okay, here it is . . . he had an early breakfast with Zoogie Cocchiaro and a shoot scheduled for ten with Tara Parker, but she wasn't sure she could make it. I don't know Parker. She's a newcomer. Probably one of his sweet nineteens. Who knows? Maybe she was my replacement."

I shook my head in disbelief. "Did you give these names to the police?"

"No. Why should I? Besides, no one, including you, bothered to ask. Does this mean you may be considering other suspects?"

I overlooked the sarcasm. "Could Brian have been blackmailing anyone?"

"Blackmailing? Oh, you mean the work for Luce? I doubt it. Brian and Luce had a relationship that went back years. She took the photos, Brian did the developing. He usually turned the negatives over as soon as he got paid. Most times, the exchange was so fast I never got a look."

I glanced at the clock on the wall, wondered if John had the prints ready for me yet, and said, "I found a safe deposit box key. Know anything about that?"

"No," she said curtly.

"What about his wife? Could she have a motive?"

"Kathleen? Who knows? I only met her twice, and each time was a disaster." She snapped at someone urging her off the phone, then said, "He hardly talked about her. But the kids, he wouldn't shut up about the kids. Belinda's fifteen, Chad's seventeen, but they seem younger. Personally, I think they're both in need of serious help. In any case, I know Brian and Kathleen fought about the kids, that's about it."

"Could she have killed —"

"Why the hell not? If the cops can suspect me, why not her? Sure. Why don't you sniff her out, Sherlock. Knock yourself out."

If only K.T. could once hear the uncensored Lurlene . . .

"Look," she continued, "I want to make sure K.T.'s okay. Is there anything else you need from me?"

I wanted to shake her up. "How do you account for the fact that Tzionah says she saw you leaving around one, an hour earlier than your estimated arrival time?"

I heard a gurgling sound, then she said, "The detective wants an accounting." For the first time I realized she sounded drunk. "Okay. Here's an accounting. Tzionah's near-sighted. She can discern the smallest variation in color on a piece of pottery as long as it's no more than three feet from the tip of her nose. Turn on the television across the room, though, and the lady has to lunge for her glasses. Besides, it was raining Sunday."

"What does that have to do with anything?"

"When I left there, my hood was up. So how'd she see me so clearly?"

The waitress gingerly tapped me on the shoulder. "We're closing," she said warily, as if afraid I might snap at her. She was right to worry.

"In a second," I muttered, then returned to Lurlene. "Do you know where Charon Centauri is now?"

She grunted. "It's amazing you make money doing this. She's in New Orleans. Far from you. Now may I be dismissed?"

Her cockiness egged me on. "One last question. Did you happen to turn Brian's body over when you found him?"

Her voice quavered slightly when she said no.

"His fly was open, Lurlene. Apparently, he was engaged in or about to be engaged in intercourse when the bullet hit."

There was a click on the other end. I finished my beer in a single gulp, tipped the nasty crew a five, and slogged back to the office. I found Jill and John lurking in the hallway. They were a striking couple, especially right then, with their dark wavy haircuts, black shirts and bloodshot eyes. Jill slapped me lightly on the side of the head. It was her way of saying she loved me. "Can't you leave a message or something? Jeez, you're as bad as your girlfriend."

I explained quickly before she could smack me again.

John pointed at Jill ominously, "You ever pull that shit on me —"

Jill punched him in the belly. "Oh, shut up, for heaven's sake. This is not about us."

I laughed. "John, now I understand why you say the woman's got to have her seven hours of zee's or she's hell on wheels."

The mood in the room lightened a bit and John handed me the first print. "Recognize either of them?" he asked with a mischievous gleam.

I shook my head. "The heavier guy looks familiar, but —"

He cut me off and stabbed at the face of one of the men. "That's Arnold Grau. The right-winger running for a Senate seat down in Louisiana. And that," he said, moving his finger to the man whose face was partially obscured by a prominent feature of Grau's otherwise flaccid anatomy, "that, my dear, is none other than Darby Stevens."

"The fashion designer?"

"And gay activist. You get a closer look at his face in the next shot. So close you can almost see the flakes of that damn faux-tan make-up he insists on wearing." He passed me the remaining photographs. "What you have in your hands would be worth a mint to either man. Matter of fact, I know of a couple of tabloids that would be happy to take them off your hands for a sum that would curl your toes."

"Thanks for spelling out my options."

I stared at the photos. What I saw was two men making love, smooth bodies entangled, muscles delineated by the force of passion, faces contorted in a primal delirium not meant for impartial scrutiny. Had Brian looked at these stolen images and envisioned profit? And had that imperfect vision ended with a bullet exploding in his back?

Chapter 5

Six months ago I convinced Tony we could afford to expand and remodel our offices. My motive was purely selfish. I wanted an office bigger than a woodshed. The one-bedroom co-op abutting our space had been on the market for almost a year. We bought it, hired an architect, and broke down a few walls. The first thing I did after the remodeling concluded was to buy a six-foot-long, forest green couch with a wealth of mushy throw pillows.

When Wednesday morning dawned, that's where I was, nestled into the cushions, my notes draping my hip like a cat. Tony woke me by banging a spoon against my Emily Dickinson mug.

"You're an ugly sight in the morning, Miller. Go home, please. And brush your teeth."

I bolted upright and blinked. My eyes weren't focusing right. I kept seeing chartreuse lines on a brick-red field. After a second or two, I guffawed. "Talk about ugly, Tony. Gee whiz, Mr. Palmer, are those ugly plaid things golfing pants?"

"You're so sharp, Pee-Wee." He hiked up his right leg and rested his foot on the arm of the couch, knowing it would rile me. His socks matched the pants. I averted my eyes. "Someone's got to keep our client base growing. I've got an appointment with the CEO of Gemini, the biotech company profiled in *Fortune* last week. Remember?"

I nodded even though I read the magazine about as often as I read the Bible.

Tony continued. "Pipitone's right-hand man may be dipping into company funds for a few extra perks, like a personal helicopter. Just my cup of joe."

As if on cue, the scent of fresh-brewed coffee wafted into the room. I left my partner behind and followed my nose into the galley kitchen.

"Whoa!" The shout came from my office. I poured a mugful, then perched on the counter to await the inevitable.

" 'They meet with darkness in the daytime and grope in the noonday as in the night.' Job, five, fourteen." Tony's voice had an amused edge.

Soon after being diagnosed with HIV, Tony assumed the annoying habit of quoting scripture *ad nauseam*. At first, the practice appeared to truly comfort him. Lately, though, I've had the impression that it's more a form of public torture. He strode over, eyes glued to the photographs clenched in his sausage-sized fingers.

I sniffed the coffee and said, "I'm thinking of blowing them up and displaying them in the vestibule, you know, dress up the place a bit. What do you think?"

"I think I'm holding pure dynamite. Where'd you dig this up?"

I told him and his eyebrows arched. "Partner, you just may have kicked your friend Lurlene off the hook. Tell you what, I'll personally go and see the detectives on the case . . . just slap these down on one of those steel-crap desks and smile real pretty. Man, it'd be fun to see them salivating all over themselves. We're talking Eye Witness News, special bulletins breaking into soap operas. Prime time TV specials. Christ. Court TV will be knocking down the door."

I snatched the photos from his hand. "Sorry to burst your flashbulbs, bud, but I don't think you and I are on the same planet right now. These," I said, waving the pictures under his nose, "may very well take some of the heat off Lurlene. But I'm not ready to destroy Darby Stevens, who may be guilty of nothing more than bad taste in choosing partners."

Tony's right eye twitched. The barb was subtle; nevertheless the point appeared to prick his conscience.

When Tony's partner on the force learned about his HIV status, he complained so long and so loud the news ended up on the desk of the Chief of Detectives. Soon after, Tony was strong-armed into an early retirement. Opening SIA was his revenge. That's where I came in. With AIDS phobia being one of the most highly infectious diseases around, a lesbian ex-romance-writer with a surfeit of funds was the best partner he could scrounge up. As much as I hate to admit it, our alliance has worked out a hell of a lot better than either one of us ever expected.

He picked up a packet of Sweet'NLow and slapped it against his palm. "Okay, fine. But let me handle this end of the investigation. I'd love to stick it to that asshole down in Louisiana."

His vehemence didn't surprise me. The last time Arnold Grau ran for the Senate, one of his television ads featured inflammatory scenes from a gay rights march, including a shot of two men necking. Both flaunted the latest in haute fairy-wear, complete with jeweled wands, sequined boleros, and tinfoil wings. The voiceover ran something like, "These are the faces of AIDS. They didn't ask for help before choosing their lifestyles. Now they want to know why America isn't willing to spend tax dollars to help them now." The visuals shifted to scenes of Grau visiting children at a Baton Rouge pediatric hospital scheduled for closure. "Arnold Grau. He'll fight for your future. And the future of your children." The ads ran exactly four days before being yanked off the air. Despite the uproar, Grau lost the election by an alarmingly slim margin. This time around his campaign was less strident but equally noisome. Yet the latest polls had him way out in front.

I took another look at the photograph in which Grau's face angled toward the camera. Tony and I are both control freaks of the highest order. A long time ago we decided to avoid pooling our energies on a single case. I was about to protest his involvement in this one, but the gleam in his eyes and the sudden color in his cheeks made me back off.

We agreed on a plan of action, then reviewed the assignments we had doled out to our small stable of freelance agents. An hour later, I swept back into my office and zeroed in on my active assignment file. I owed Abigail Whitman an update about Julie Reed. She answered groggily. From the quickly muffled conversation on the other end, I gathered she was still in bed. And not alone.

"Nursing old wounds?" I quipped, then winced.

Abigail made a sloppy sucking noise and I pictured her drawing deep on a cigarette, her skeletal fingers clenching it like a joint. She ignored my teasing comment and asked brusquely, "Any progress?" Her voice had the raspy quality that comes from a lifetime of heavy smoking.

Right then it struck me that I'd choose Julie Reed's company over Abigail Whitman's any day of the week. Or time of the night. But it was Whitman whose three-thousand-dollar check topped my in-box.

"Well, we found her," I said. "She's in Provincetown, performing under the name Julie Rush —"

"Fantastic!" She whispered something to the unnamed bed partner, then said, "Finally. When do I start collecting?"

I rolled my eyes. "Not so fast. We explained all that when you first approached. Civil suits —"

"Yeah, yeah, civil suits are hard to collect on. Only ten percent of all claimants collect, blah, blah, blah." Her voice went soft all of a sudden, like an unexpected bruise spot on a firm apple. "I need that money, Robin."

I sat up straight and ran a hand through my hair. Tony was right. I needed a shower. "Abigail, there's no guarantee you'll be able to recover a dime. You know that. By now, Julie could have blown the whole wad. But at least we finally have a name and a location, so we can start checking bank accounts, vehicle registrations. You're just going to have to be patient a little longer."

"Hold on . . ." Rustling sounds, then the clink of glass. "Darlin', I gotta tell you I'm getting a little desperate here. Aphrodite's isn't drawing the same crowds any more. I barely made last month's payroll. Of course, paying you guys didn't help matters. Then, two nights ago, my bartender quit. After all these years, I'm back behind the bar pouring drinks. When I tell you I need the money, I'm not kidding."

Abigail had been sober a little over sixteen months. For her, mixing drinks had to be like negotiating through a mine field. I promised to do my best, then hung up.

Jill arrived a few minutes later. I dragged myself across the hall. She glanced up and grimaced. "Christ. You look like shit."

I work with such kind, soft-spoken individuals. "Thanks, love chicken," I said sarcastically. "I just got off the phone with Whitman. The lady's getting testy."

Her eyes brightened. "The only one who uses my pet name is sugar poop, so watch it, Miller."

"John's nickname is sugar poop? God, I hope K.T. never loves me that much —" I stopped myself, felt my eyes fill. Shifting gears like Andretti, I said, "Update me on Julie."

She cloaked the sudden seriousness in her eyes and gestured at the computer screen. "I can't move much faster. I picked up the search first thing this morning. Still nothing. No records at the DMV, so as far as I know the BMW's evaporated into thin air. I called the county assessor's office. No real property registered to Julie Ryan, Reed, or Rush. I did manage to locate a bank account for a Judith Ruppert in P-town. The account opened the day after Julie skipped New York, so maybe that's another alias. If it is and she's stashed the money there, all we need is to get the writ of attachment to the bank, but I doubt it'll be that easy."

She spun her chair around and faced me again, her expression so earnest I backed away. "Forget this for now," she said quietly. "Have you heard from K.T. since last night?"

"No." I hoped my tone would dissuade her from continuing. No chance.

"You do know that this has nothing to do with your relationship, right?"

I shot her a warning look and retreated to the door. "I'm going home to shower. I'll be there an hour or so. If you find anything before then, give me a call."

Outside, the air surprised me. Late June, yet a cool breeze swept the streets that smelled sweet and earthy. If I could have closed my eyes and ignored the car horns blaring, the hiss of traffic, and the clinkety-clank of rollerbladers scraping over concrete, I might have imagined myself in the country. I paused for a moment, just long enough for a bus to spit a cloud of exhaust in my direction. Coughing, I detoured down one block and walked home along Prospect Park West. Maybe it was the job or maybe just the city cacophony, but I felt downright edgy.

A woman with cheeks so brightly rouged they beamed from her pale face like brake lights headed toward me, her hands outstretched. I gritted my teeth, retrieved change from my pants pocket and dropped it into her palm before she could weave me into yet another tale of sorrow in a city with too many, then I broke into a trot. I wanted to be home.

The phone was ringing when I swung open the door. I scooped it from the hook, noting that my stomach had managed a quarter-turn.

"You're not an easy woman to track down."

I couldn't place the voice.

"Julie Rush," she said, obviously sensing my hesitation.

"Hey," I said as if I had fully expected her call.

She laughed. "Oh, we are cool, aren't we? You must be a better heartbreaker than my ex. We had a date, or don't you remember?"

How could I have forgotten such a voice, so breezy, sexy and full of fire? I perched on a stool and sighed, a smile settling on my face. "I had business to attend to. Sorry. Maybe we can reschedule."

"I bet you had business. And a pretty, red-headed business she is."

The smirk evaporated from my face. K.T. She knew about K.T. I tried to sound unruffled. "Riddles so early in the morning. Talk about being unkind."

"Talk about K.T." Her tone had shifted slightly, bore a hint of challenge. And something else. Excitement.

I bit a cuticle nervously, then said, "I never said I was unattached."

"No. That's true. But the implications, my dear. Oh, the implications."

I felt myself blush and resented the response.

"I met your friend last night," she said lightly. I could barely hear her over the thump of my heart. "I'm off Mondays and Tuesdays and I met a . . . let's say a fan . . . at the Pied for a few drinks. Tell the truth, I was hoping to find you there. In only minutes this nouveau, pretty-faced dyke had me yawning so hard my eyes teared. So I excused myself and locked myself into a bathroom stall, hoping she'd get the message and disappear by the time I emerged. Imagine my surprise when all of a sudden the outside door bursts open and this woman runs in crying. I peek out and see this copper-haired fox with fine, fine legs hunched over the sink, hyperventilating. Well, you weren't around and she was, and I was intrigued. I zipped up, readied myself for the rescue when another woman had the gall to storm in. I pressed myself back into the stall and decided to eavesdrop. Seems your girlfriend's convinced you two are heading into splitsville, fast."

Her silence felt assaultive. I couldn't think fast enough. And I couldn't swallow.

"Not so glib now, are we?" she asked.

Suddenly I didn't care if I blew Whitman's case or not. I had to find out what K.T. had said. I asked her and she harrumphed, a little aborted laugh that told me she was in control and knew it.

"Here's what I know. You disappointed her. Let her down when she needed you. You don't understand her. You resent her relationship with Lurlene. What else? Oh, yes, she wants to have a child and you're not ready for that kind of commitment. How did she put it? Robin Miller raise a child? 'When hog meat don't attract flies.' I take it she's not from New York?"

My eyes widened. Raise a child? What the hell?

"The woman was fairly hysterical, understand. I had the sense the dam had just burst, you know what I mean? She was all over the place. The worst part was that her friend kept spewing Hallmark cardisms at her. Are they lovers, Robin? I couldn't tell."

"No." I wanted to scream. Instead I kicked the cat's water bowl across the floor.

"Someone else came in to pee around then, so they quieted down. Still, I heard enough to realize who she was. Given our encounter on Sunday, I'm assuming you're not particularly despondent over this relationship's demise. So, to answer your earlier question, yes, I am willing to reschedule our date. When are you getting back up here?"

By then I was leaning over the sink, ready to upchuck. "I don't know, Julie. Soon. Soon. Can I call you back?" I took down her number, my hand trembling as I jotted down each digit.

In her silence I could hear a bell buoy clang.

"Is it foggy there?" I asked inanely, a heavy numbness stealing over my limbs.

She hesitated, then said, "Yes . . . God, Robin. Did I misread this whole thing? You sound really upset."

Upset? Nah. Not Robin Miller.

"No problem, Julie. Just surprised, that's all. I'll call you."

"Sure. I'm cool," she said, sounding anything but. "I want you to know I wouldn't have gone to the trouble of tracking you down if I'd thought you were serious about her. The impression I got —"

"Julie."

"Right. You'll call."

She hung up. I shuffled into the shower and let the hot water knife my shoulders until the heat turned into pain, then I gritted my teeth and waited until the pain changed again. Soon I felt nothing.

"Coffee?" The fluty voice drifted in from the kitchen.

I closed the photo album. "Wha — oh, no thanks. I've had more than the recommended daily dosage already."

I was in Kathleen Fritzl's apartment, just five blocks away from Brian's condo. Still somewhat shaken from my earlier conversation with Julie, I was struggling for the right interrogative approach.

Kathleen's appearance had surprised me. The woman had not aged well since the time of the photograph in Brian's bedroom. She was too thin, reedy rather than willowy, and her face was gaunt. Dark brown hair in a high-fashion blunt cut, gap-toothed smile. Her best feature was her bright saucer-shaped eyes, accented by pale blue eye shadow and a trace of mascara. The deep commas marking the corners of her mouth told me the woman had to be a frequent smiler. But you wouldn't guess it from the strained, remote expression she carried now.

She reentered the room carrying a plate of cookies. "No fat. Fruit sweetened," she said politely, as if I worried about such things.

I refrained from requesting Oreos, with fat and sugar, please, and thanked her for agreeing to see me.

"You piqued my interest. I have to confess I contacted Detective Chinnici after our first phone call. He advised against this meeting. Obviously, I ignored him."

Chinnici was in charge of the investigation. Tony had warned me about his distaste for private operatives. When I called Kathleen earlier I had offered up as much of the truth as I could spare. I wanted to make sure she'd see me even if Chinnici told her to blow me off. It seemed the tactic had worked.

"You were very forthcoming on the phone. I appreciate that, as much as I appreciate the plight of your client." She selected a cookie carefully, took a bite, inhaling slightly as she chewed. She was a crumbless eater. Instantly I distrusted her.

"Your children are very attractive," I said, referring to the photo album she had thrust at me soon after my arrival.

"You want to know why I showed that to you."

I nodded.

"To answer your as-yet-unasked questions. Brian and I never divorced because we still shared a common obsession. Our children." She shifted back into the wing chair. Audrey Hepburn, I thought all at once. A far less attractive version, sure, but the ilk was one and the same. Cultured, studied. Slightly affected, yet undeniably gracious. Her home was modestly decorated, Shaker simplicity. Neat and precise as a starched doily. Kathleen had money. So much money she could afford to be understated.

"Do the children inherit?"

Her eyebrows knitted together. "Do you know who I am?"

"Do I —"

"Kathleen Wallace-Fritzl." She waited. I felt dumb. "Sorry, I guess that's a sign of vanity, supposing everyone has heard of you. Quite humbling, actually, to remember all this —" She waved her hand. "All this amounts to so little, doesn't it?"

She retrieved a second cookie, emitted a single crumb. I started to like her a little more.

"Most of my photography, unlike Brian's, is considered art. I know how that sounds, but I'm not communicating anything you wouldn't find in a critical summation of our works."

I glanced around, knew then what had been troubling me since I arrived. The walls were largely blank. No photographs, no artwork, nothing more than a few light switches and a cherry-toned bookshelf that displayed esoteric art and philosophy books. The only human touch were the athletic and academic trophies won by her son and daughter. She watched my gaze and grinned slightly.

"We're a family of achievers."

"How come your photographs aren't showcased?"

"The way Brian does? I don't need such an ostentatious display in my home. My photographs are in galleries. I specialize in landscape photography . . . you might even recognize some of them, if I had them here to show you. I'm afraid prints of my Cape Cod series have even appeared in those ubiquitous poster shops that have the audacity to call themselves galleries. But we're not here to discuss that, are we? You're trying to exonerate your client. Understandably, you probably suspect me and half of New York City. Anyone but this woman Brian was seeing."

"Did you know Lurlene?"

"We met. Three rather inauspicious occasions. Once in a restaurant, another time at the Whitney, and then again at Chad's private school. Brian and I had scrambled our schedules. But if your point is, was I aware of their sexual relationship, the answer is yes. I knew of her, the way I knew of the others. Including that choleric neighbor of his."

"Tzionah?"

"Yes." She wore a simple peach silk blouse. Now she unbuttoned the cuffs and meticulously folded them twice.

"Did the affairs disturb you?"

Her head turned to the left. The profile struck me as being at once aristocratic and turkey-like. I kept the observation to myself.

"The affairs, as you call them, started even before our marriage. It was a condition of our relationship that I accepted from the first." She stood up, ambled behind the couch on which I perched. "He was charismatic, and I was a plain-Jane with too much money and talent to attract any men I could trust. On our first date Brian told me right off that he did not believe monogamy to be a natural state. Although he could be monogamous for long stretches of time, he would never forgo what he perceived as being his innate right to sleep with whomever he chose, whenever he chose. His honesty was refreshing. And the sex was superb. So I accepted his terms. He was an attentive lover, and it was satisfying to be with a man not intimidated by my skills."

Her tone betrayed no hint of resentment, nor dislike. I shifted around, saw her idly dusting with her palm a mantle that held no dust. As if sensing my gaze, she turned and shrugged. "Not many women understand. I will say this for that potter woman. She wanted Brian on her terms, and only her terms. When he refused, she closed the door, so to speak."

She stepped toward a Sony rack system. "Do you mind?" I said no and she dropped a CD in. A second later, Moussorgsky's "Pictures at an Exhibition" boomed into the air. I watched Kathleen hug herself, her eyes brimming, a bitter smile curling her lips. "Our song," she enunciated. "Very romantic, in a unique way."

She returned to the wing chair. "The second reason we never divorced," she said simply, "was that we still loved each other. Quite strongly. Brian preferred to tell other women I was the beast who barred his way to a second, happier marriage. The truth was I was a convenient excuse. We rarely slept together anymore, but ask any of his lovers where he spent the holidays. Always with me and the children. Always." Her chin jutted proudly. "Did Tzionah tell you Brian complained of how rarely he saw Lindy and Chad? Of course she did. How else could he have explained the frequency of his visits here and to our home in Truro? Sometimes I suspected Brian used up his entire allocation of honesty during our courting years."

The thought seemed to please her. I asked, "Do you believe Lurlene murdered your husband?"

She pushed the cookie plate toward me. I relented and tried one. It tasted like a no fat, sugar-free cookie. A fine hockey puck.

Kathleen steepled her hands and said, "I'm afraid I do. She never seemed stable to me. Brian told me she had suffered some kind of sexual abuse as a child. A terrible, terrible lot for any woman, and one that scars deeply. She was erratic, moody, manipulative. I know that after the first few times Brian felt uncomfortable about her seeing Lindy and Chad." She puckered her lips, looked pensive. "In truth, she seemed jealous of the attention he showered on them, actually became rather vindictive on one occasion that I know of personally. Told Brian that we babied the children. Tried to convince him that there was a limit on how much a parent should sacrifice for a child. That said a lot to me. For both of us the children's welfare comes first."

I couldn't argue with her description of Lurlene. And the fact that she knew so much about Lurlene bespoke an intimacy between her and Brian I hadn't known existed.

She stroked her neck and said, "I'm sure a jury would take into account her history —"

"It won't get that far."

Her lips twitched, as if she disapproved of my manners.

I changed the subject. "Do you know who inherits Brian's estate?"

"Yes. Of course. Our children are already well cared for financially. My parents saw to that. And I certainly have no need of additional funds. I should also explain that Brian's estate, as you call it, is hardly a fortune. Last time we discussed such matters, I believe the grand sum, including his photographic equipment, came to less than a quarter million."

I didn't bother to inform Kathleen that people in this country had been killed for leather jackets, never mind a quarter-million dollars.

"Who inherits?" I asked as a violent crescendo of strings sliced through the air.

Kathleen rose up, sailed toward the stereo and lowered the volume. "Brian had a close friend die from AIDS, so ten percent or so goes to GMHC. Another portion, I think twenty percent, goes to his niece. She just turned seven, so I doubt she's involved. The remainder goes to Tzionah."

I felt myself rubberneck at her from across the room.

"Tzionah Stein?"

"That surprises you? I suppose the police might react similarly. Frankly, the thought hadn't crossed my mind until you asked." She fingered her temple as if a headache were coming on. Or maybe I was just projecting. "It's because of the child."

"The child?"

She frowned. "She didn't tell you? Well, I guess I'm not surprised. In some ways, it's to her credit that she's ashamed."

Tzionah hadn't struck me as the type to be ashamed of much, especially not of giving birth to a child out of wedlock. I told Kathleen the same.

She rolled her eyes. "Of course not. It's the nineties, for heaven's sake. Married, single, gay, or rock star — having a child is all the rage. No. I'm talking about hospitalizing the child. Lurlene wanted Brian and I to do the same with Chad." Her lips tightened till they were pale slashes. "My son's extremely sensitive and a bit high strung. Lurlene acted like that was a crime. The reality is, the woman could never understand the artistic sensibility. My son's a talented poet, a mimic, a songwriter. Like many teenagers he has a tendency to get morbid."

She crossed her arms and paused, a dare in her voice only a fool would have ignored. When I didn't comment, she continued. "Their baby was born with a host of problems, not the least of which was respiratory distress syndrome. The brain damage was severe. Still, the doctors expected him to live at least into his teens. Apparently that wasn't sufficient for Tzionah Stein. I suppose for some people a child must live a fixed number of years before he or she is worth the effort of rearing them."

My head was swimming. "You don't have to answer this, but I have to ask. Where were you when Brian was murdered?"

She blinked. "In Truro. The police summoned me home. I'll be returning there in a day or two with Brian's ashes." Her neck muscles constricted and she looked away. After a moment, she continued. "His papers specified that I rent a sailboat with the children, sail out till we discover a whale . . . a great pastime of ours . . . and then scatter his ashes. If there's no whale, we're to repeat the trip every day until one materializes. Lindy and Chad are staying with neighbors for now. Anna Parulski and Stephen Alsace. Feel free to call them, if you must." She gave me the number. "We were barbecuing when the news came."

"You left the children with neighbors?"

Her expression turned colder. "Anna and Step are

very capable, and Brian's murder has been hard enough on the children without dragging them into this dark Gotham." She clutched her stomach and shook her head, eyes suddenly wide. "Are we done? I'm afraid I've given you as much information as I can for now. I hope for your sake that Lurlene's innocent, or the court system lenient. As for me, I just want to return home to my children and get away from this God-awful city."

I left her swaying to Moussorgsky. As soon as I was outside, I made a beeline for the nearest pay phone. Anna Parulski picked up right away. She confirmed Kathleen's story, provided a fine mix of detail and divergence that convinced me her alibi was probably solid. The next phone call went to Tzionah. Her answering machine informed me that she would be out of town for the next several days.

To paraphrase Alice, things were getting curiouser and curiouser.

Chapter 6

Apple blossoms carpeted the backyard. In the early morning light, the moist air reflected a pale pink and smelled almost candied. I spun in place, creating an eddy on which the blush leaves swirled, and kicked out from the hip. Again I pivoted, this time kicking in the opposite direction, my palm slicing out at a right angle. The shouts lay buried in my throat. It was five in the morning, and I had crept into the backyard via the basement outlet. Beth, Dinah and Carol were no doubt still in sweet domestic slumber. But I was battling with myself, had been for hours.

Now sweat beaded on my forehead, even though the touch of cool air minutes earlier had raised goosebumps along my arms. I liked the efficient snap of my limbs as I ran through my routines, the way it shut out thoughts, memories, like the ones my damn therapist insists on probing with the zeal of a Nazi scientist.

Anyway, it was my own fault. When I returned home yesterday afternoon, nothing went right. K.T. wasn't at the cottage, hadn't called in, and apparently had written me off. Jill had turned up zilch on Julie Rush, and the bull's eye painted dead center on Lurlene's butt hadn't budged a millimeter. Around dinner time, I realized it was Wednesday night. Therapy night. I had canceled my remaining June appointments prior to leaving for P-town; nevertheless Vivian Mauer squeezed me in. Right away, before I could tell her about my case and its impact on my relationship with K.T., she started in on my mother.

Stamp kick, knifehand strike. Yaaah! I let out an unintended howl and glanced guiltily toward the ground-floor windows. No movement inside. I switched to jumping jacks, focused on breathing, but then something distracted me. Sparrows flitted around the bird feeder hooked onto the rear fence. I stopped and watched them, and that's all it took. I broke.

My mother was diagnosed a few months ago as having lymphoma. I got the news from my brother, Ronald. The prognosis was three to five years, if the chemo worked. Ron and Barbara, my sensible CPA older sister with bad taste in men and an aberrant punk haircut, immediately flew down to Florida to see her. They're the good children. Me, I stayed home and continued the pretense that life had set in motion almost exactly thirty years ago: poor Robin, faux orphan.

To say the relationship with my parents was never great is a gross understatement. After my sister Carol died — "at my hand," as my family never let me forget — my father stopped talking to me and my mother entered a blank-eyed twilight zone. Unlike my father, however, she acknowledged me, the way she would have any stranger who happened to reside in her home and depend on her for sustenance for a decade or so. The unspoken and unrelenting rules were: never mention Carol's name, never address Daddy, never cry, and for heaven's sake, don't make loud noises. We also had to downplay the fact we were Jewish. (Shhh. Daddy wants to forget the holocaust.)

My insomnia commenced a month after Carol's death.

When I turned eighteen, my parents packed up Ronald and moved to Miami. I stayed behind with Barbara. Ron had a brief but lucrative career as a burglar and hold-up expert, then moved back to New York — Staten Island, to be exact — wed an innocuous woman, had a seemly number of babies and became a locksmith. He could have stayed a crook, though, and my folks still would have adored him. After all, he never knew Carol, hadn't even been conceived until after she was dead and buried. In our family's mythology, that made sweet Ronnie a Perpetual Innocent. I hated the son-of-a-bitch until just a few years ago.

I made the obligatory, hypocritical annual trip to see my parents up until my father passed away in 1985. Oddly, the contact between my mother and me became even more sporadic afterward, as if she no longer felt compelled to compensate for his toxic silence and could finally drift into her own uncommunicative renouncement. So when I got the news about her, I didn't know how to react. After all, I had been motherless for so long that her impending death seemed somewhat anticlimactic. At first.

Then Vivian started dissecting dreams, ordering me to uncross my arms and legs as I sat opposite her, reminding me to breathe when I somehow managed to momentarily forgo that particular bodily function. At some point it hit me. My father, remote even at the moment he died, was gone forever. I couldn't yell at him anymore or shoot him withering looks when I arrived in Miami wearing my dykiest clothes and scuffed combat boots. An earthquake had destroyed the road between us long ago, and it was far too late to ever find my way home.

Next Monday my mother was coming to New York to start a second round of treatments at Mount Sinai. The timing was worse than lousy. In little over a week, July 4th would be here. The anniversary of Carol's death. A real red-letter day in my personal calendar.

Therapy had ended with me biting a fingernail down so far it hurt. No answers. No cathartic sobs. No pat, pat on the back or a there, there. Just a hell of a lot of questions and more pain than my body wanted to bear. I came home, made the mistake of knocking on my housemates' door, and entered their living room. Gershwin's "Someone to Watch Over Me" was playing in the background while Beth sat in a rocking chair, holding tiny baby Carol — my dead sister's namesake — against her chest. Dinah stood behind her, massaging her shoulders. I lasted half a minute.

Now I watched the birds peck at the feeder, sat down on the hard, splintery deck and cried. I'd like to say it helped, but I'd be lying and I try to save my lies for my professional life.

I waited for the beep. "Hey Luce, this is Robin Miller again. If you ever visit earth again, I'd appreciate a call back." This was my third message. Luce Lorelli, the detective who had worked with Brian Fritzl, was pretty damn reliable so I was surprised she hadn't returned any of my calls. I hung up, turned up the brightness on my home computer and retrieved my case file. Mallomar, my chubby blue-eyed calico, took that as an invitation. She leapt onto my lap, pawed me insistently, then graciously offered me her belly. How could I resist?

Five minutes later, I was still serving time as a cat vassal when the phone rang. It was Jill. "Did you forget about us, oh great one?"

"You, never. Tony, I don't know."

She laughed, a good hearty sound as soothing to me as white food. Vanilla ice cream. Pot cheese and noodles. Sour cream on potatoes.

"Hey, are you listening to me?" she shouted into my ear.

"Yeah," I said, dropping Mallomar off on my way

down to the kitchen. "I just remembered that I skipped dinner last night. What do you think about bacon and baked potatoes for breakfast?" I put down the cordless and switched to the kitchen phone in time for Jill's response.

"For you, not bad. I'd expect Twinkies and a Yoo-Hoo."

Oh, the power of suggestion. I went for the Twinkies double-time and asked, "What do you have for me?"

"On which case? You have a choice."

I surprised myself by saying, "Julie first."

The hesitation on the other end told me Jill was equally surprised. "No problem," she said, a little warily. "I did a fine bit of detecting this morning. Remember how our initial skiptrace deadended in Chicago? Well, I went back and ran another trace using 'Judith Ruppert,' the name on the bank account in Provincetown. It correlates to another city Julie lived in. So then I ran a full trace on Judith Ruppert, starting with the county index of vital statistics."

"Did you do a bit of time traveling?"

"Big time."

"And?"

"It's her real name, Robin. Julie Reed came much later, after high school. But she was born Judith Ruppert, to Edna Ruppert, single, age sixteen. And, get this, Edna also changed her name twice, first to Edna Free and then to Edna Isles. Sound familiar?"

It did, but I didn't know why.

"Edna Isles is the name of her inn. Julie's mom runs a lesbian bed-and-breakfast in P-town."

Twinkie cream squirted onto my chin. I fingered

it off, said, "Bottom line, please," and made myself an iced coffee.

"Julie's got plenty of cash stashed in another Massachusetts bank. But from what I can decipher, all of it predates Abigail Whitman."

"No recent deposits?"

"Yeah. A few, none over nine hundred dollars. Hardly a bank roll. Doesn't matter, though. Money's money as far as the courts are concerned. Should I send the writ of attachment?"

I licked icing from my fingertip, puzzled. "No. Something's not right here. Let this slide a couple of days until I can figure out what's bothering me."

Jill lowered her voice. "How good-looking is this woman?"

I slammed the refrigerator door. "What kind of asinine question is that?"

"That good-looking, huh?"

"Jill, enough. You got anything else for me?"

"You mean on that other case? The one involving the best friend of your devoted, and damned attractive, lover?"

I frowned. These days, I wasn't sure how to define my status with K.T. "Lover" seemed pitiably off course. I said, "The case involving Lurlene Hayes, yes."

Jill sputtered at my gruff tone. "Look, I don't know what's going on between you two, but —"

I stopped her before she marauded into my life any further.

"Okay," she blurted, clearly annoyed with me. "Strictly business. Fine. I can do that." She muttered, "Asshole," under her breath, then said, "I located Charon Centauri's New Orleans address. I tried calling her yesterday, but she was 'on retreat.' From your description of her, I wasn't sure if that meant she had beamed onto Jupiter or just cashed in some frequent flyer miles for a trip to Tahiti. Which, in case you're interested, is where I'd like to be at the moment."

I couldn't stay annoyed with Jill long. When it came to sarcasm, she was an artist. Strangely, the more she sniped at me the more convinced I was of her good intentions. I lightened my tone. "Anything else, love chicken?"

"I caught Charon in this morning. She hasn't left New Orleans since May. I asked her about June twenty-first, and she said she was at a psychic's retreat. Five minutes ago I confirmed her alibi, so she's out of the game."

I shrugged. "One down, twenty to go."

"Twenty-two. You have a message from Tony. With much regret, he's dropping the investigation on Grau and Darby Stevens. This morning CompTek's Junior Captain summoned Tony to his side." CompTek was our number-one client, and its overzealous twenty-six-year-old president was Tony's biggest fan. "He insisted that Tony fly out to the California site personally to check on their security system."

"Had he made any progress?"

"Some. Darby Stevens and his last boyfriend broke up sometime in February. The apartment belonged to his ex, so Stevens moved out. He's been staying with a friend ever since. Dale Waterson, Upper West Side. She's fifty-two, a former marine, and very eccentric. Anyway, about two months ago Stevens rented a suite in, of all places, Washington,

D.C. At the Marriott on Pennsylvania. The account's open, so he can come and go as he pleases. Coincidentally, that's the hotel of choice when Grau's in town. Tony said their schedules overlapped on six weekends."

I jotted down the information. "Any mention of where the lovers spent Sunday?"

"Sure enough, and here's the eyebrow-raiser. Grau was in New York City for some primo photo opp with New York church officials. Supposedly, he took an afternoon flight home, but I haven't confirmed that yet."

"Keep trying."

"I will."

"How about Stevens?"

"The doorman saw him leave the building around ten a.m. He hasn't been back since."

"I don't suppose you've had a chance to make any calls about Tzionah Stein."

"The incredible wandering potter? Unfortunately, no. Between you and Tony snapping at me, I've barely had time to go to the potty. But enough about me, have you tried to locate K.T.?"

I crunched into an ice cube and made it clear that it was time to disconnect. The last thing I wanted to do was talk about K.T. Or think about K.T. What I really wanted, I realized with a start, was to scamper back to bed and succumb to a good, long fantasy in which Julie Reed had star billing. Instead I hung up and went back to work.

The case offered plenty of innuendos, but so far the only evidence I could bite into and chew pointed at Lurlene. I opened the yellow pages. According to

Lurlene, Brian had planned to meet two models the Sunday he was killed. Someone — probably the same person who had attacked me in Brian's studio — had torn out the appointment sheet listing their names, and I had better find out why. I settled down on a kitchen stool and dialed.

Zoogie Cocchiaro answered right away. I told her who I was and asked if she could meet me later in the day. She was gravel-voiced and a little jittery. I waited until she finished prattling about what a shame it was, how talented Brian was, don't it make your brown eyes blue, and other assorted banalities. Then I interrupted, "So when can we meet?"

"Well, I'm trying to get a few jobs in —"

"Any time's fine for me, even a few minutes between shoots."

"Oh, for sure, but see, it's just impossible. Can't I just do this, you know, over the phone?" Her tone held a hint of valley girl.

"Okay. Quick question. Did you have breakfast with Brian the day of his murder?" Say yes, please.

"Break —" Again, she halted mid-stream. I wondered if she was on drugs or just naturally spacey. "Have you talked to the police about all this?"

Interesting response. I scratched my nose and asked, "No. Have you?"

Silence.

I stood up and walked to the bay window. Zoogie was nervous. Maybe she had seen something suspicious. Or was there another reason for her restraint? I repeated the question.

"I don't have to do this, do I?" she said, sounding

age thirteen. "I mean, how do I know you're who you say you are, huh? Right? This isn't official. This isn't anything."

She wasn't spacey at all. She was just plain defensive.

"Zoogie, let's meet. I promise you —"

"Meet? No. I don't think so. No. Besides, I canceled breakfast with Brian."

"When did that happen?"

"Sunday morning. Nine. Man, this whole scene's making me zippy. I mean, I coulda been there, you know?"

I began pacing, bumped into the corner of the stereo cabinet, and instantly changed gears. "You like music, Zoogie?"

"Music? Sure, yeah."

"Ever listen to *Red, Hot + Blue*?"

She didn't answer. "Look, I got an appointment in twenty minutes and I can't be late. The competition . . . damn, I don't have to do this. This is hard, really hard. I mean, he was going to make me . . . fuck . . . I mean, make my career. You don't understand, okay? I'll call you later, when I can pull it together, all right?"

I started to recite my number, but she disconnected before I hit the fifth digit. Redialing netted me a busy signal. I circled her name, then tried the second model. Tara Parker was more poised and less cooperative. Like Zoogie, she was on her way out. I figured ten o'clock must be the roll call in the modeling world. She was obviously reluctant to meet me, but I was too persistent and she was too rushed to argue for long. We made an appointment for nine o'clock Saturday morning.

I was having such a productive phone day, I redialed Jill. "Hi, love hawk, it's me again. We have any freelancers available?"

"Love hawk. I like that. So tell me, why the sudden interest in our loose cannons?"

I told her about my conversations with the models, then added, "I want tails on both women. Twenty-four hours. Observation only."

"Madwoman Popo's hurting for funds."

I laughed. Madwoman was a raven-haired giant with a penchant for leather and blood-red eye shadow, ideal for forays into the world of grunge. "No, thanks. Anyone more discreet?"

"Eddie may be free."

"Better. Do what you can." I gave her what I had on the models — home addresses, phone numbers, and modeling agencies — then I hung up and headed upstairs, sidestepping a tackle by my cat Geeja. My office made me feel claustrophobic. I shut off the air conditioning and opened the windows. A stale warmth rushed in. I had a nagging suspicion that tears were building somewhere inside my orbs so I sat down and stared hard at my unwavering, Disney-blue computer screen.

Time to face facts, Miller.

K.T. had chosen Lurlene over me, had allowed her friend's plight to put a wedge between us. More than thirty-six hours had elapsed since our last conversation, despite the fact that she had to know how worried I was. This case was kicking my butt three different ways to China, but Lurlene was her priority and there was only one explanation. K.T. had given up on me. Dinah was right. Long after I'm a footnote in K.T.'s romantic history, Lurlene will still be around.

I remembered the first time I met Lurlene. We were outside K.T.'s restaurant, the day after a heavy snow storm. Lurlene sneezed and K.T. instantly pressed the back of her hand against Lurlene's forehead, then adjusted her friend's scarf with a motherly zeal I had never known. At the time, her caretaking had amused and moved me. I thought, here's a woman who knows what it means to care for someone. Later, as the three of us ambled through Central Park, K.T. held both of our hands, breaking contact only once, to scoop snow from a tree branch. I had braced for the inevitable snowball, but instead K.T. had raised her hands toward us and offered a taste of the snow as if it were the finest confection she had ever known.

Okay, K.T., I almost said out loud, I'll solve this damn case, then you and me are going to have one hell of a showdown. I pounded on the keyboard so hard my cats scampered from the room. Their claws etched the wood stairs as a list flickered onto my screen.

Lurlene may have been the cops' prime suspect, but she sure wasn't mine. As I ticked off the names Arnold Grau and Darby Stevens, an unwelcome mental picture sprang instantly to mind. Those photographs could cost Grau his political career and when it came to motives, few were as compelling as saving one's own ass. Even if it turned out that he and Stevens had solid alibis for Sunday afternoon, there was always the possibility the murderer was a hired hand.

I considered Tzionah Stein next. Her reticence about the child she and Brian had conceived and her sudden departure from town sure didn't earn her any brownie points. Besides, the woman stood to benefit financially from Brian's death and, by her own account, was home at the time of the murder. Thinking that she could have also been behind the darkroom attack, I boldfaced her entry.

Right below her name was Kathleen Fritzl's. I had a hard time believing in her complacency regarding Brian's infidelities, and her thinly disguised narcissism disturbed me. I made a note to probe her alibi further, then typed in the names Zoogie Cocchiaro and Tara Parker.

I downed the rest of my iced coffee and pulled up my "Loose Threads" list. I wanted to sew them into the fabric of the case, but the threads didn't match. I needed more information. A lot more. I tried Mel first, but she was in court. Then I dialed T.B. The bureaucrats on the other end bumped me around for a full minute, then he came on. His voice and cadences were too reminiscent of K.T.'s.

"Any news?" he asked hurriedly.

"I have the same question and no answers."

He cursed under his breath. "I don't mean the goddamn case, Robin. I mean K.T. Have you heard from K.T.?"

As I recounted my conversation with K.T. from a very distant Monday night, my stomach kicked up its contents.

"They must be so scared," he muttered. "I keep praying one of them will call me." T.B. was a nice guy, but right now I didn't want nice. I wanted news.

"What are you hearing internally?"

"The cops don't know K.T.'s involved. As far as they're concerned, she's on a camping trip with her boyfriend. With Ginny and Larry. All the uniforms in his precinct knew Larry was going to be out of pocket this week. My brother-in-law won't like being pulled into a phony alibi, but Ginny can handle him."

"Who told them about the trip?"

"Who do you think? K.T.'s my sister, for Christ's sake. Thank God the guys at her production company backed me up. Meantime, have you made any progress?"

I gave him the facts.

"Not much," he said dismissively.

"Not much? I'm tracking down other suspects. Tzionah Stein, for instance —"

"You've got less than you think, bella. Hold on. I'm going to transfer you to a private line." Mozart's Jupiter Symphony played for a full minute before T.B. picked up. "This is strictly confidential, Rob. Okay? I haven't called because, frankly, my focus isn't on you right now. Not that I don't think that you're good at what you do —"

"Get to the point."

"The bullet didn't kill Brian. The slug cracked a rib, did some internal damage, but the vic could've survived." He was whispering. I pressed the phone to my ear. "Remember that missing tray in the darkroom? The vic — I mean Brian — didn't knock it off the counter as he collapsed. It could've happened that way, but it didn't. Someone poured the shit down his throat. Bleach fix. Burned his guts so bad, they pretty much disintegrated. Lips looked like smeared butter, that's what one of my buds here told me. On the q.t., of course."

I was furious. "How could you keep this from me?"

"Shit, Rob, not everything's about you. I just found out this a.m. Apparently, some of the brass aren't so sure about where my family loyalties end and my professionalism begins. Can't say I blame them, considering this conversation."

"Could this help Lurlene?"

There was a deep intake of breath on the other end. "Doubt it. Her fingerprints are on the tray."

Of course. She had been working as Brian's assistant. "Any other prints?"

"Brian's and an unidentifiable."

Good. A mysterious third print could instill just enough doubt in a jury to save Lurlene's ass. "Where'd they find the tray?"

"On the floor."

"Right? Left? On top of the body?"

"Man, Rob . . . I didn't ask . . . there was so much —"

"Fine, fine. Was he shot first?"

"Looks that way. Why do you ask?"

My mind raced ahead and I felt annoyed with T.B. for meandering in my dust. "How far was the gun when it went off?"

"Estimated distance, six feet. *Now* will you tell me what you're getting at?"

"One shot?"

"Yeah." He was getting impatient.

"From Brian's gun?"

He grunted. "How does my sister stand you? Yeah, from Brian's gun."

"And the gun had other bullets in the chamber?"

"Yes, again."

"And they still think there was only one person involved?"

"Yes ma'am. And the perp's name hasn't changed a syllable."

I rolled my chair back and glanced outside just as a battery of firecrackers exploded in a neighbor's yard. I slammed the window, turned on the a.c., and asked, "What about the photo in the tray and the undeveloped film they found?"

"Standard work product. No significance there."

"And no I.D. on the model in the photograph?"

"I didn't ask."

"Any intelligence on the pantyhose?"

"Oh right. Sure thing, Rob. L'eggs, petite. Control top. C'mon, no one's straining to read the fine print on this case. The headline says it's Lurlene. And that's the way they like it. The only ones interested in digging further are me and you. And let me tell you something . . ." His voice assumed a stage whisper. "My focus is on finding the legal loopholes. I've been in touch with your friend Mel and we're exploring tricks of the legal trade. Disruptions in chains of custody. Stuff like that."

It was my turn to grunt.

"Fine, Rob, but while you play Dick Tracy, I'll focus on the real world. 'Bye."

I stared at the phone and felt my cheeks simmer. T.B. was leaving me out in left field, not that it was hard to understand why. In a smaller, saner city, this murder might have been front and center. Here, it was just another pothole in a road on the verge of collapse. T.B. thought he was being practical. In my eyes, he was just being dumb.

From the new facts I had, the murder didn't sound premeditated. After all, why would someone first shoot Brian, then drop a perfectly functional and loaded gun only to pour him a chemical cocktail? A second shot would have been more efficient. And cleaner. My belly started to tingle.

I tried to imagine the chemical scorching my tongue, running down my throat like liquid fire. A shiver stopped the exercise dead in its tracks. The murderer must have wanted to cause Brian as much pain as possible, so much so that risk no longer mattered. I wondered if the bleach fix had left its mark on the murderer. It could have easily burned skin, stained clothes, eroded shoe leather. Poisoning was sloppy.

Another question surfaced. How could I be sure that the finger on the trigger belonged to the same person who had coldly watched Brian's lips dissolve in the wash of bleach fix. Maybe two people were involved.

I unlocked my lower drawer and extracted the hanging file holding the negatives from Brian's studio. As I placed it on the desk, something slipped out and clanged to the floor. It was the plastic bag containing the silver make-up case I had found in Brian's bathroom. I picked it up and examined it closer. The case appeared to be antique, the silver tarnished. Fingering the embossed cover through the plastic, it struck me that the motif wasn't just ornamental. There were so many curlicues I hadn't deciphered it at first, but now it leapt at me: the letter *S* scrolled around the octagonal case like a snake about to strike.

I didn't have to look into a mirror to know that the smile on my lips was not pretty. It was time for some field work. A couple of phone calls later, I had my overnight bag packed, my ATM card ready for a quick withdrawal, and one foot out the door. I wasn't even surprised when the phone rang. I avoided Geeja's tackle and Mallomar's forward body roll and dove for the receiver. "Yup?"

"Robin Miller?"

I hate when people do that. I wanted to say, "No, Mitch Miller. Follow the bouncing ball, asshole." Instead I grunted yes.

"It's Kathleen Fritzl."

I straightened up. She sounded odd, like she had been crying. "What can I do for you?" My tone was deliberate.

She coughed, started to say something then stopped herself abruptly. Finally, she said, "Please drop your investigation," as if she were asking me to pass the salt.

"Excuse me?"

She repeated herself, this time with a little edge in her voice. Her voice sounded rough, almost masculine.

I ripped the box of Twinkies out of the cupboard. "Care to elaborate on that request?"

My question seemed to unsettle her. A few seconds passed before she continued. "Lurlene's guilty. I know it. Don't ask how. Please, let justice be done." She hung up before I could respond.

It was almost eleven. And I was out of Twinkies.

My trip would have to wait. I had a house call to make.

To get into Kathleen Fritzl's building, an occupant had to buzz you in. I figured Kathleen wouldn't be real thrilled to see me so soon, so I resorted to subterfuge. I arrived at her address wearing generic khakis, a wide-brimmed cap, and carrying a box of long-stemmed daisies. I rang her buzzer first. No answer. I stepped back and glanced up at her apartment window. A shadow behind the curtains disappeared suddenly. Okay, so she wanted to play games. My inquisitiveness became determination.

I read the names next to the buzzers. Bertha Markowitz sounded about right. Sure enough, an elderly woman answered. I shouted "Florist!" into the speaker. A few seconds later I was on the third floor, placing a box in the hands of a sweet, white-haired lady with a cluster of moles under one eye. She began chattering right away, clearly thrilled to have an unexpected visitor. I smiled, said, "From a neighbor," and left her feeling pretty satisfied.

Then I hopped down to Kathleen's apartment. I knocked and stepped away from the peephole. I'm not good at impersonations, but I tried my best to imitate Bertha's babble.

At first I thought I had blown it, then I heard the lock click. I pressed my shoulder against the door, which opened too quickly. I stumbled into the room and turned to face —

A six-foot tall boy who so resembled Brian I gasped.

He stood there, one hand still on the door knob. He looked more perplexed than worried. A moment later he blinked and his eyes focused on me with understanding. He said, "You're the detective my mom warned me about."

"And you must be Chad." I extended my hand. He stared at it as if I were proffering a glass of spoilt milk. "Mom home?" I asked inanely, trying to obscure the fact that I had more or less just barreled my way into this kid's apartment.

"She went down to the precinct."

That's when it struck me. Chad and his sister Belinda were supposed to be in Truro. So Kathleen had lied. Not nice.

"Where's your sister?"

"She's asleep," he answered defensively. "You can't wake her. The radio's on."

I didn't try to follow his logic. The kid had obviously taken his father's death hard. He looked like a B-movie zombie — gray skin, sunken eyes, thin hair that clung to his scalp in clumps. Despite his height, Chad looked closer to thirteen than seventeen. The oversized Jefferson Starship sweatshirt he wore bunched around his wrists. The item must've belonged to Brian. He had pudgy cheeks, moist, puppy-dog eyes and thin, tight lips. I didn't have to be a descendent of Albert Einstein to know that my presence agitated him.

"Mom wouldn't like this, no, not at all," he said, more to himself than me. All this time he had been holding the front door open. Now he swung it back and struck a pose I associated with Superman: legs spread, arms crossed manfully across his chest, chin jutting. Except Chad's chin was weak, his chest shapeless, and the legs protruding from his gym shorts hairless and wiry. If he decided to get macho on me, I'd have to hurt him.

"I hear you think Lurlene's innocent," he asked, looking like he could care less. "How come?"

I sat on the couch and gave him a *USA Today* blip on the case. All at once his face paled and his head whirled toward his left. Whatever had attracted his attention escaped mine. He looked panicked, his mouth twisting in an ugly expression. "You better go, lady."

I stared in the same direction he had.

Chad approached me stealthily, smacked his lips like he needed water, then asked, "Did you hear something?"

I had the feeling he was daring me to answer in the affirmative. I didn't oblige him.

"You better leave now, little lady," he said in a voice reminiscent of John Wayne in *True Grit*. Fighting a smile, I stood up and then I did hear a sound, but from the opposite direction. I turned and saw a waif of a girl staring at me from a shadowy hall.

"Lindy, go to your room. Immediately!" Chad sounded enough like his father that Belinda obeyed instantly.

"Wait," I shouted. She paused, seemed to consider the situation, then approached me. She stopped short of leaving the hallway entirely. She was no more than 5'2" and probably weighed less than one hundred pounds. A shadow cut a diagonal across her face. Even so, I could tell she had been crying. Now she hugged herself and shivered.

I could feel Chad's gaze burning through my back.

Just days earlier, these kids had lost their father to a violent death. I was out of line here. I muttered, "Sorry," and retreated to the front door.

He snapped it open, then said defiantly, "I knew you weren't Bertha. She pops the *B*."

I paused to look at him.

"I may be seventeen, but I'm smarter than you think." His eyes were red and glassy and his breath sour. I thought, Kathleen should invest in a case of Listerine for this kid.

I turned again, but he stopped me in my tracks.

"Lurlene's guilty. I know 'cause I saw her. That's what Mom doesn't want anyone to know. *I was there.* I saw her. She shot my dad, the wicked witch with the ghost bonnet. I hope she fries."

Nice kid. Maybe I'd have my tubes tied.

Chapter 7

My room at the J.W. Marriott in Washington faced Pennsylvania Avenue. I parted the curtain. The Washington Monument was ablaze in unrelenting sunlight. Tourists scrambled toward it over meticulously mowed grass that shimmered in the heat. Even with the air conditioning on high, I was sweating. D.C. does that to me.

I pressed the phone closer and waited for Jill to take me off hold. Four hours had lapsed and still Chad's parting words rung in my ears.

Jill returned. "They're standing by their story, Rob."

Before leaving New York, I had asked Jill to contact Anna Parulski and Stephen Alsace, the neighbors who had supposedly been with Kathleen and the kids on the day of the murder.

"They insist they all spent the day barbecuing. Cape Cod beef and bliss. Kathleen and the kids didn't head down to New York until after the cops called. I asked them if anyone could corroborate their story and Parulski reluctantly gave me the name of their butcher. That was him on the other line. The guy swears they came in on Sunday with both kids. He opened up especially for Father's Day. Mitch the Butcher said he thought it was real nice the family was gonna barbecue. Told me they picked up a dozen dogs and three shell steaks. He sounded like the real thing. Went on about how butcher dogs are way better than the crap you buy in supermarkets. He's right, by the way. Of course, the nitrates will kill you —"

"Jill."

"Right. So the kid's lying."

"Maybe. But why?"

"First of all, we know the kid's not exactly the next-door neighbor type. Second, Lurlene was shacking up with his dad. For most kids, that would be enough. Then add in the fact that Lurlene supposedly tried to drive a wedge between him and his father. Think about it, Rob. Chad already had plenty of reason to hate Lurlene and now she's the prime suspect in his dad's murder . . . and *you're* the bitch trying to get her off. The kid obviously wanted to throw you a curve. Even if it meant lying. And remember, Kathleen said he was an artistic type. He probably considers lying to be the same as poetic license."

"Very neat. But let me ask you this. If he's so loosely held together, how do we know if he's not the murderer and Kathleen's just covering for him?"

"What's his motive? Besides, the mother might be willing to cover, but why the neighbors, the butcher and the candlestick maker?"

"What candlestick maker?"

She ignored me. "Okay, maybe the kid fought with his father over something, I don't know, maybe it was about Lurlene. So Brian's standing there in his dark room developing some photograph and the kid decides to kill his father, *his father*, mind you. You think he's not going to unravel completely? And what about Kathleen? From the way you described her, she sounded pretty damn calm. Think she could pull that off if she knew her son was the murderer."

"It's possible, Jill."

"Sure, it's possible. And it's also possible that your friend Lurlene did the dirty deed herself. Or that nutty potter who's skipped town. And let's not forget the photogenic boys whose trail you're sniffing out even as we speak. Who knows, Rob, maybe *I* killed Brian."

Jill was right. The bottom line was that I still didn't have enough evidence to shine the light in anyone's eyes. I rubbed mine wearily. It had been a long day. And the damn sun just wouldn't set. I shifted the phone to my other ear and said, "Look, I'm beat. I better catch some z's before I go the next round."

"Good idea. By the bye, I contacted Stevens' office

and then called the hotel right before you got there. You'll find this interesting. The word is he flew to Paris last Sunday. Unexpectedly. A night flight, so he could've committed a little mayhem before taking off for Paree. He's scheduled to arrive in Dulles late tomorrow. I couldn't squeeze the room number out of the desk clerk, but I tried."

"Thanks, you've been really great this week."

"I'm always great. You're just too much of a shrew to notice it most days. Anything else before I drag my weary bones back home to my neglected sugar poop?"

"Yeah. Solve the case for me."

"No problem. Call me after your next break-in."

I crashed into bed. I needed every inch of its king size. For the next fifteen minutes I thrashed around. My body and my head were not communicating. Every muscle screamed for sleep, my eyelids were slamming into my cheeks. Yet my brain was percolating. Why had Chad lied to me? And was it really a lie? Maybe I was way off course and Lurlene really did kill Brian.

I sat up. My gaze collided with the mini-fridge. I unlocked the Pandora's Box. Amazingly, the chocolate milk didn't jump me. Nope. This time I went straight for the Kahlua. Then the vodka. Later I switched to amaretto and orange juice, with a Famous Amos chaser. Sometime around eight, the sun had pity on me, the booze set in, and consciousness slipped away.

The good news was that I didn't wake up until after seven in the morning. The bad news was that I didn't wake up until after seven in the morning.

Losing even an hour in an investigation this complex could mean the difference between success and sucking mud. I plunged into the shower, hurriedly donned clean duds, and scrubbed my mouth with Listerine. Sleep hadn't helped much. I still felt like hell. And I had dreamt. Sometimes I think that's the root of my insomnia: dream phobia.

One dream had K.T. dead and cut up by a motor boat. Another had Lurlene sleeping with Chad. But the last one, the last one was worth the price of admission.

Julie Rush and I were in a movie theater. Some thriller's playing. She reaches over and grabs my thigh. I move her hand to my zipper. Her eyes turn toward me, surprised, but I'm too busy watching the movie. A woman's crawling through a darkened apartment. A killer's nearby. You can feel it in the audience. We're all holding our breath. Then Julie runs a nail over my zipper. Tooth by tooth. I can feel it like a line of fire. I want to gasp, but don't dare. There are people all around us, and I want her so bad I'm hurting. Our eyes still haven't met, and I'm watching the woman on screen lean against the door, breath ragged, pale breasts heaving under a nightgown. The knob's turning above her head and now Julie's pulling the zipper down, slow, in time to the breathing of the woman on screen. I look down. I can see my lower belly, ghostly in the reflected light, and a line of pubic hair. Julie eases a finger down. I want to explode. The man's hand is coming around the door and the woman is palming her breasts, so full, the color of milk, and Julie is touching me now, playing with me slow, easing inside. Finally she's whispering. *You want this. Go ahead, pretend you don't notice. It's a turn on. Besides, I know.* And she's so right. I'm grinding on her fingers, gasping out loud, so wet, so slippery, so hungry, and then the knife comes out and plunges into that sweet pale breast.

That's when I woke.

Life sucks.

Breaking into a hotel room is pretty easy. Especially for someone who lies well. I convinced the front desk I was an irate office assistant, sent from New York to pick up an important package from Mr. Stevens's hotel suite. I made it sound shady and worth a round of gossip at the next staff meeting. I also insisted that Stevens had checked in early. As the clerk consulted her computer screen, I snatched the room number. Next, I called housekeeping and requested that an extra robe be placed at once in the master bathroom of Suite 868. I waited down the hall, by the ice machine. An older, red-haired woman exited the elevator pushing a cart of fresh linens and toiletries. A neatly folded robe sat on top. She slipped a card key in the door's computerized lock, then swung it open and left it that way as she proceeded to the bathroom. I slipped into the front closet.

After what seemed an eternity, I was alone in Stevens's suite. From the number of personal accessories in the room, it was clear that the suite functioned as home away from home. I headed for the drawers. The man was neat. Folded his socks. Arranged his shirts by color. In the desk I found ATM receipts and credit card slips for meals at local restaurants. I jotted down the credit card and bank account numbers. The real treat was in the bathroom. From John Feyre I knew Stevens always wore cover-up so I wasn't surprised to discover more cosmetics on the counter than I've owned in my entire life. But the bonus was the silver hair brush, a match to the make-up case in my pocket.

So Stevens had been in Brian's studio. The question was when. And why?

I now had enough chips in my pocket to force a show-down with Stevens and Grau. The photographs alone had indicated a possible motive. With the make-up case clearly pointing to Stevens, opportunity also seemed possible.

I snapped a shot of the cosmetics counter, then exited the bathroom. I paused at the bedroom closet. Sometimes people leave extraordinary information in their jacket pockets. I slid the louver doors apart and starting fingering Stevens' handsome collection of suits. I found a packet of rainbow condoms, assorted match books, and an unsealed envelope containing a check for $25,000 made out to cash. Issuer: Arnold Grau.

Interesting.

Maybe my assumptions were wrong. What if Stevens himself had hired Luce Lorelli to photograph his lovemaking sessions with Grau? But why? Certainly, as a top fashion designer Stevens had more than enough financial security. Blackmail simply didn't make sense. And if he was the blackmailer, why would he have wanted Brian dead?

Because Brian knew too much.

I suddenly thought of Luce Lorelli. Why hadn't she returned any of my calls? With a shiver, I replaced the envelope in the jacket pocket.

There was laughter in the hallway. Distant. I tilted my head toward the living room area. The voices were approaching. I glanced at my watch. Ten o'clock. Still early in the work day. Stevens wasn't expected for hours. I squeezed my eyes shut and listened. Shit. There was a distinct swish, the insertion of a card key, and then a click. Stevens had arrived. Feeling trapped in a B-movie skit, I slipped into the closet, between an ironing board and an oversized magenta robe that smelled of Cling. The outside door creaked open. I stifled the ill-timed urge to laugh. Maybe K.T. was right after all. Maybe romance writing wasn't so bad.

The voices were clearer now. Two men. And it didn't take me long to guess the identity of Stevens's mystery guest. The great Arnold Grau himself. And he sounded downright jovial. "I've missed you, Darby. This was the longest, son-of-a-bitching week of my life. And what a week."

Sloppy kissing sounds.

"We've survived the worst, A.G., I'm sure of it."

"Wish I had your confidence. My wife's been on me. 'Why can't I come to D.C. with you?' Ten times a fuckin' day. Like our marriage really meant somethin'. Sex was never great, you know, and since you . . . well." There was a smacking sound, then the clink of glass. "Too early for a real drink. Damned unhappy about that, I can tell you. I've barely slept a wink since Sunday. A shot of J&B would take me just where I need to go."

The sound of rustling clothes, then Stevens's voice, husky and seductive. "How about this instead? Where will this take you?"

"God," was Grau's strangled response.

My eyes widened. I wasn't real pleased with the direction of the conversation. I almost shouted, go back to how bad this week's been. Give me the details. But for Christ's sake don't start making out.

"Darb, how do you do that to me?" Grau sounded sincerely puzzled. "It's goddamn fire. Right through me. Oh yes, that. Damn. Damn."

"You're still fighting it, aren't you? There's a part of you that hates how good I make you feel." Stevens's tone had turned challenging.

"Fuck it, man. Not now. Don't talk."

"But I want to talk. I want to make sure you know it's me that's touching you. Me. Darby Stevens. Fashion designer. Grand faggot of the north." He laughed, a tight, unamused sound. "How's this feel, Senator Grau?" Taunting. I could almost see him gritting his teeth.

"Man, what more do you want from me? I've put my marriage, my career, my whole fuckin' life on the line for you."

"Not enough, Arnie."

Grau groaned. I had the impression that Stevens had not stopped caressing him for a single moment. "What the hell does that mean? Oh, lord. You're somethin' else. C'mon."

They were moving closer. An instant later their silhouettes were visible on the other side of the louver doors. Stevens had one hand hooked inside Grau's trousers. The other was on Grau's chest, pressing him against the front of the armoire. I started to squirm. How the hell was I going to get out?

"Tell me, A.G., does this . . ." Grau's body slammed backward. "Does this mean enough to you?"

Grau was nodding rapidly, his eyes tightly shut. "Oh yes," he whispered.

Stevens yanked down the politician's pants. His legs were pale. I averted my eyes right before Stevens dropped to his knees. "Enough to admit to our relationship? Publicly?"

My eyes darted to Stevens, who was rubbing Grau's penis between his hands like it was a magic lamp and he was waiting for a goddamn lavender genie to pop out. Maybe this was what it was about. Political blackmail. A magnificent outing.

Grau grabbed a lock of Stevens's sandy blond hair in his fist. He snapped Stevens's head back and dropped to his knees so that they faced each other, their expressions etched by excitement and anger. "Didn't we go through this before?" Grau demanded. "Aren't we done with that game?" He gestured toward the closet and I jerked back. "Do you have someone new stashed in the closet, Darby? Another fuckin' photographer? Are you still trying to force my hand?"

Darby shook himself free. "Goddamn it, Arnie, no. Do you think I'd make the same mistake twice? I'm just as worried about those damn negatives as you. I don't want to hurt you any more than I have. I swear."

It was getting harder to breathe evenly. I wanted

a tape recorder and a small posse of big women with bigger guns. I pressed my nose against the closet door.

Stevens had moved to the bed. He removed his starched white shirt deliberately while Grau looked on. His gestures were elegant, measured. It was like watching a ballet. He ran a long-fingered hand over his chest. His muscles could have been carved from marble, so perfectly were they defined. He stood and kicked off his slacks. In the distance, Grau pressed a hand against his abdomen, his jaw slack.

Stevens turned so that his butt faced the closet. "This is what I'm offering you." One leg bent at the knee, the other stuck straight, a hand poised on the left hip, Stevens's body was glorious.

Grau tore off the remainder of his clothes. I closed my eyes.

"Take me," Stevens ordered quietly. "This time take me the way you like me to take you. Then tell me if I'm holding anything back."

"What about the photographs?" Grau asked, breathlessly.

I almost shouted: Yeah, what about them?

"It's over. Brian's dead, isn't he? And Lorelli's not going to talk. I fixed it, baby." And with that, Stevens spun toward the wall and braced himself. "C'mon. Show me what that bitch of a wife of yours has been missing all these years."

Grau stomped toward him. He bent his mouth to Stevens's neck, bit him, then asked, "How much did you pay her to keep quiet?"

"I didn't have to." Stevens's neck arched as he

strained to look Grau in the eye. His hand stretched backward to stroke Grau's thigh. "I love your softness. Your stomach against my back . . ."

"And this," Grau muttered, pumping against him so hard I heard the smack of flesh.

"Yes, baby."

Grau's tone changed suddenly. "If you didn't pay her, then where's the check?"

"In my jacket. Where you left it."

"Let me see."

"Now?" Stevens sounded stunned.

Grau paused, then all at once he lifted Stevens with one hand and slammed him toward the bed. Grau's thick body moved against him hard, rhythmically, his groan the howl of wind over an open field. After what seemed twice the length of an eternity, he collapsed on Stevens. By then I was pressed against the back wall of the closet, breathing as hard as the two men. Abruptly Grau's voice stabbed the air. "Now, Darby. Get me the check."

"It's nice to be trusted," the younger man replied, then practically spat the word — "Politicians!"

Stevens rolled out from under Grau and headed toward me. I tried to grab an iron from the top shelf, but didn't move fast enough. The door swung open and Stevens shouted, "What the fuck?" An instant later his fist landed on my jaw.

I fell against the wall, the metal legs of the ironing board skinning my forehead. Grau shouted, "Again?" and ran toward me.

"I swear A.G," Stevens sputtered, "I know nothing —"

"Fuck you!" Grau shouted, grabbing and tossing me into the room like a sack of mulch. My knee cracked against the bed frame. Pain ripped through my back.

Stevens was on the far side of the room, dressing rapidly. Grau seemed unaware of his nakedness. He kicked me in the hip, ordered me to stand, then kicked me again before I could comply. He bent toward me, reached for my neck with his beefy hands. But I had had enough. I took a deep breath and slammed my head into his scrotum. He howled across the room.

"No one gives a shit about who you fuck," I yelled at the top of my lungs. The sound made my head hurt. Truth be told, one of my top goals, besides escaping from this hotel room with all limbs attached, was blotting out the memory of their recent encounter. But it was hard to do, especially with Grau dangling right before my eyes. Stevens extended his hand, nudged Grau behind him. His stance was more protective than offensive.

He said, "I've never hit anyone before in my life . . . but I'll do it again if you don't tell me what the hell you're doing here."

My hip felt like fire, my jaw throbbed, and I could feel blood beading on my forehead, but instead of weeping — which I wanted desperately to do — I stood up, half-smiled and pretended to adjust an ear piece. With a studied nod to myself, I carefully enunciated, "It's in control, fellas. Gimme five." I took a few steps back, patted the wallet bulging in my jacket pocket, and hoped Grau and Stevens were too agitated to notice that the only wired part of me was my nerves. "I'm a detective," I said in my Tyne Daly voice. "NYPD." I flashed my P.I. license so fast, the boys barely had time to blink. "You're under suspicion for the murder of Brian Fritzl." So pleased was I by their shocked expressions that I went ahead and read them their rights.

By the end, Grau was as white as porcelain. But Stevens's eyes were smiling. "You almost had me. Almost." He turned to Grau, who was struggling into his clothes now, clearly expecting an onslaught of D.C. police and reporters. "She's conning us, A.G. Look at her. She's no cop."

Grau dropped his pants and stared at me, his insolence slipping back into place. I didn't care as long as both men kept their underwear on and weapons out of sight.

"Sit down," Stevens said, clearly in control again.

I glanced at the bed and shook my head.

"Let's call the police," Grau blurted, sounding like someone who thought he was a Big Man in Town.

Stevens shot him a look that spoke volumes. Grau deflated instantly. He shook his head sadly and finished dressing in silence. "It's another world," he muttered to himself.

"Right you are, darling. Maybe now you'll understand." Stevens cupped his hands around my shoulders. "Why don't we start from the top. Who sent you?"

If Stevens was the murderer, he was surprisingly composed. I wondered if there was a weapon nearby that I hadn't discovered in my search. In any case, there were two of them and one of me. The odds were not good. I decided to talk Stevens's language. "Look, from what I've heard, you and I had the same motive. I'm a member of ACT-UP —"

Stevens guffawed. "That's a good one. Look, hon, I believe you're gay. You have the right . . . aura. But you're not here because you're committed to the good fight." His tone turned grave. "And that's what concerns me. Again, who hired you?"

Behind him, Grau grunted. "Shit, shit, shit. You said this was over, Darby . . . dammit."

"Shut up, Arnold."

They exchanged fiery glances. Something was off here. Grau's eyes had widened. He was scared.

Stevens looked back at me, scratched his clean-shaven cheek pensively. His fingernails left furrows in his make-up. In the tracks I could see the ridges of a scar shaped like a lightning bolt. Our eyes met. His mouth twisted in an unsettling smile. "Gift from a former john. Before fame smiled on me. But you probably knew that already. Luce certainly did."

Clearly Stevens assumed I knew more than I did. The question was, how could I use that to my advantage?

"It was mentioned," I said casually.

"What else did she mention?"

I decided to sit. The appearance of confidence was critical. "Enough to be here. Enough to know your relationship started a little over two months ago. And that most of your time together has been spent in this suite. Enough to know that some pretty hot photographs were obtained right here." I patted the bed.

Stevens sighed. "You have the negatives, don't you?"

I nodded. "In a safe-deposit box. Along with a note indicating my trip here, and instructions to distribute the photographs widely if I happen to meet my maker a little earlier than I'd hoped."

Grau closed his eyes, pinched the bridge of his nose and whispered, "I told you, Darby. Without the negatives, we're sunk."

Stevens grabbed Grau's hand and squeezed it. "Curse the day you met me, huh?"

Grau started to nod, then stopped himself as Stevens drew the back of his hand along his jaw. The corners of Grau's mouth turned down, his expression sad, resigned. "Not really." Tears welled up in his eyes. Without another word he exited. A second later I heard the refrigerator door open. "Anyone care for a drink?" he shouted.

Stevens forgot me and hurried outside.

Why were they willing to leave me alone? I could have a weapon. Use the phone. Christ, I could even open the damn window and shout my head off. I started doing rapid-fire calculations. They all ended up in the same place. These men weren't killers.

I found them sitting on the living room couch, holding hands. They heard me approach and looked up. Stevens asked quietly, "How much do you want?"

"How much did Brian want?"

They appeared puzzled, glanced at each other first, then Grau said, "I thought you said Brian wasn't interested in money."

"He wasn't. Believe me, he wasn't." Stevens looked more upset now. "Did Lorelli give the negs to you?"

I made my chin jut out. "Why don't we talk about that? What'd you do with Luce?"

"What'd I do?" Stevens asked. "For Christ's sake, she's just across town. Why don't you ask her yourself?"

"What the hell are you talking about?"

"Luce is at the San Raphael."

"Luce is in town?"

"As if you didn't know. Now why don't you just tell me what your scam is?"

I ignored him and crossed to the phone. Neither man tried to stop me. I got information, then dialed the San Raphael. The front desk put me through right away. Luce picked up after four. I kept my eyes on Grau and Stevens as I spoke. "Hey, Lorelli, it's Miller. I'm standing here with some friends of yours. In a locked hotel room. Any suggestions?"

"Robin, that you? What the hell are you talking about?"

"I'm at the Marriott with Stevens and Grau," I said, then added in a whisper, "Any reason I should worry?"

"Sure there is," she answered hurriedly. My back stiffened. "Grau's a pompous, bigoted asshole and Stevens is as twisted as my Aunt Bea's intestines. And his make-up smells like cheap bubble gum. Any other questions?"

I had forgotten how sarcastic Luce could be. I sat down on the end table, rubbed my hip and cut to the chase. If these men wanted to kill me, fine. At least Luce would have my death on her conscience. I smiled at the thought and said, "Talking about make-up, I found a make-up case belonging to Darby Stevens in Brian Fritzl's studio. Not to mention a pretty assortment of photographs. What I'm asking is, are these men responsible for Brian's murder?"

Grau shot up from the couch, started to protest, but Stevens shook his head, slapped Grau's behind, and whispered, "Down boy. It'll be fine."

Meanwhile I could hear Lorelli's tut-tutting on the other end. "You're still pretty junior at this."

I gritted my teeth. Tony had once considered asking Lorelli to join our operation. I warned him that if he did I'd leave skid marks on the office carpet. I said, "Get to the point, Luce," and dabbed my forehead with a sleeve.

"Your boys are guilty of some pretty funky coupling, but murder isn't one of their fetishes."

"Want to tell me the whole story?"

"I'd love to, pal. Especially if you're picking up my hourly tab, but right now, I have an Amtrak train to catch. Unreserved seat. Some of us can't afford to travel first-class, you know." Luce's business ran mainly in the red. She made at least one money dig at me per phone call. "Call me when you get home, tenderfoot. *If* you get home," she added with a chuckle.

I hung up, stared at my blank-eyed hosts, and waited. Stevens broke the deadlock. "Before I say anything, just tell me, is that all you want . . . an explanation? Proof that we didn't kill Brian?"

"Bingo."

Grau downed the rest of his glass. From the way his Adam's apple bobbed, it must have been a real smooth sherry.

Stevens said, "Fine. First of all, Brian and I were friends."

I heard Grau snort. So did Stevens. Irritation rippled over his features then disappeared. "We slept together once, Arnie," he said to Grau, then to me, "After a photo shoot of my fall line. For *Vogue.*"

I forgot to be impressed.

"He seemed delightful. Open-minded, exciting. Macho, yet surprisingly insightful. All he wanted was a taste of the flip side. That's how he put it. The 'flip' side." He tried to suppress a grin, then relented. To Grau he said, "He was an absolute beast."

Grau's nostrils flared. "Don't talk like that," he snapped. "You sound —"

"Queer?" Stevens asked. "Mincing?"

Grau headed back to the refrigerator. Clearly, this was a relationship designed in hell.

Stevens issued a perfunctory apology and continued. "Attitudes like those of my mate here are what propelled me into activism. And fame. Amazing what you can get away with when you're rich. Even so, I've found that many of my dearest colleagues have a distinct line drawn into their acceptance levels. As long as I dress like a real man, speak like a real man, design like a real man, and refer only obliquely to what us real men do in the back room, why then, I'm perfectly suitable company. But God help me if I want to be myself, whatever that happens to be on any given day. Brian, though, wasn't like that. He was truly open. To all kinds of sexuality. And that was one of his problems."

By now Grau was seated next to Stevens again. He reached out and squeezed his partner's knee reassuringly. Stevens patted him back and smiled. Glancing up at me, he said, "I can see by your expression that you've underestimated Arnold. So did I. Bigotry, like homosexuality, doesn't have one face."

They leaned toward each other, lovers again. I bit off the sarcastic remark ready to spring from my tongue and let Stevens continue his self-impressed babble.

"Brian and I had little contact after our one-nighter. Some time later, I heard rumors about him that were, well . . . distressing would be putting it lightly. Time passed, the rumors faded, and one day we met again on a flight here. April it was. I was in town for a debate on National Public Radio. Gays in the military. An ideal topic for a fashion designer, don't you think? My handler must have thought the topic was gays and the millinery."

The joke was old and my patience was wearing thin. Stevens seemed oblivious to both.

"My opponent was the esteemed Arnold Grau from Louisiana. Brian happened to have a local shoot nearby, and he was so damn charming I finally said, what the hell, and agreed to meet him for dinner." To Grau, Stevens said, "You were such a bitch that day," then to me, "He was infuriating. Jerry Falwell couldn't hold a flaming cross to him. Arnie raised bigotry to a new high. But the odd thing was, how he looked at me. I've been queer since infancy. And the one thing I'm confident about is knowing when a man's turned on to me. And there he was, this supreme bigot, practically panting at me."

Grau had narrowed his eyes and began shaking his head slightly, as if freshly stunned by Stevens's words.

"So that night, Brian and I were dishing . . . we were both a little high and a lot randy. Luckily, we were in public. Anyway, he leans over and says to me in this real sexy whisper, 'Why don't you lure the honorable Mr. Grau into bed and photograph the whole damn incident?' " He paused. "I thought the idea was a hoot. Then, when I returned home, the scheme just got under my skin. I mean, why the hell not. This bastard —" Grau flinched at the word. Nevertheless Stevens repeated it. "This bastard was running for a Senate seat. So I called Brian and he put me in touch with Luce."

Now Stevens stood and crossed to the window. He parted the curtain and stared outside. After a moment, he looked back at me. "The problem was, and you may not believe this because I barely can — I fell in love with him."

Grau cleared his throat.

"I was stunned by what A.G. was like when he dropped his pompous, right-wing bullshit."

I pictured Grau kicking my hip and raised an eyebrow.

Stevens said quickly, "You haven't seen him at his best."

No shit.

"I contacted Brian and asked him not to release the negatives to Lorelli. Brian called me a chicken. He said he'd wait and see. His exact words were, 'When you stop thinking with your dick, you'll thank me.' A few days later he started pumping me for money, said he wanted to see how far I'd go to protect Arnie. Meanwhile Lorelli wanted her bill paid up. I refused. No money until the negatives were handed over to me and all photographs destroyed. The three of us spent weeks arguing over the phone. Then I decided to level the playing field. I'd heard that Brian had come on rough to a couple of models, so I conducted my own investigation. Saturday I went to see him. He was mighty pissed, but he finally gave in. The negatives were to be sent to me this week, after I sent him and Luce payment for services rendered. The only problem is that by Sunday, Brian was dead."

He reached for Grau's glass, took a sip and shuddered.

"And you took off for Paris," I interjected.

"Not really. That's the line my office is handing out. In fact, I've spent most of this week negotiating with that amazon friend of yours."

"Luce?"

"I was convinced she planned to bank on the negatives the way Brian had, and she was convinced Arnie and I were murdering thugs. Only yesterday she confirmed my alibi —"

"Which is?"

"I spent Sunday in Delaware with some of my favorite queens. The point is that last night Lorelli called a truce. On her terms. She handed me the set of photographs she got from Brian, and I paid her bill in full. A paltry seven-fifty. I almost laughed out loud. I was so relieved I hired her to locate the negatives for me. And now you show up."

His story rang true. I excused myself, secreted myself in the bathroom to wash my face and collect my wits. When I exited, I told them my half, or as much as I felt like sharing. In the end, I promised to burn the negatives. There was a cost, though: I wanted the dirt on Brian.

The men stood. Stevens squinted at me and said, "He raped one of the models I work with. Don't ask who, I vowed to keep her confidence. She lives in New York. If you look hard enough, you'll find her."

My hands ice-cold, I reached for the door.

Stevens raised his voice. "One more thing. From what I hear, she wasn't the only one."

Chapter 8

A thunderstorm stranded me on the runway for over an hour. By the time I made it back to Brooklyn, I was sopping wet, dosed up on Advil, and starved for food and information. I decided to satisfy both by treating Luce Lorelli to dinner at La Paulina's, an Italian restaurant in the heart of Bensonhurst. The food there is intense and the waiters aggressive. I argued with pug-faced Dominic about the suitability of tomato vodka sauce on penne versus shells, then I ordered the snapper in a scampi sauce and ruined a beautiful friendship. Anthony hurried over to try to change my mind, even kissed his fingers as he described the osso buco, but I was implacable. He shrugged in Dominic's direction, clearly dejected. That's when Luce arrived.

She sized up the situation instantly, winked at Dominic, and ordered the stuffed artichokes, a cold antipasto, penne puttanesca, extra olives, and a side of fried zucchini. Anthony brought her a glass of Chianti and her own basket of bread. Steam rippled up from the crust. The one thing Luce Lorelli and I share is a passion for food. Tonight she had bested me.

Five-seven and a solid one-seventy, my colleague is a handsome woman with a one-sided smile and a reluctance to talk about anything personal. After five months of contact, her sexuality remains a question mark.

We took turns ripping leaves from her artichoke. It was so good and sucking so much fun that neither of us spoke for five minutes. Finally Luce drew the plate toward her, expertly scraped the choke from the heart, and said, "You've earned your first question. Shoot." She didn't raise her eyes.

I buttered a slice of bread and asked, "Did you know Brian Fritzl was a rapist?"

The fork halted at her bottom lip. "Come again?"

I gave her the details of my earlier encounter.

When her fork clanged to the plate, I knew the shock was real. "It's hard to believe. Brian was such a character. A real tease. But I can't —" She stopped herself. Her doe-brown eyes suddenly looked bruised. "Never underestimate people," she muttered enigmatically, then said, "One time, we were at this place in the city. Real chi-chi. Can't remember the name, I knew I'd never go back. Brian took me there in return for a personal favor. There was this woman there, real sexy in a skinny way. Know what I mean? One of those boy-thin models with a moody face. She sees Brian from across the room, lets out this rabbit-like squeal and hauls ass out of there. It was a real scene, could've been embarrassing, but Brian laughed it off. 'One of my girls,' he goes, like he was feeling indulgent. I said something to him, like, 'I didn't know you were so popular,' and he said, 'Ah Luce, the ladies all love me. Just sometimes they need convincing.' I didn't think anything about it then, but . . . who knows?" She flicked the edge of her fork. "Damn."

We waited until Dominic cleared the table and presented the antipasto.

"How often did you and Brian work together?" I asked.

"All the time. The standard stuff — adultery, insurance fraud, you name it. I took the photos, Brian developed them. I sometimes suspected he got a kick out of the work that I sure as hell don't, but I never questioned it 'cause whatever his reasons, the guy was an asset to me. About a year ago, he suggested we open a joint safe deposit box and use that as a dropping point. The system's worked real well."

A piece of provolone caught in my throat. I told Luce about the safe deposit key I found in Brian's office.

She smiled. "Found one, did ya? Were the real dicks around at the time, or were you just visiting?"

Rule of the game: never admit to breaking and entering.

"Just visiting," I said.

"Remember the number?"

"Forty-something."

"That's Brian's personal box. Ours was thirty-two."

"Same bank?"

"Just a few feet apart. He said it was his secret stash, even Kathleen didn't know about it."

She waited expectantly. I didn't disappoint her. "Monday morning?"

I watched her roll a piece of prosciutto around a sliver of melon, then pop the masterwork into her mouth. "Cost you more than a meal."

I reached for my wallet.

Luce growled. "I may be hungry, Miller, but I'm not desperate. Let's see what happens Monday." Her eyes sparkled maliciously. "Then we'll talk compensation. Meantime, we eat."

Dinner lasted four hours. Around ten o'clock, Luce and I undid the top buttons of our jeans and split three desserts. As I spoon-dueled with her over the chocolate hazelnut meltaway, I caught Dominic watching me intently. He gave me a thumbs-up. I went home in much better spirits.

The lights were on downstairs so I decided to give my housemates a chance to see my uncharacteristically content countenance. I knocked and someone inside shouted, "Enter at your own risk." I obliged. They took turns enveloping me; I was surprised at how good it felt, body aches notwithstanding.

Beth took a step back and all at once reached out and tilted my head, her nursing instincts in rapid ascension. "Nasty bruise you got there, buddy."

Without asking permission, she raised my shirt and began palpating my midriff. She interrogated me for a few minutes, then said, "Ribs seem fine. I'd rate it a four on the calamity scale."

Dinah didn't look amused. For that matter, neither did Beth. I tried to trip a different conversation wire by proceeding to Carol's bassinet and emitting godmotherly coos.

"Give it up, Rob," Dinah ordered, more brusquely than expected. I cocked an eye at her, realized she wasn't feeling especially playful, and planted myself on the couch. At some point Beth disappeared and returned with an ice pack, Motrin and a bottle of iodine. Even with her ministrations, the full update took less than twenty minutes.

Dinah stopped pacing, aimed a finger at me and said, "Great business you're in, kid. Meanwhile, you're screwing up your whole damn life. You *do* know why K.T. isn't calling, right? She can't depend on you. There's always some case or some reason you have for pulling back. You don't have the time or stamina it takes for the personal —"

Beth broke in before I could. "For heaven's sake, don't you think Robin's been beat up enough today. Lay off the psychobabble and look at your friend. She doesn't need a goddamn lecture."

Dinah's gaze ricochetted between us. "Great," she huffed, then stormed out of the room.

My cheeks were on fire. I turned to Beth and asked, "What the hell was that about?"

Beth ran a hand through her spiky blonde tresses. "It's been a bad day all around. Sorry you had to step into our pile of doo-doo." Her smile was feeble.

"Care to elaborate?"

Just then Carol turned over in the bassinet, discharging a sputtering sound like a balloon in sudden air-release. Beth pointed at her daughter and smirked a little sadly. "My baby just said it for me."

"Ah. Parental bliss."

"Mostly. Really." She sounded defensive. I stayed quiet. "You know we're fine, it's just we hardly see each other anymore. When Dinah's got the baby in the morning, I'm at the hospital. Then I come home and Dinah's first client arrives two minutes later. The other day, her eight-o'clock cancelled and I was jubilant. And sex . . . well, don't ask."

"Believe me, I won't."

"It's been three months. Three months, Robin. I'm ready to climb the walls. I mean, before Carol, maybe we'd have a short lull. Three weeks max. But three months?"

Did I ask?

"So tonight heaven sends us a gift. I mean, if ever there was manna, this was it. Two minutes after Dinah's last client left, Carol fell sound asleep. Even the em-eighty some juvenile delinquent exploded in our recycling can didn't wake her. I think, hallelujah, time to visit the promised land, and what does my honey do? She starts analyzing me. How she understands *why* I need reassurance, how we're going through a classic case of the new-parent syndrome. She's sitting there, analyzing how Carol's presence in our lives has transformed us from lovers into mothers, and all I could think was how badly I wanted to strangle her."

I bit my lip to keep from smiling and grabbed Beth's hand. She puckered her mouth, sighed, and slumped against me.

"Such problems."

She laughed. "And you, poor baby, walked right into our drama. Bet you expected something different. Like in the old days. The two of us watching some dumb sitcom, eating Haagen-Dazs, and just waiting for the chance to smother you with our aggressively loving attention."

"Ooh, it sounds so good."

"Matter of fact, it does." She stood abruptly, patted Carol's exposed and very pudgy thigh, and slipped through the sliding parlor doors. A second later she yelled, "Find something dumb on the tube." I hit the remote, surfing until I found a repeat of "Mary Tyler Moore" on Nickelodeon.

"How about a hat-tossing Mary?" I shouted back.

"Perfect."

We spent a few hours rummaging through seventies sitcoms, fisting popcorn and M&Ms, before Beth fell asleep on my shoulder. I didn't leave until almost four in the morning, when Carol woke up, Dinah descended bleary-eyed and repentant, and I was hit with the awful realization that I missed K.T. far more than I had thus far admitted.

Saturday should have been my day off. But no such luck. Tara Parker had said she'd meet me at her apartment building promptly at nine a.m., so I showered, dolled myself up, even tweezed an eyebrow, and drove into Manhattan. There was a parking spot right in front of a Greek diner. I took it, ordered three cups of joe, no sugar or milk this time, and headed over to Jane Street. I was fifteen minutes early, so I flipped the lid on coffee number one and started gulping. The building was five stories tall. A glance at the buzzers told me there were three occupants per floor. Next to number twelve I found Parker's name followed by a slash and the name Abrams. Their mail box was empty. I jammed the buzzer and waited. Thirty minutes later I was still standing there.

Parker had blown me off.

I dropped a cup into the waste basket, placed the diner bag on the floor, and peered into the hallway. The apartment doors abutted each other. Breaking in would be real risky, especially on a weekend. Besides, I was feeling lazy. I retrieved my coffees and headed for the nearest phone booth. No one was in my office, no surprise there, so I dropped a second quarter and dialed Jill's home number. John answered, groaned, and handed the phone to Jill. She, at least, was cordial.

"I really like my job," she said, "but can't I have a day off now and then?"

"Sure. Then is fine. Now, I have some questions. Did the freelancers check in yesterday?"

She hesitated. "Oops. I forgot to call them." She made big with the excuses, but she didn't have to. In some ways, I was relieved she wasn't perfect. Gave me more leeway. I forgave her, felt really good about myself, and decided to drink the remaining coffee with a hot bagel. Afterward, I walked over to Zoogie Cocchiaro's apartment on West 19th Street. We didn't have an appointment, so of course I found her home. She buzzed me up and I skipped inside.

Zoogie was wearing a lemon-yellow halter top and dungaree shorts that barely made it past her butt.

She was young, salon-blonde, and too thin. With make-up and soft focus she probably was a knock-out, but right then she looked like half the kids strolling through Washington Park. Except a lot more high-strung. She lit a cigarette as soon as the door closed behind me. I took the time to check out the decor. Clearly, her career to date had not been stellar. The furniture was spare — most of it smacked of an Ethan Allan purchase made by a mother a good fifteen years ago. The stereo had an eight-track deck. The music blasting from it was unrecognizable.

"A Monster is Loose," she pronounced from behind me. My head pivoted in her direction. The cigarette wiggled between her lips. She sounded like southern California, but looked like pure Brooklyn. "Do you know it? Toxic Water's the group. What do you think?"

"Interesting."

She smiled. It made her look pretty. "My mother says the same thing."

I wasn't pleased by the comparison, but I figured it was a start. "She must be a smart woman."

A shrug. "I dunno. She's good, though. Better than my pop."

I had one last coffee, lukewarm and on the verge of congealing. I offered it to her. She didn't seem to mind. She sat down cross-legged in front of the couch, which was draped in a white sheet and littered with throw pillows which only half-concealed the glistening spokes of a few errant springs. I joined her on the floor.

"Where are you from, Zoogie?"

"Bensonhurst. Originally. The last ten years I lived in L.A. with my dad. He's an actor, a cool dude but not much good at the parent thing. Last year, I got my first modeling job and then, I dunno, I ended up back here. It's been kinda cool, though. My mother's been righteous, y'know, writing letters for me, driving me around." She lit a second cigarette.

"How old are you?"

"Guess."

"Twenty-three."

"Seventeen. Cool, huh? My agent says my look's really in these days." Her smoker's cough made her sound fifty. When she finished hacking, she rubbed her eyes with one palm and asked, "So, you a cop or what?"

I flashed my license. "I'm a P.I."

Her smile broadened. Maybe she could make it as a model after all.

"I've kept your name from the cops. I didn't have to. Matter of fact, I'm risking my career by protecting you. But that's not your concern. All I want from you is the truth. What happened on Sunday? Did you keep your breakfast appointment with Brian?"

The smile collapsed. She stood up, exposing more of her tush than I needed to see. I wanted to buy her knickers. She flipped her hair, crossed the room, said, "No. Brian canceled," and started drawing circles on a filmy window pane with her index finger.

Whrrrr. Wrong answer. "The other day you told me that you were the one who canceled."

She spun around, stared at me quizzically, then shrugged. "I made a mistake."

"Now or then?"

"Whatever."

The cigarette tip brightened as she took a deep

drag. Her skin looked pallid, her dark brown eyes frightened. I had to break through. "Zoogie, I'm going to tell you something no one else knows. Not even the police. But I'm going to trust you. Okay?" She shot me a furtive look.

"Brian raped one of his models."

Her back was toward me. Even so, I could tell she had stopped breathing for an instant. She moved over to the stereo, knelt in front, lowered the music, then rose slowly. One hand holding the cigarette to her lips, the other clutched to her stomach, she muttered, "I knew it."

"Knew what?"

"Knew it, that's all."

"C'mon, for Christ's sake."

She glared at me, but I wasn't the focus of her anger. "He was such a pig."

"How'd you meet?"

"At a shoot for *Seventeen*. My big breakthrough, you know. Okay, it was a group shot, about ten of us, but Brian picked me out, okay? Told me I was the standout, the one who'd make it to the big time. I was ga-ga for him. Who wouldn't be? Even my mom was impressed. I mean, Brian Fritzl shot some of the biggest talents in the business, and he was pursuing *me*. A week later, he took me and my mom to dinner, then another time he showed up here with a portfolio of his photographs. He spent an hour, all business, talking to me about poses, make-up tricks, things no one else knew. He said if I learned what he called the fuck-you attitude, I could be the next hot-shit model."

She stabbed her cigarette against the wall, then licked a fingertip and wiped away the ash.

"What happened Sunday?"

"I went there all right. He had a spread ready for me, bagels and lox and shit like that. But neither of us ate. Man, was he on. Music blasting, camera clicking away, just like you see in the movies. I mean, the fans were blowing and my clothes were whipping around me." She had closed her eyes and begun to sway, a dreaminess descending over her features. My breath caught. She looked gorgeous. "Then Brian stopped shooting and began circling me. He looked kind of funny so I giggled, and then he said he had a hunch he wanted to play out. Told me to take off my pantyhose, said my skin was more cream than cream and he wanted to capture the real thing. I was kind of shy, I mean, pulling down my pantyhose like that was so strange, but then he came over and just whipped them from my hands. He balled them up, kinda, and kicked them, almost angry-like. Then he hiked up my skirt and told me to straddle the stool. The position made me, you know, nervous, he was standing so close, so I said something, like I better get going and he gave me this righteous smile. Told me not to worry, that I was a queen and he was just my servant." Goosebumps erupted on her skin. She shivered and said, "It was kinda spooky, how his voice changed." Her eyes focused on a spot over my shoulder. "My mom's going to be home soon."

"Your mom lives here?"

"Kinda. She's a flight attendant. She crashes with me when she's in town. I really don't want her to find you here."

"What happened, Zoogie?"

She went over to a coat closet, rummaged in a

jacket pocket, retrieved a new pack of Virginia Slims and ripped the plastic with a manicured fingernail. I repeated the question.

"That's it. Really. I mean, I kinda knew where things were heading. He stroked my cheek, told me I needed ripening, how he could take me places no one else could. I can guess what woulda happened if my mom hadn't come by just then."

I concealed the leap in my interest. "Your mom interrupted?"

"Yeah. I had kinda borrowed her uniform for the shoot. It was Brian's suggestion. She went ballistic on me."

We both heard the keys in the front door at the same time.

Zoogie said, "Shit," and lit the cigarette. I turned to say hello. Zoogie's mom had to be my age, but we were from two different worlds. She was five-seven, decked in a tight-fitting American Airlines uniform, and looked like she was ready to walk the plank in a Miss America pageant. Her name tag identified her as Cherie Cocchiaro. She had dark brown hair and strong hands. From the way her eyes sparked and nose flared as I explained my presence, I guessed she had no trouble expressing anger.

She didn't bother to introduce herself. She wheeled her flight bag to one side of the room, removed her jacket, then quietly asked me to leave.

"I can understand how you feel, but Zoogie may have been the last person to see Brian alive and —"

She spun around. "Do you think I give a flying fuck about men like him, huh? I deal with that type every goddamn day. My fucking husband's the same way. You know what that fuck was doing when I came into his studio, huh? Did Zoogie tell you that?"

"Mom!"

"He was dry-humping her from behind, his fucking hands on her breasts —"

"Mom!"

"I wanted to rip his eyes out. Believe me, if I'd known there was a gun in that fucking place, I would've shot him myself."

"Did you?"

She laughed bitterly. "Get the fuck out of my house."

The lady meant business. I started to back away, but not before I noticed an ugly burn on her right ankle. Even through the hose, I could tell the skin was blistered. She followed my gaze, said, "Some asshole spilled his coffee on me."

I started to ask another question, but she stopped me cold by snapping up the phone and stabbing 911. I got out of there before the call went through.

Saturday afternoon passed in a blur. I lunched with Dinah and Beth, had the honor of receiving Carol's cheesy emissions not once, but twice, then went upstairs, took an uneasy nap, woke up, and spoke in rapid succession to Mel Olsen, Jill, my sister Barbara, and finally K.T.'s brother-in-law Larry, who had just arrived home from backpacking in the Adirondacks and now deemed it necessary to lecture me about how stupid T.B. and I were for keeping information from the real cops. He pissed me off, so

I told him I had lied to T.B. The truth was, K.T. had last called me from Minnesota and they were heading west. Payments were being made in cash, and they were using the names Maud and Alice Smith.

I hung up, took four Advils and a bath, and hoped the day would end not with a bang but a whimper. That's when the phone rang again.

"You dressed yet?"

I smiled at the voice, said, "If this is an obscene phone call, you better start moaning," and finished toweling myself.

"Sorry to disappoint, but it's only us, Spoon and Moon, otherwise known as Amy and Carly, two of your closest and most forgiving friends." Carly's voice was buried briefly under traffic noise. "We've left the Poconos behind and are ready to boogie big-time. Wanna join us?"

"You're in town?"

"Sweetheart, it's Gay Pride weekend. Where else would we be?"

Shit. Gay Pride. I'd forgotten. "I don't know, you country girls are always doing something exciting, like planting bulbs or basket-weaving."

"It's June, the bugs are biting, and my hiney needs a workout. Are you and K.T. up for some action?"

At the mention of her name, my stomach turned. "I'm solo tonight."

There was the slightest pause. "So, it'll be like old times. I'll save all the slow dances for you. You know how Amy and I hate to lead. C'mon."

"Well . . ."

"I'll buy you a Yoo-Hoo."

Good friends know how to play dirty. "You're on. I'm steam-cleaning my sneakers right now."

I rummaged through my closet, found a white shirt with no stains and a pair of chinos with pleats intact. Then I put on Tina Turner, danced around in a pair of relatively unscuffed shoes, decided this night might work out after all, and headed out the door. The annual women's dance was being held at Manhattan Community College, off the West Side Highway. It was ten o'clock and the streets were swarming with festive lesbians of all shapes and sizes. By the time I finally found a parking spot, I had fallen in lust twelve times and in love once. I was a wild woman on the prowl. I bought a roll of Mentos and trotted toward the front door.

Auburn hair billowing in a sticky Hudson River breeze, Carly stood outside the entrance. She was decked out in black silk and red-hot lipstick. Amy wore a low-cut blouse the color of blush, white stirrup pants, and a pair of neat pumps. We kissed, hugged, and agreed to exchange no facts. The arrangement made me giddy. Inside, the building throbbed with music and pre-march hormones. The three of us never made it to the dance floor, we just began moving in place.

Someone grabbed my butt, too hard for me to enjoy, and I spun around to be on the receiving end of a boozy kiss from my client Abigail Whitman. She screamed in my ear something about wanting to cash in on Julie's ass, then her bloodshot eyes focused elsewhere and the skin across her cheeks seemed to tighten. Capillaries threatened to burst. I followed her gaze to where a young brunette stood. She was talking to a good-looking Hispanic woman who had one hand resting on the brunette's hip.

"Motherfucker." It was Abigail. She sliced her way across the room and began shouting at the two women. She raised the back of her hand to the brunette, threatening, and I jolted forward. Before I made it there, the two of them had melted into the crowd. Carly found me there, standing open-mouthed, and made me dance with her until my toes hurt. After a short break, a woman behind me started a seductive hip bump and I made her pay for it with a good, heavy sweat. She invited me home, I declined and moved on to the next gyrating body.

By twelve-thirty, I had snubbed three ex-lovers, danced with one, and broken up with someone I had never slept with. I ran into Mel Olsen at one point, warned her away with a kiss that told her I was reckless and horny and not looking for talk. It also told me that I had better get my ass home. I rounded up Carly and Amy and told them it was time for food or sex. They understood instantly. We started shimmying toward the front door when I saw her. The face made my heart skip a beat.

The last time I had seen it was on a piece of photographic paper disintegrating at the bottom of a stop bath. In Brian Fritzl's darkroom.

Chapter 9

I left Carly, Amy and my car behind and followed her on foot. She was even more striking in person. Tall, maybe five-ten, with just enough flesh to drape her bones like a satin sheet. Her skin was the color of toasted marshmallows, not burnt, just golden enough to entice the tongue. Her eyes were emerald green, her lips full and coral-pink. The cleft in her chin was the designer's final flourish. Accompanying her was another woman who, though she faded by comparison, was no plain jane. A good five inches shorter than her friend, she had muddy-red, shoulder-length hair, expertly permed. She was stocky, broad where the black woman was thin, curved where she was angular. They were both dressed simply, dungarees and GAP shirts, little jewelry and no make-up. The black woman also wore an old-fashioned vest, complete with pocket watch.

They strolled uptown chatting quietly, their hands laced and heads bowed together in what seemed an intense conversation. I didn't want to lose them. The nearest subway was in the opposite direction. Betting on a hunch, I flagged a taxi, slapped a twenty into his palm, said, "Listen to me closely, and you'll have the best fare of the night," then instructed him to idle up the street slowly. My instincts paid off in two blocks. The shorter woman waved down a cab, and they hopped in.

"Now, follow that cab." Before he could laugh, I reinforced the order with a second twenty. Then I checked my wallet. I had forty left. I leaned forward, my hands braced on the bullet-proof divider, my heartbeat ringing in my ears. The pounding accelerated as the taxi in front of us weaved through traffic and made a sharp left onto a block I recognized instantly. I didn't even wait for it to stop. I yelled, "Stop," removed a ten, and got out. Sure enough, the women were headed toward a building at the far end of the block. Tara Parker had come home.

It was after one and I was feeling ornery, otherwise I might've waited until morning which, as it turned out, would have been a mistake. I followed them into the building, smiled real sweet as they unlocked the door, pretended to search my safari-style jacket's eight pockets for my keys, and muttered something about how great the dance was. I even flashed the neon lambda stamped on the back of my hand. They smiled back, held the door open for me, mumbled something like, "Have a good march."

I climbed the steps, barely keeping pace with them, waited till they reached door number twelve, inserted the key, and then I took the last two steps in one jump and said, "Hey, aren't you Tara?" like her name had just dawned on me.

The stocky one was suspicious. If her distrust hadn't been directed at me, I would've said, "Good girl." Instead, I flipped my license for the second time that day, and grinned real wide. "Robin Miller. We had an appointment this morning. Remember?"

Her partner looked ready to deck me, but it was Tara's reaction that interested me most. I could almost see the moisture evaporate from her lips and bead up instead on her forehead. She averted her eyes and scampered into the apartment like a puppy just speared by a porcupine. I tried to follow, but a fat palm ended up dead center of my chest.

I had never used tae kwon do on an innocent, but right then I was tempted. I sliced my arm up and moved past her with a look that said, don't even think it, and made myself real comfortable on a love seat that faced into the room. It was a nice apartment, furnished in pine and natural fabrics. The art on the walls, all signed oil paintings, provided the only color. There were three of them, all depicting African women and painted in bold strokes of vermillion, black, green and lavender. I crossed my legs slowly and counted to ten. Then I took off my jacket because I didn't like feeling myself sweat.

Tara had disappeared into another room and her

partner's attention kept bouncing between me and what I assumed was the bedroom door. She finally made her decision and left me alone.

I made a beeline for the desk. A stack of bills lay under a paperweight. I didn't have time to memorize the credit card numbers, but I tried. The message pad near the phone had a number scribbled on it that struck a familiar note. I used a pen to jot the digits on my palm. There was a *Gaia Guide,* one paged marked by a Post-it. I flipped it open to the heading Provincetown. Five different inns had been check-marked. Intriguing. More intriguing was the checkbook in drawer number-one, with notations indicating trips on Monday and Wednesday to two different doctors. I made a mental note and went to open another drawer when I heard footsteps approaching. I lunged for the couch.

As they exited the bedroom I caught a glimpse of two hefty suitcases, ready and waiting to go. Those babies had been packed way before I arrived. They disappeared behind a door. I looked up at Tara and stopped feeling smug. This lady was disintegrating fast. She kept her eyes lowered as her lover gingerly sat her down on the love seat, pushed in next to her, and reached for her hand. She shot me a look filled with venom. "Tara neglected to tell me about your phone call. By the way, my name's Cindy."

I nodded. "Sorry about meeting this way —"

"Cut the shit."

Cindy was direct. I like that in a woman. "Fine. I'll get to the point. Tara was —"

A gurgling sound made me halt. Tara said, "I think I'm going to throw up," and ran out of the room again.

Cindy watched her go and then exhaled deeply. "Just tell me what you want."

"First, no one else knows who Tara is . . ."

"What do you mean?"

"Her photograph was found in Brian Fritzl's darkroom the day he was murdered. The police didn't find it interesting. I did."

"So?"

"She had an appointment to see Brian at ten o'clock the same day. Approximately two to three hours before he was killed."

She waved a hand at me. "None of that means shit, and you know it."

"Cindy . . ." The voice was Tara's. I turned around. She was leaning against the wall near the bedroom door. She raised her chin and tugged on the points of her vest. "Maybe it's better this way —"

Cindy jumped up, angled her head at Tara in a clear warning. Tara paused just long enough for Cindy to interrupt. "Tara was never there —"

"I was, hon."

"I said," Cindy enunciated with meaning, her eyes fixed on her lover's, "you were never there."

Tara shook her head, reluctantly submissive. "Fine. But it's just a matter of —"

"Justice." Cindy bit off the word. The two women exchanged a glance that excluded me, then Tara's gorgeous green eyes filled and she smiled weakly. She mouthed, "I love you," and joined her partner. They sat down opposite me, hands linked, a formidable roadblock to the truth.

I tried a different approach and got the same answer. Yes, Tara had had one photo shoot with Brian; however, the exact day of the shoot could not be recalled. If she had in fact scheduled a second session with Brian last Sunday, she had forgotten it. She and Cindy had spent the day at the Metropolitan Museum of Art, followed by a picnic lunch in the park. They spent the night alone, watching videos of old B movies. Cindy quickly elaborated: "The Blob" and "It Came From Outer Space." The dialogue was rehearsed, even Cindy's interrupts. No matter how hard I tried, I couldn't budge them. When the clock struck two, my resolve weakened and I stood up.

"You ladies planning a trip out of town?"

For the first time in nearly an hour, Tara's poise slipped and a ripple of alarm disturbed Cindy's resolute calm. They answered no at the same time, but neither one of them was convincing. It didn't matter. I had seen the suitcases. And the destination.

"Well," I said, lifting my jacket from the couch, "don't. If I can't get an answer out of you, the cops will." I rifled through my wallet for a business card. "Unless you call me before I call them."

Tara reached for the card, but Cindy pulled her back. Again, they had a silent conversation, one that made me envious of their relationship. Tara said, "That won't be necessary."

I didn't bother asking why.

When I walked into my apartment, the kitchen clock said it was three-twenty-four. I had five messages. I put the a.c. on high, fed the cats for the fourth time in twenty-four hours, tossed back a refrigerated Kit-Kat bar, then hit play.

T.B.'s call was first. He was pissed at me for "giving K.T. up." Apparently, brother-in-law Larry had bought my nonsense about K.T.'s phone call and had notified the detectives working on the case. T.B.

was working on a strategy to throw them off course, and he wanted to meet me tomorrow at four. Which was today. I glanced back at the clock. A little more than twelve hours from now. If he didn't hear from me, he'd expect me at the same cafe where we had talked the day after Brian's murder. It was a command performance.

T.B. should've been an actor.

His call was followed by one from Detective Mario Chinnici. I was expected to call his office "at my earliest convenience." I knew cops and knew the subtext. Chinnici knew I had been withholding and was now gunning for my ass. I started wondering if it was time for me to take my act on the road again.

The next call was from Carly and Amy, ordering me to call them in Pennsylvania as soon as I got in. One ring would suffice. I took care of that before the message finished. I had one hang-up, then the final phone call, which began with a rush of canned disco music.

"Hey, it's Julie. I know you probably didn't expect to hear from me again, but I just can't stop thinking about you. So happy Gay Pride, and all that. And if you come back into town, please, please, look me up. No commitments or anything. I just think, well, you know what I'm thinking. All I can say is, ouch."

I went to sleep. I didn't even stop to brush my teeth.

Five hours later I cursed and grabbed the phone from the cradle. Dinah and Beth tried to convince me to go to the march. I wasn't interested. In fact, I was barely conscious when they called from downstairs. But I didn't have time to linger. I got up and sleepwalked through my morning routines. I was feeding the cats when I noticed the ink smears on my palm. Damn it. I had forgotten to write down on paper the phone number I had copied at Parker's apartment.. The digits were something-zero-eight-two-nine-something-four-something-seven-zero. Or eight. I wrote them down, slapped the Post-It onto my pocket notepad and poured the coffee.

Right before Dinah and Beth left I exchanged car keys with them and explained my plans for the day. Afterward, I packed a couple of suitcases and headed out. It depressed me that the cats didn't seem surprised to see me go.

I loaded my housemates' new Toyota hatchback, checked to see that no neighborly thieves had witnessed my boldfaced act, then walked over to the office. Naturally, there were two messages waiting for me from Detective Chinnici. Call, and call at once. K.T.'s brother-in-law had churned the detective's waters like a pro. I used Tony's private line to dial Jill. Our conversation was short and efficient. As a lark, I dialed Tara Parker's number. Of course, no one answered. Same response at Tzionah Stein's and Kathleen Fritzl's. The birds had flown the coop.

Feeling lonely for suspects, and with more than three hours to kill before I needed to head into the city for my meeting with T.B., I dialed into an information network. I didn't amass much data. Tara Parker's credit was good. Tzionah Stein owned a 1990 Mazda sedan with a license plate number I couldn't run a trace on without an assist from the NYPD. Kathleen Fritzl was listed in every social register imaginable. Zoogie Cocchiaro and her mother were not.

I had one more task to perform before leaving the

office, identifying the doctors listed in Tara Parker's checkbook. That's when I hit paydirt. Dr. Emanuel Cora was a gynecologist located right on Parker's block. The second doctor was Margaritte Bonner. I had a little trouble locating her at first, but locate her I did. Dr. Bonner was a psychologist employed at the Rape Intervention Clinic on West Twenty-Third.

Ten to one, I had found Brian's last victim.

T.B. was pacing in front of the cafe when I arrived. He glanced up at me, sighed visibly, and signaled to the waiter. It was our friend Mike, the waiter who had served us last Monday. He didn't seem annoyed with me, so I assumed he and T.B. had ironed out their earlier misunderstanding about their respective sexual preferences. I sat down. Mike leaned over and whispered, "I don't care that he's straight. I've overcome that obstacle before," then proceeded to pull the chair out for a flustered T.B. I ordered a Caesar's salad with grilled chicken and T.B. asked for a plate of pasta, no sauce or butter.

"My stomach's upset," he explained. To give the guy his due, he looked like crap. "I'm going to make this fast, because I don't need to be seen with you. My boss called me this morning, on a Sunday, threatening to can me. Larry wouldn't even talk to me after last night, but Ginny threw a hissy-fit and promised to leave him if he didn't at least hear what I had to say. So I told him about Tzionah Stein —"

"You what?"

"C'mon, Rob. We discussed this. She's one of your top suspects —"

"Operative word there is *one*."

"I had to send Larry sniffing in another direction."

"That's why I gave him Minnesota."

"Fine. And I gave him Tzionah. Before you bite off my nose, let me tell you what my well-connected, brown-nosing brother-in-law found out. Tzionah Stein's in Wellfleet. Don't interrupt, and close your mouth. I don't need to see your fillings. Apparently Kathleen Fritzl doesn't know everything there is to know about the dearly departed. So, if you stop muttering, I'll take you out of the dark."

I quickly averted my eyes and began toying with the salt shaker. I wasn't the only one in the dark. T.B. still didn't know about my activities in Washington. Or Brian's sexual attacks.

"Tzionah Stein inherited a nice parcel of land in Wellfleet. Four acres. Ocean view. Fritzl bought the property for a song some fifteen years ago. It's now worth half a mil, give or take a hundred thou."

"That's a pretty generous bequest for an ex."

"The will was drawn up a few years ago, when the heat was still on. The lawyer said Brian talked about changing the terms but never got around to it."

"Convenient."

"That's what Larry said. He's also impressed by how fast Stein's moving. Right before she left town, she met with an architect about designing her dream house."

"You have an address for her in Wellfleet?"

He shook his head and leaned back as Mike served our meals. The handsome waiter with the good buns said, "Some friends of yours were down here the other day."

T.B. and I both turned puzzled faces to him.

"You know, the cops."

We both intoned, oh, with no interest shown. I hoped Mike would take the message, leave us the parmesan cheese and peppermill, and go. No such luck. He cranked out the pepper slowly and said, "They were real impressed with my recall. About that hit-and-run I told you about. Other people here, the waiters, customers, one guy was a lawyer, none of them remembered anything but how that white sedan came barreling around the corner . . ."

I zoned out while Mike replayed the graphics of the now infamous hit-and-run. T.B. was more indulgent. He nodded his head and ignored his pasta. I dug in. Mike cited estimated speed, type of bumper, day and time, almost to the exact minute of impact. I crunched into a garlicky crouton and stopped. "Repeat that last part."

Mike had one of those big-dimpled smiles. He repeated himself and I thought, I may owe him one. Maybe I'd introduce him to one of my single male friends. A cute one.

"What about the occupants?"

"Occupants. There were two. The driver had real short hair and the passenger had, you know." He pretended to flip his nonexistent locks with the back of one hand. "Real long hair. I couldn't make out color."

"Sex?"

"I prefer men," he said, then winked at T.B. "Especially redheads."

T.B. squirmed.

"License plate number?"

"Funny. I got the last two digits, but I'm a little dyslexic. It was three-seven-oh. Or something like that."

A customer at a nearby table shouted for service. Mike apologized for the interruption and left us.

T.B. broke into my thoughts. "What was that about?"

"You didn't get it, did you?" It was his turn for illumination.

"The hit-and-run took place at five past one. It made a sharp left this way, leaving Prince Street. *Prince Street*. Brian's block. Right around the estimated time of the murder. Get it now?"

He guffawed. "So, of course, it was the getaway car."

I speared a thick wedge of Romaine and shoved it into my mouth. Chewed. Then smiled. "The last three numbers on Tzionah Stein's license plate are three-oh-nine. Mighty close. And . . . did I mention this? The car's white? Comments?"

T.B. stood up, grinning. "I have a phone call to make."

I used the time to finish his pasta and pay the check. I left before he made it back to the table. The only problem was, I didn't know where to go. Returning home or to my office could land me in the arms of one Detective Chinnici. I toyed with the idea of driving straight to the Cape, but I was tired and needed a quiet place to think. Somewhere no one would expect to find me.

I drove to my sister's.

Barbara's a CPA and looks, dresses, and eats like

one. She lives on West 89th Street, between Columbus and Amsterdam, in a two-bedroom apartment loaded with dark-wood Victorian furniture and antique-framed paintings by dead men with Latinate names. She makes a shitload of money and wears pantyhose on Sundays. I had only four reasons for loving her: her punky haircut, the two amethyst-triangle earrings she wears in her left ear as a tribute to me, her dismal track record in the romantic department (equal to, if not surpassing, my own), and the fact that she's the only one in my family who ever bothered to treat me like a kid.

The doorman called ahead, so Barb was waiting for me at the elevator. She had on pink, fuzzy slippers and, I hate to admit this, a house dress. She would have called it something else. Matter of fact, she did.

"Before you say a word, it's a Mother Hubbard, very stylish, and if you call it a house dress, I swear to God, I'll ram my slippers down your throat."

Okay, so there a fifth reason for loving her. She hefted a suitcase from one hand and said, "Please tell me you're not moving in."

I laughed and told her the truth: "The mob's gunning for me, and the police think I killed Hoffa."

"Oy. Some people have sisters. I have torture."

"You love it." I trailed her into the apartment. As always, my first response was to speak in hushed tones. "Is this a library, or a home? And what's with the lights? You saving on electricity?"

"It's peaceful, you nincompoop, no wonder you don't recognize it. Peaceful. P. E. A. —"

I killed the spelling lesson by hitting the power button on the television remote. Barbara lunged for it. "C'mon, Sis, I want to see if I made the news." She didn't buy my explanation. She knew my real mission was to get on her nerves.

She replaced the remote in the carved mahogany box that sat at the upper-right corner of the coffee table. "Did you eat yet?" she asked.

"Yeah, but since when does that matter?" I sniffed the air. Something was cooking. "What's in the works?"

Now she smiled fully. "Put your bags in the guest room. Neatly, please. Then join me in the dining room."

I did as I was told, took a moment to call my housemates and check my messages, then marched into the kitchen and moaned. "Oh, you got to be kidding." I wasn't sure if I was staring at a meal preparation or a science experiment. Scales and metal scoops lined the counter. Barbara's a little on the hippy side, by no means fat, but she approaches meals like obstacles to be conquered. A chunk of chicken the size of a pack of cards and the color of winterized skin laid on top of scale number one. A fistful of overcooked rice topped a piece of wax paper on scale number two.

"Why can't you weigh that stuff before cooking it?"

"I did. I just wanted to double-check."

"Tell me, oh great and accurate one, how are you going to split the bounty?"

She laughed, sliced the chicken thinly, spread it over the rice, sprinkled both with soy sauce, and walked toward the dining room. I followed reluctantly. "Don't tell me you have one of those things ready for me?"

We passed through the swinging doors. George Gershwin was playing softly in the background. The Tiffany lamp of roses and lilies glowed over a cherrywood table set for two. Barbara's spot was marked by a cloth placemat and napkin, sterling silverware, and a goblet of white wine. Mine had a plastic mat, no utensils, and a peanut butter and jelly sandwich. Barbara waited expectantly for my laughter. I surprised us both by turning damp eyes toward her and saying something stupid, like I love you. Then I got back to normal and ate my third dinner in two hours.

I cleared the plates, tossed mine in the trash can, and washed my sister's. She measured out the coffee, a feat at which she is unrivaled. "So," she said, "This works out well." Her tone was suddenly stilted, which should have warned me about what was coming. "Ronald's picking Mom up at the airport at ten —"

I flattened my palms on the counter. "Don't start."

"She's dying, Robin."

I left the room. She followed me. It was after eight. I considered driving home.

We faced off in the living room, in front of the fish tank. "All I'm asking," Barbara began, "is that you come to the hospital once. That's all. We're checking her in for a few days and then Ronald's going to —"

"Do whatever Mother wants. I know. Ronald's a good boy. And you're a regular, what would she call it, a *ba-ala busta*."

"I'm not a housewife."

"Well, I'm the murderer. Remember."

We stared hard at each other. Barbara broke eye

contact first. She focused on the fish. Another of her fetishes. Her bookcases contain two shelves of reference guides on tropical fish. The fish tank itself is nearly eight feet long. There was one, bright yellow and black, whose body curled through the water like a reel of film. I blinked and moved to my sister's prized Regency armchair. The lattice work cut into my back.

Still mesmerized by her fish, she said quietly, "She's never used that word."

"Did anyone have to? It's too late for this, Barb. I know you mean well, but —"

"But what?" She strutted over, knelt, and hung onto my knees. "Are you going to wait until she's dead, huh? The way you did with Dad. You're a grown woman now. It's different."

I leaned back, tilted my head away. The chair was made for interrogations. I stood up.

"The only thing different is that I don't need her."

"She needs you." She spoke to my back.

"She has you and Ronald."

"She asked if you were coming."

I couldn't afford to turn around. I said, "Tell her I'm hunting down a murderer. She'll understand." Then I went to bed. Barbara didn't pursue me. I guess that's another reason to love her. She knows when to stop.

Barbara left for work before I rolled out of bed. I wrote her what I considered a mushy note that she'd call a letter of harassment. She left me a set of keys and a Weight Watcher's muffin, ready for nuking. An hour later I was outside the Chemical Bank on Broadway, handing Brian's safe deposit key to Luce. She wore black baggy trousers, a cream poet's blouse, and a nicely tailored blazer stabbed with a silver pin. I had never seen her look so good and I told her so. She flipped the compliment off with a wave of a choice finger, warned me that my check better not bounce, and left me outside.

I grabbed a coffee and a newspaper from a corner deli. Brian's death had hit page three last Monday. Today, the murder was history. I was reading the lead article about the Supreme Court's decision to uphold abortion rights when Luce exited the bank, her leather satchel bouncing merrily on her generous hip.

"Treat me to brunch at some place pretty," she said by way of greeting.

We compromised on Big Fat Sam's, a breakfast-only restaurant that smelled like burnt bacon and wilted onions. The table at the rear was small, private, and the film of grease coating it thin. I unfolded a napkin and Luce laid the goods on top. There was a copy of Brian's will. I read the key passages, confirmed what I already knew, with one exception, and tossed it into my briefcase.

Luce smeared a thick wedge of butter onto her rye toast. "Any surprises?"

"Not really. Tzionah Stein's the big winner. Kathleen and the kids inherit his photo collection —"

"Not those I bet," she said, pointing the butter knife at the vellum-wrapped packet that came next. I slipped out a stack of eight-by-ten glossies, groaned, and put them face down.

Luce stabbed a fork into the heart of her sunny-side-up and said, "From the quality, I'd say the photos weren't his."

"I don't know, they're better than most porn shots." I had a bad taste in my mouth so I stole a piece of Luce's toast.

"Keep going," she said.

I lifted a thick, legal-size vinyl folder sealed with a velcro closure. I plucked it open. The first item I retrieved was a black-and-white photograph of Tzionah and an infant, clearly taken in the hospital. Tzionah was in a Beth Israel patient gown, the baby cradled in her arms, cocooned in blankets. Shadows circled her eye sockets; she must have been crying before the photo was shot. Her cheeks still glistened. The way she held the baby was odd. Close to her belly, her rough hands flat against the infant's body, yet she appeared somewhat detached. From the left-hand edge of the photograph, disembodied hands extended toward her. I cleared my throat and swallowed.

I reviewed a copy of the boy's birth certificate next: born August 2, 1990, at 3:32 p.m., weight 5 lbs, 1 oz, named Nathan Thomas Stein, father Brian A. Fritzl. The medical files on the child were extensive, including the signed forms that signaled the couple's decision to keep the infant hospitalized indefinitely. Apparently, the physician who delivered Nathan had been dead set against the decision. There were other legal and financial documents, including Brian's living will, a rubber-banded collection of stock certificates, correspondence with a place called AMI of Massachusetts involving son Chad, two letters from his daughter Belinda, and assorted correspondence with women in cities ranging from Tokyo to Tampico, Mexico. Luce handed me a suede box containing an odd collection of jewelry. An emerald earring. A strand of pearls. A gold pin.

I looked up at Luce. "For this," I said, holding up a hollow gold medal Brian had won in some college photography contest, "for this you expected a fancy brunch?"

"Hey, you've got the will. The porn collection." She tapped a box of three videotapes. "Who knows what you'll find in those. Maybe a snuff film."

I snagged her wrist, stopped the fork from entering her mouth, and said, "Not funny."

She shook off my hand and bit into a thick slab of bacon. "No shit. Let me tell you something." Her elbows planted on the table, she leaned sharply toward me, her voice a harsh whisper. "I worked with that son-of-a-bitch for years. Ate dinner with him. Exchanged birthday presents with him. One New Year's, I even kissed him on the damn lips, hugged him like he was one of my best friends. So don't you start telling me what's funny and what's not, okay? This man conned me."

After breakfast, I stopped at a bank, paid Luce in cash, and returned uptown. I sat on the couch and stared at the fish tank for twenty minutes, felt my breathing go zen on me, and understood my sister's hobby for the first time. But the unnatural calm unnerved me so I retreated to the primo leather chair in Barbara's minuscule den and dialed my office.

"Serra Investigations, Jill Zimmerman speaking."

"Hey, it's me."

"Sorry, Mr. Serra is away on business right now. May I help you?"

"Jill, it's Robin."

"Yes. We've had an excellent track record in missing persons. Can I make an appointment for you?"

"What the . . . wait a second . . . is a Detective Chinnici there?"

"Of course. Friday will be fine. Can I have a phone number please, in case we need to cancel."

I gave her my sister's number, told her I didn't expect to be there long, but I'd check in later. "Give Chinnici my regards. Tell him I'm expected any minute, okay? But if he drinks any of our imported coffee, you'll be docked a week's pay."

"Thank you for calling." She hung up.

So my office and home had to remain off limits. Time to weigh my options. My list of suspects had narrowed, but so had my information avenues. For all I knew about K.T. and Lurlene, they could be in Nova Scotia by now. Or in handcuffs. Zoogie Cocchiaro and her formidable mom had probably sicced a posse on my tail. Tzionah Stein was in Wellfleet, and Kathleen Fritzl's current whereabouts were unknown. Meanwhile, Tara Parker and Cindy Abrams were no doubt sunning themselves somewhere in P-town. I turned on the radio. A heat wave was moving in. The forecast for the next three days was hot, humid and overcast. Even with the a.c., I started to sweat. I strolled through the apartment, stopped in front of the fish tank and watched a turquoise fish swim upside down and make a cute O with its mouth. Screw it.

I had my laptop, pocket modem, luggage, and a hefty wad of cash. I wrote my sister a second note and made for the open road.

Chapter 10

I held a Yoo-Hoo in one hand and four aspirins in the other. The headache was bad, and my mood was worse. I had arrived in Provincetown around seven, only to learn that the cottage had been rented to someone else. K.T. had canceled the last two weeks and pocketed the refund. So, grinding salt into an open wound, I was footing the bill for their escapade.

It was a Monday night, the week before Independence Day, and I was in one of the hottest vacation spots for lesbians, gay men, curious straights, whale watchers, Bostonians and skunks.

Three hours, a bike rental and two grand later, I found a suite at the Watermark Inn on the East End of town. I had been forced to use my agency's credit card, which meant sooner or later Detective Chinnici would travel the data highway to my doorstep. I downed the aspirins and fantasized about taking revenge on the woman who had been my cherished lover up until one week ago.

I had a bad night — tossed in bed, read, walked on the beach, sat on the deck, paced. I fell asleep when I didn't want to, about an hour before sunrise. When I woke up, it was almost noon. Fog beaded up on the suite's glass sliding doors. I rolled them aside and let the warm, salty wind settle on my skin and hair. Horns moaned, buoys clanged, seagulls swooped. I hugged myself and leaned against the door jamb. For the first time in my life, I hated how much I loved this town.

I closed my eyes. The sounds carried me back to Fire Island, the first time K.T. kissed me. Her gentleness. Her fire. How, when I pushed her away, stunned and terrified by the power of my response, her lips swept the edge of my lobe. "Tremble in my arms," she whispered in a voice that melded with the wind. "You've never been this safe before." She tightened her grasp, rocked me slowly, my heartbeat a roar between us, and then kissed my face countless times. Finally she said, "I've been to the ocean enough times to know that patience has astounding rewards," and she had walked away, leaving me angry and aching and amazed.

I moved back inside, the doors still open onto the bay. Last night I'd stopped for groceries, so breakfast came fast. Strong coffee, scrambled eggs, and a toasted bagel. I ate slowly. I didn't want to face the day. Or the facts.

My life with K.T. was over. I played with my food, thought, it doesn't make sense, what K.T. and I had . . .

I stopped myself from continuing. Whatever happened with this case, whether or not I saved Lurlene's ass, K.T. had chosen a path that led away from me. And I had to let it go. I pushed away my plate. The first step was solving this damn case. I cleaned up and fetched my computer from the bedroom. I set the laptop on the desk, plugged in the pocket modem, and went to work. Or tried to. Five minutes later, my hard disk crashed. I could've cried then, but if I had I wouldn't have stopped. I gathered my things, slipped on my windbreaker and left the suite. There was a pay phone a quarter-mile down Commercial Street. I dropped in the coins, dialed information, and then called collect to John Feyre's Manhattan photography studio. I used his wife's name, but John caught on quick.

"Robin? Is that you?"

" 'Fraid so."

"Jill hoped you'd call. That detective's been a real pain in her ass, but she's getting revenge. She sent him on a goose chase he won't soon forget. By the way, you're supposed to be in Louisiana working on a top-priority investigation. The client's a hotshot politician. Very hush-hush."

"I appreciate the mirage, but did she have any news that could help me solve the case I'm really on?"

"Not that I know . . . all she's doing is trying to buy you, K.T. and Lurlene some time." I winced at the combination of names and switched the phone to my other ear. John was saying that Jill had contacted Tony and brought him up to date. My partner had wisely decided to remain on the West Coast.

"I better go. Tell Jill I'd like her to find out where Tzionah Stein's staying in Wellfleet." If she's still there, I thought, but didn't add. I gave him the information on the plot of land she inherited and my number at the Watermark. "I'd also like her to do some follow-up work on Zoogie Cocchiaro and her mother. Tell her to call me as soon as she can."

"Fine. Watch your back, buddy."

"I'm trying."

I didn't return to the suite. A fine mist was falling and the wind was soft, hesitant. I walked until my hair was thoroughly wet, my sneakers damp, and then I reversed directions. Back at the suite, I toweled off, spread my papers on the carpet in front of the deck doors, and started scribbling notes.

Estimated time of death: between twelve and two.

Opportunity? Tzionah Stein, Lurlene Hayes, Tara Parker. Possibly Cindy Abrams. If Kathleen's alibi stood up, she was in the clear. And it appeared that Zoogie Cocchiaro had been rescued in time by her mother. But that burn on her ankle still bothered me. Could it have been caused by the bleach fix?

Motive? The same three names came out on top.

Preliminary interviews/evidence? I summarized the facts. I circled the words *hit-and-run* and *rape*.

I uncrossed my legs and cracked by neck. I felt pretty confident that Tara Parker was here in town. The question was, where? I shuffled papers, found my notepad and peeled off the Post-It. I ran a finger along the telephone number I had copied down at

Parker's house. Of course. The first three digits were 508, the area code for the Cape. I pulled out a phone book and checked the digits against those of the five inns that had been marked in Parker's *Gaia Guide,* but life's rarely that simple. There was no match. I dialed all five inns, asked for Tara Parker first, and then her lover, Cindy Abrams. The couple had not checked into any of them, at least not under their own names. Who knows? Maybe they had chosen another destination altogether.

I wasn't ready to give up. Or to remain planted on my butt in a town I love to roam. The main part of Provincetown is all of two miles long. Ninety-nine percent of the shops, restaurants and bars line a single street. Experience has taught me that if someone you know is lodging within a ten-mile radius of P-town, ten to one you'll meet them walking down Commercial Street at least once a day.

Mist had gathered into a driving rain, cold and sharp and smelling distinctly of fish. A chill flickered down my back. Okay, so walking was out. I flipped up my collar, shook out my ragged locks and straddled my rental bike. I had a P-town guide with me. I took off for the nearest inn and started searching for Tara Parker in earnest. Sometime after four I acknowledged that my plan wasn't working and my hip and jaw still ached, but at least the exercise had kept me moving and my brain occupied for a few hours.

I returned to the Watermark, took a long, hot bath, then slipped into my warmest shirt — a flannel baby I've owned since college — and a dry pair of jeans. The rain stopped around dinner time, so I decided to walk through town. I bought a Katherine

Forrest mystery at Womencrafts and, for no reason whatever, a ceramic mug studded with a handle resembling a breast. At Napi's I dined on stuffed mushrooms, blackened swordfish, cajun rice and a slab of hazelnut cheesecake.

You may be surprised about where I ended up, but I'd be lying if I said I was. I stood outside the Lighthouse Café, where Julie Rush performed. Her act was off that night. I shrugged to myself and rambled by. A finger snagged my jacket collar.

"Please tell me you're looking for me and not that hirsute female impersonator I alternate with."

Because God is cruel, Julie was even more attractive than I had remembered. Her sun-kissed tresses hung loose, framed her face and broke over her shoulder in soft waves. She had amazing green eyes. How had I forgotten that? They shone like deep-sea water illuminated by high beams. Her skin, tight and tan, glowed. And her mouth was a killer. The upper lip had a distinct edge, shaped like a flattened capital *M*, and her bottom lip seemed ready to pout. Or kiss. I fought against lowering my gaze past her neck, so certain was I that her bounty extended below her clavicles.

I swallowed and, despite my foul mood, smiled. "Would you believe me if I told you I was just passing through town?"

Oh, Lord. She puckered her mouth, her eyes squinting knowingly. The woman was gorgeous.

"It's great to see you again. Let me get rid of these." She waved a stack of flyers for her show. "And then, maybe you'll let me buy you a drink."

I didn't say no.

The streets were stranger-bumping crowded and

the atmosphere manic, the way it usually is in P-town after a day of rain and hotel-room fever. Julie attracted a lot of attention as we strolled through town, all of it from women. I hate to admit it, but it made my hormones hop. I was wondering how Tom Jones's wife felt as women had pitched brassieres at her husband's feet when Julie hooked her arm into mine, pointed with her chin and said, "The place over there's pretty quiet."

We walked in, Julie took an employee aside, and five minutes later we were seated at a primo table, on the far end of a pier that jutted into the gurgling waters of Cape Cod Bay. We ordered Mexican coffees and fell silent. The tension between us was palpable.

I cut it. "Have you seen —" The sigh was involuntary. "My friend. Have you seen her around town?"

Julie lowered her face, rubbed a hand over her forehead as if the question concerned her and said no.

I nodded, muttered, "Fine," and stared out at the water. Small boats bobbed as the tide rolled in. It was a dark night. No stars.

"Where is this going, Robin?" Julie asked.

I faced her, shook my head for no reason, and shrugged. I was lonely, reckless, and sick of my work. I thought, fuck it, and said, "Julie, I'm a private investigator. I was hired by Abigail Whitman to locate you so that she could collect on a civil suit she won by default several months ago . . . apparently you skipped town and changed names, which seems to be a habit of yours. My agency's supposed to issue a writ of attachment on your bank accounts and any other assets I can identify. I've been holding off, in violation of my professional obligations, because . . . well . . . because. By telling you this, I've just blown every known rule in the P.I.'s book of procedures, not to mention etiquette."

The waitress came with our coffees. I accepted mine eagerly, gulped the burning liquid and ordered a bourbon, straight up, before the waitress had gone two paces. My goal was two-fold — drowning the sick feeling in my gut and evading the shocked expression on my companion's magnificent face.

"I thought you were a writer," she said.

"I am, or was, but this is how I earn my keep now. Don't ask why. Better minds than mine have contemplated that question with no success."

"Abigail Whitman's a nut."

"And she says you're a golddigger. Unfortunately, the facts seemed to bear that out." I ran over the details of the case.

"That bitch. Christ." Julie scraped her chair back from the table. And away from me. She looked royally pissed. "Let me tell you something, I left town because that woman scared me. And yes, I've changed my names a few times — which, by the way, is not a criminal offense — but not because I was scamming people. I'm an artist. Over the years, I've tried different acts. When they didn't work, I'd pick a new name, a new town and a new persona. And by the way, my mother has changed her names a few times and I don't ever recall the cops —"

"I'm not a cop."

"Right." She took her first sip of coffee. I was already on the bourbon and feeling a little annoyed that I was the only one experiencing guilt. "Okay,

Robin. Okay." She appeared to be having a dialogue with herself. "I had an affair with Abigail Whitman. I happen to be attracted to older women."

I frowned. She didn't notice, which was just as well.

"Sometimes those women have been pretty comfortable, but I sure as hell didn't nail them for their trust funds. I have better taste . . . and morals . . . than that. I made some dumb choices, women who saw me as a young appendage to flash in public to prove their, I don't know. Is there an equivalent word to *virility* that applies to women?"

I didn't answer. I was remembering how I had felt about the lesbian fans who had scampered after her as if they were seagulls and Julie a ferry boat. Dodging my conscience, I asked, "What happened in Hawaii?"

"I met Abby on a bike tour. On Haleakala."

"I've been there," I interrupted. She sent me a faint smile and I crumbled into my chair.

"So you know. I was depressed. This woman lawyer had just dumped me, told me I had served my purpose, whatever that meant. Abby was equally miserable. Lonely, I guess. And getting sober had been tough work. We met at a rest stop, started to talk. I didn't really find her attractive, but her need was so . . . what's the right word? Compelling. Something about it touched me deep. And, as it turned out, the sex was hot."

A heat flash singed my cheeks. I adjusted my posture, focused on a schooner slicing its way through the bay.

"I felt as if I could make a difference in her life. Sounds corny, doesn't it, but that's the truth. She offered to take me back to New York with her, give my career a boost. I had been in Boston, Chicago, L.A., San Francisco. Even Dallas. I thought, why not? Maybe it's time for New York. New name, new act, new lover. Abby has this bar . . . well, that much you know. It was doing lousy then, losing business, especially with young dykes. She had a fifties concept of bars. Dark, boozy. I got into it, you know, suggesting changes, sprucing up the place. Before long she made me a partner. I didn't ask for it, the idea was solely hers. Actually, that was the first thing that made me worry. She seemed to want to *own* me, take control of my life. I told her I didn't want to run a bar, I wanted to get back into performing. She said I could do gigs at the bar, so I went along with it."

"She bought you a BMW?"

"Yeah. But I gave it back before I left New York."

I straightened up. "You didn't take it with you?"

"Hell, no. What the hell would I do with a BMW? You know how many times that car was broken into? And the cost of maintaining the damn thing was outrageous. You don't believe me, ask around town. My mode of transportation is a Huffy. A nice model, but certainly no luxury vehicle."

I started to worry my bottom lip. "Go on."

She proceeded to flip each of Abigail Whitman's accusations on its ear.

"Why didn't you fight the lawsuit?" I asked.

"Hard to fight something you don't know about."

Of course. She had changed names again, left town. And when it came down to it, finding Julie while the lawsuit was in contention had not been in

Abigail's interests. She had won the case by default. Only afterwards did she have a solid reason for tracking Julie down.

"Near the end," Julie said, "she started getting really nuts. She had spent more money on me than she had been able to afford. The cost of impressing me, I suppose. One day she demanded that I pay her back. I have some money banked here in town, but that's my security blanket. I told her, no way, I never asked for anything from her. But she got wild. The first time she hit me I said to myself, time to get out of town, kid. I found someone interested in my share of the bar. I sold it, gave her the money and ended the relationship."

She laced her hands in her lap, swung her feet onto the rail and sniffed. "She went on a binge." She glanced at the glass in my hand. I put it down. "Got real sick, throwing up, shaking. The works. I stayed through the night and the next day she asked me to go to AA with her. I did. I lasted another week, then some friends helped me get out of town without her knowing. She's right about two things. When I left, I went out of my way to make sure she couldn't track me down. And I did take a few pieces of jewelry she had given me. As birthday presents. Believe me, I'll be happy to give them back."

A gay male couple strolled on the sand. They embraced openly, kissed. Julie reached over, placed her hand on my arm.

"I'm not saying I'm an angel," Julie said. "I like sex, money and success. I want it all . . . and Abby offered to help me get there. The bar was convenient and she was fun, at first, but I never promised her roses, if you know what I mean. I never used those soft-focus words — forever, love, commitment. She was my lover. That's all. Eventually she was more trouble than distraction, and I booked."

Despite the alcohol, I felt unpleasantly sober. I leaned over the table and said, "You're going to have one nasty legal battle on your hands. She has a judgment against you for a quarter-million."

Julie laughed. "Great. There goes my Huffy."

I scratched my chin, feeling like an ass, and abruptly excused myself. There was a pay phone outside the bathroom. I called Jill, gave her the news. I didn't appreciate the way she guffawed, and I chewed her out for a solid five. It felt good. She ignored me, tried to discuss the Fritzl investigation, but I cut her off. "Not now. Call me in the morning. The point is I want you to contact Mel Olsen, tell her about Julie's situation and see if she can help us out."

"Help *us* out?"

"Just call her. And tell Abigail that if she wants to get her ass out of debt, she had better come up with a new scheme because this dyke plans to stay between her and Julie's assets."

There was no response for a moment, then she said, "Rob, I know this has been a hard week, but you're in this too far —"

"Send John my regards."

I hung up and returned to Julie, who looked surprised to see me. I commented on her expression and she admitted that she had expected me to leave her and her problems in the proverbial dust. The thought had never crossed my mind.

"Let's take a walk," I said, my hand reaching for hers before I could make it stop. We strolled toward the West End of town, past the last shop, and around the curve where a quiet residential area starts. We held hands, bumped, but we didn't talk until we had almost reached a Cape Cod home painted the palest shade of lilac, with a rose trellis out front.

Julie hesitated. "I live here."

I faced the house. Whoever owned the place was a magnificent gardener. Golden-yellow sunflowers marked the property's edges. At the heart of the garden arched a massive, bleached whale jawbone, encased in lavender, morning glories, and flowers I couldn't identify. I hadn't noticed any of this the night I had camped myself outside to spy on the woman whose hand I now held. I said, "I know. You're staying here with a 'friend.' I . . . observed you one night. Before we met."

She didn't look annoyed. "What did the 'friend' look like?"

"A marine."

"Oh." She smiled and arched her eyebrows. "That didn't work out."

"But she's letting you stay here?"

Her head tilted in puzzlement. "It's not hers."

Oh boy. "So you're staying with someone else."

Her long fingers stroked her neck. "As a matter of fact, yes."

"Fine." I shook my head as reinforcement. "Fine. Guess we better keep walking."

She stayed put, held my hand tightly as I took a step. I turned around. "It's my mother's place, Robin."

"Oh."

"Oh."

"She's staying in Hyannis tonight."

"Oh."

"Right."

We stood there, staring at each other.

"Good God," she said, a massive grin illuminating her face. "You're going to make me do it."

I didn't ask her what she meant. I knew just what she was talking about, and she was dead right. These bones have jumped many a limb, but at that moment they were as immobile as those of King Tut.

She steepled her fingers by her mouth, her eyes seeking confirmation. The woman read body language like a pro. The next thing I knew she had me pressed against the rose trellis. If there were thorns, I didn't know it. Her palms pinned my shoulders back and her mouth started a slow, torturous path down the side of my neck. I groaned.

She whispered, "Honey, this ain't nothing yet." Her body moved closer. "I'm not going to make love to you, Robin Miller. No. What we're going to have is sex." I could feel the moisture of her lips on my earlobe. I tried to find her mouth, but her head wouldn't move. "Hot, raw, heaven help me, I'm going to die, sex. Do you understand?"

I nodded, squirmed.

"Good."

She was wearing a scarf, draped loosely around her neck. Now she slipped it off with one hand. "Stay," she commanded. I started to protest and she placed one finger on my mouth; the look she landed on me was downright salacious. An earthquake could have hit then and I swear, I would not have moved. She bound my wrists and tied them to the trellis.

The situation hit home right about then and I

shrugged. "Hey, this is kind of public, don't you think?"

"Yes, I do."

She brushed her lips over my forehead, her tongue darting across an eyebrow, sliding to my ear. "You know what I want? I want to fuck you, right here. Now." She punctuated the words with a hand rubbing hard along the inside of my thighs. "Do you want that?" The pressure increased, the fingertips digging in. "Do you?"

My voice caught in my throat. I wanted her, God knows, my body ached for her hands, but I couldn't say yes.

She moved back, narrowed her eyes, bit her bottom lip. One hand played with her top shirt button, her gaze riveted to my eyes. My focus was her hand. A fingernail scraped the button, teased it for a slow eternity, then flipped it through the buttonhole with flair. She wore no bra. Her cleavage was tan, smooth, and her breasts promised to be full. The next button was undone and so was I. I forgot about the restraints and jerked toward her. She smirked. I watched the tip of her tongue run along the edge of her upper teeth. She opened the rest of her shirt. She didn't touch herself, didn't even move apart the fabric. All she did was close her eyes and tilt her head back, her hands flat against her thighs. She drew them closer, rubbing the crease where leg met hip, and I found myself grinding against the trellis.

Almost at once she was on me again. This time she ran her mouth down the center of my neck, over the buttons of my shirt, the zipper of my jeans, and then she knelt there, her head against my thighs. She bumped me with her chin, edged her way in. My scalp scraped the trellis, discovered a thorn. I yelped just as she growled, "I smell you," and then, to herself, "oh, God."

I bore down, tried to find her, responded, "Goddamn it, fuck me," my voice and words belonging to someone else and coming from the core of me. She rose, her body angled so that one nipple, one pink and thick nipple, ran along my clothes. Her moans were loud. Julie did not give a damn about making sounds, attracting attention. She used her teeth to open my shirt, stared at me without touching for far too long, then reached behind me and undid my bra in one motion, her knee knowing where to find me, but disappearing whenever I tried to ride it.

The scent of roses became intoxicating, mingled as it was with my own body's musk. I rocked against the trellis, lost in sensation, delighting in the pain of craving and not receiving the satisfaction it was too early to want. Julie's palms circled my erect nipples, first soft and then her fingers clenched down hard, followed by her mouth. She drew me in, rhythmically and just a little too rough. It was as if she had tapped a nerve that ran from my tits directly to my clitoris. My body throbbed as if her mouth were already there. Ready to burst I begged her to take me. She just laughed. "No," she said. "I want you screaming."

"Fine." I raised my voice.

She edged away. "You think I'm joking. I'm not. I want you screaming. Screaming. And then I'm going to fuck you like you've never been fucked."

I don't know how long we were there. At times, I swear, I came close to losing consciousness. All I know is that shortly before dawn, a howl ripped from me that drowned out all other sounds.

Chapter 11

Morning came and went. Afternoon rolled around. I kicked my legs off to one side of Julie's sag-in-the-middle bed. Clothes carpeted the floor. Only four items were mine. Neatness wasn't one of Julie's assets. She remained in bed, knees jammed up near her chin. In the full daylight I was able to appreciate more fully the beauty of her athletic musculature. If I had been an artist, I would have rushed to my sketch pad. But I was a detective, albeit a sluggish one, and I had a murder to solve.

I dressed swiftly, noisily. At some point last night,

Julie had made it clear to me that she sleeps like the living dead. When she didn't so much as flicker an eyelid, despite the nasty seagull screeching its head off on the deck right outside her room, I believed her. I tied my sneakers, rubbed my slightly bruised wrists, shook my head in amazement and stood up. I contemplated morning-after protocol and decided that, under the circumstances, a polite note would be blasphemous.

I opted for a clean exit, except I couldn't remember which door opened onto the hallway. I picked the wrong one and got a shoe box in the head. The second time I made the right selection and escaped without incident. I went downstairs, paused at the bottom landing to admire an oil painting of Cape Cod Bay, and was about to exit when a voice rang out.

"My baby's been busy again, I see."

I turned around. The woman standing there was an older, heavier and tougher version of Julie. Her hair was cut short, blown back from her face. She wore no make-up, not that she needed any. It had been a long time since I had had to introduce myself to someone's mother after a night of outrageous sex. I hesitated to extend my hand, attached as they were to my scarf-burned wrists, but habit won out. She laughed and grabbed it in both of hers. Her grip was impressive.

"Tell me you're the writer."

I acknowledged her guess with a nod.

"Thank God. Julie's been obsessed about nailing you."

The blush started at my forehead.

"Ha! I thought that would get a rise out of you.

I'm Edna, by the way, Julie's infamous mother." It struck me that she was probably in her early forties, not much older than most of my best friends. "Come on in. I've got coffee and fresh-baked muffins. My own concoction. A little banana, a lot of walnut, and a chocolate core that's almost as exciting as sex."

Like mother, like daughter. In keeping with my own tradition, I accepted the offer.

"So how'd you and my daughter get together?"

I didn't hold back. She only interrupted once, to pronounce Abigail a dried up, drunken and malicious old bitch, then she kept her opinions to herself until I finished. She didn't seem to mind that I had started out by spying on her daughter. All's fair in love and work, I suppose.

She separated the muffin top from its base and dug her teeth in the latter. I followed suit. She wiped her mouth and said, "What other cases you got? It sounds like a fascinating job."

I surprised myself by talking about Brian Fritzl's murder, outlining the details of the case. She was a sharp listener. Her questions were right on the mark, her observations astute. She would have made a damn good detective.

"Describe this Tara Parker to me again." She didn't miss a beat as she measured out a second pot of coffee. I repeated the description, embellishing this time, partly because I suspected that Edna Isles was a lesbian aficionado and would appreciate it.

"Light-skinned black woman, killer green eyes. Body that stretches from here to Hong Kong?" She replayed my words, adding her own spice. I shook my head. "I may be off, but she sounds like a beauty who's biked by here the last two nights. Around six o'clock. You know, one trail head is just a mile from here. Hang around till then and you can check her out. The worst thing that'll happen is she'll please your eyes. But don't tell Julie I said that. I have a feeling she's gonna want you for herself. At least for a while."

By the sardonic grin on Edna Isles's face, I gathered she was issuing a friendly warning. For my part, the prospect of Edna as comrade was far more palatable than that of future mother-in-law. I took a second muffin and pretended our silent conversation had not happened.

Edna, however, was on her own track. "Julie's a free spirit . . ."

Mildly irritated, I said, "Then it's a good thing I didn't propose marriage last night." The truth was I had K.T. on my conscience. I didn't want to think about her, but there she was, and the more Edna emphasized her daughter's vagabond ways the more I contrasted her with K.T. Don't get me wrong. Sex with Julie had demonstrated that out-of-body experiences could be downright physical. And fun. But good sex — scratch that — fabulous sex was still just sex, and K.T. had taken me to a place way beyond that.

I cut Edna off, thanked her for the coffee and the tip on the sexy biker, and headed back to the Watermark. The phone was ringing twenty minutes after I walked in. I finished updating my daily log, including a note about my appointment with Tara Parker, and picked up.

"Finally." Jill sounded exasperated.

"What's up?"

"What's up, she asks. What's up is that I've been

trying you since early this morning. From a damn phone booth. I've been in and out of the office seven times. If the cops are interested enough in you to be watching me, they must think we're both loco. Which you certainly are. Not to mention inconsiderate. I've been envisioning your body cut up and battered, and if it's not going to be at my hand I'd rather you stay whole until —"

"You're wasting money."

I won't bother repeating her next seven words. "Fine. You want brief, how's this. The police have figured out that we're pumping smoke clouds and are not real pleased. In the future, we're going to have a much harder time getting cooperation from them. Despite Tony's connections."

"Did you get a location on Tzionah Stein yet?"

"Sure did, and she's a popular lady these days. Amazingly, someone at the NYPD agreed with you about Stein needing a closer look. T.B. and I talked an hour ago and the rumor is Stein's about to get a visitor or two, so if I were you I'd stay away from Wellfleet. And you should tell K.T. —"

"I haven't seen her."

"Have you looked?"

"If she wanted me to find her, she'd know what to do. The lady's quite resourceful." I reminded Jill about how K.T. had handled the refund on the cabin, then I changed the subject. "Anything new on Zoogie Cocchiaro?"

"Nothing on Zoogie, but her mom's a wildcat. Used to work for American Airlines, until she slapped a first-class CEO who pinched her derriere. She's been on the U.S. Air shuttle to Boston ever since. That's it."

"Not much."

"I'm dancing as fast as I can, boss."

The operator interrupted us.

There was a clang of change and then Jill said, "I'm sick of this phone. One last message. Your sister called. She wanted to know if you had kidnapped one of her angel fish."

I laughed, said, "Of course, I need all the help I can get," and ended the conversation with Jill on an up note.

I jangled the car keys in my palm, weighed the wisdom of driving straight to Wellfleet, and decided I could reach out and touch my prime suspect without spending a dime on gas. I cradled the receiver in my hand and dialed Tzionah Stein. It was almost three o'clock, but my prime suspect sounded like it was midnight. I identified myself and waited for a pin to drop.

"I won't say I'm pleased to hear from you," she finally said. "Especially not while I'm on vacation."

"Is that what you're calling it?"

Icy silence.

"Are you planning to move Nathan into the new house with you?"

A sharp intake of breath and then she spat back, "What a bitch. How dare you —"

"You were so forthcoming when we first met, I was surprised to learn about your son, never mind the inheritance."

"I didn't know about Brian's bequest. And my son is none of your business."

"Let me lay this out for you . . . you had a damn good motive, not to mention the opportunity, for murdering your ex-lover. Under the circumstances, your life is my business. So tell me, whose idea was it to hospitalize Nathan?"

"This is absurd, but I certainly don't have anything to hide. The decision to hospitalize Nathan was mine. He was . . . and is . . . *my child.* Brian was never under any obligation to us. I'm not saying he wasn't involved, because he was, but we understood from the first that the decision to carry to term was strictly mine to make. Once Nathan was born, Brian was right there for me. It was difficult, of course . . . however, we each fully acknowledged our limitations. Brian was, in the end, a realist, though he sometimes needed a push, the way Lurlene was with him about Chad. You see, unlike his oh-so-noble-wife Kathleen, I'm well aware that a child's sometimes better off with professional help. But . . ." She coughed. "I can't believe I'm doing this. I think that's enough."

"What will you do with the money, Tzionah?"

"Hire a hit man to knock you off and restore my life to its previous order."

"Interesting answer, Tzionah. Good thing I'm recording it for posterity."

For some inexplicable reason, she hung up. Her timing was perfect. I had a biker to catch.

I rode past Julie's place and coasted toward the West End breakwater. The sun had drifted west, the heat had eased up, and a delicious wind was coming in with the tide. My muscles felt loose and my legs a little rubbery as they kicked the pedals. I walked out onto the rocks, white acorn barnacles crunching under my feet. I squatted, fingered the moss, and listened to the slap and gurgle of the waves. No one else was around. I gazed into the bay's depths, watched the strands of eel grass swaying in a slow dance, then my gaze caught on my wrists. K.T.'s birthday was tomorrow. Her presents — including a gold bracelet, an 1820s recipe book, an antique frying pan and five cards — had been left at the cabin along with some of my clothes. I wondered what she would do with them.

It was half past five. I rode up toward the salt marsh. There were quite a few bikers heading home from the beach, and a few riding toward the dunes. I parked myself where I could see the traffic going in both directions. Fifteen minutes later I took a swig from the water bottle and saw her. Tara Parker was the last woman in a pack of five, but she was the only one wrapped tight in white latex. She bent into the hill, the muscles in her calves in sharp relief as she drew ahead of the other bikers. I hopped back on my rental and followed her. She rode with a vengeance. Not fast so much as hard. She stood up on the pedals and slammed her heels down rhythmically.

If we had been on an open trail, she would have lost me at once, but Commercial Street narrowed quickly, Tea Dance was letting out at the Boatslip, and soon we were both half-walking, half-riding through town. She stopped at the Portuguese Bakery and bought two flippers, a fried sweet bread dough that makes my mouth water and my stomach upset. She shoved them into her backpack callously, without even pinching off an end.

We turned up toward Bradford. The place she and Cindy had checked into wasn't listed in any guide I owned. It was a private home, with a small coffee-stained sign in the front window that read "Rm to Rent." Paint chips fell from the shutters. The lawn was burnt. The red cat on the front steps was heaving up a hairball. This wasn't a vacation spot. It was a hide-out. I felt my temperature rise as I called her name.

She spun around, her mouth opened but emitted no sound.

I leaned my bike against the fence and stepped forward. "I know. It's a small world."

"Shit. I knew someone'd been following me." Her hands trembled as she locked her bike onto the porch railing. "What do you want?"

"The truth, Tara. That's all."

She plopped down next to the cat, rubbed its head lightly, and asked me to sit. The next thing I knew I had a flipper in my hand. I softened my tone. "If Brian tried to hurt you —"

A long delicate hand fluttered toward me and stopped. I waited. Tara said, "I can't talk about this, not yet. Okay?"

I planted my elbows on my knees and stared out at the lawn. A plaster birdbath had blown over and cracked. The fragments were still visible in the brown-edged grass. "Some place you guys picked."

I thought I heard the beginning of a laugh. "We thought we'd be anonymous here." The irony in her tone wasn't lost on me.

"Did you guys drive up?"

"No, we took the bus. Why?"

I was thinking about the hit-and-run. I asked, "Car in the shop?"

Nonplussed, she answered, "We just didn't feel like renting again. It adds up."

I bet it does. Note to mental file: *contact rental agencies near Parker's apartment.*

She lifted the cat, flopped him on his back, and rubbed his belly and leg joints. The creature hummed like a mini-fridge. I asked, "What's his name?"

She shrugged. "He's a stray. Gorgeous, isn't he?" She stroked him so tenderly I had to look away.

"Tara, just tell me this much. Did Brian attack you?"

Her lips tightened. A muscle running along her jaw jumped twice. "I never expected —"

A new voice broke in. "Thought we left you in New York."

Tara's lover squeezed between us, but did not join us on the steps. She turned her butt toward me and said, "We have reservations at seven o'clock, hon. You better go inside and shower."

"Baby, don't you think —"

"Tara, we've discussed this. Please."

I stood up. Clearly, I needed time alone with Tara. Without her overprotective lover around, the woman would eventually talk. I said, "Can we have one more moment? You can stand right inside and clock me if you want."

Cindy eyed the two of us, stuck a finger an inch from my left eye, and warned me, "You have exactly one minute." To underscore the point, she set the timer on her Casio. Before disappearing indoors, she kissed Tara on the cheek and whispered instructions in her ear. Tara hugged herself tightly in response.

A second hand ticked in my head. I talked fast. "If I promise to keep your confidences, *whatever* they may be . . ." I paused for emphasis. "Will you agree to talk with me? I won't go to the police. I won't mention your name. But anything you can tell me could help me save an innocent woman's life. Please."

Tara glanced toward the house nervously. I had tickled her conscience, I could see it in her eyes. Still staring at the porch, she muttered, "I'm going to have to talk to someone else first . . ."

I said, "Fine." Patted her back like an old friend.

"I bike every afternoon at the same time. Meet me tomorrow evening, around four, on the Beech Forest Bike Trail, near Clapp pond." Then she drifted off.

I would have followed her, but Cindy barred my way. I tipped an imaginary hat toward her — every woman should have such an overbearing lover — and picked up my bike. I pedaled back up Bradford, crossed on Conwell, and huffed my way up to Race Point. The sun was setting and the wind was wild. Sand pitted my bare legs. Terns scampered along the shore line, gulls skidded over the whitecaps. Dusty miller, a furry gray-green plant, and seaside goldenrod crowded the dune's crest. Slowly the landscape slipped from golden to a dusky purple. The temperature dropped.

I kicked the bike stand, debated the wisdom of squeezing in a visit with Julie before her ten o'clock show, and raced back into town, but when I reached Julie's house fatigue overwhelmed me. I ended up outside the pizzeria Spiritus, a greasy slice resting on my palm, tomato sauce dotting my T-shirt. I had two, followed by a hot fudge sundae with extra nuts. After an hour, people-watching bored me. I gave up my prized seat on the bench and walked. Outside the Lighthouse Cafe, I paused. Women were shouting, "Rush!" I glanced at my watch. As luck would have it, it was just after ten.

I locked up, climbed the stairs, and stood outside the door. Through the crack I caught Julie in her performance duds. She strutted across the stage, a Bette Midler with the good looks of Michelle Pfeiffer. A young gay man with a goatee dragged a steel stool to dead center. Julie straddled it, legs spread, planted one palm on the cushion in between those magnificent thighs, and angled forward so the fullness of her breasts were available even to those in the back row. After a deep and nerve-rattling intake of breath, she belted out, "Someone to Watch Over Me." She made it sexy, sad and slightly over the edge. I shivered.

Last night that woman had driven me crazy. Tonight she made me feel incredibly alone.

Back at the suite I turned on the radio. I wanted music without words. I couldn't find classical, so I settled for elevator tunes. I sat down at the kitchen counter with a cup of coffee and my case notes. Something was nagging me. Why was Tara Parker so afraid to talk to me? And was Cindy's protectiveness selfless? I picked up the sheet with the phone number I had copied down at Parker's house. If I was right about the area code, only two digits were missing. I pursed my lips, figured why the hell not, and decided to run through the different combinations. I irritated a lot of Cape Codders that night. But the thirteenth call made my jaw drop.

I hadn't talked to her in days, but I had no doubt about who was behind the polite, nasal drawl on the other end of the line. "Kathleen Fritzl?"

"Yes? Who is this?"

I hung up. So Parker had contacted Brian's wife. Why?

The first thing I thought when I awoke was, today's K.T.'s birthday. The second thing was, I've met the murderer. We've talked. We may even have touched. But what really bothered me was that the murderer had kept her edge over me. Not much longer, though. I could tell by the way my nose itched. I ate breakfast, dressed and went down to the pay phone.

Jill answered right away. "I made a trip to the I-SPY boutique and bought us a bug detector. I've checked the phones and we're clean. However, the rest of my news isn't so good. No one's said anything to me, but I have a hunch your location is not an unknown to Detective Chinnici. His last phone call came late last night and he was so congenial, something must be up."

"Fine. Maybe the NYPD's solved this thing and I can come home."

"Solving it might mean Lurlene Hayes is headed for Riker's."

I didn't respond. Jill got the message. "So you still haven't heard from her."

"Tell you the truth, Jill, I was hoping K.T. had contacted you or T.B."

"Sorry. Her family's as much in the dark as you are. T.B.'s state of mind has gone from worried to frantic. No one can get a peg on her. Even I've tried. The car she borrowed from Otto has vanished. No credit trace, no bank withdrawals, no calls. Nothing."

My eyebrows furrowed. "T.B.'s not thinking Lurlene would harm her, is he?"

"I don't think so . . . still you've got to admit her silence has been mighty thorough."

What if Lurlene were the killer? Or if the killer had a reason for disposing of Lurlene? Could K.T. really be in danger? I said, "I don't think they've gone far. They'd be crazy to squander the cash they got from the refund on the cabin on transportation. The smart thing would've been renting a place for a month or so, eating in, laying low." Who knows? They could be staying less than a mile away from where I stood. Still, I felt a quickening in my pulse. I had let my pace slip. And I didn't want to interrogate myself about the reason why. I told Jill about my meeting with Tara Parker and the phone number that had led me to Kathleen Fritzl's auditory channel. "Seems I may have some traveling to do."

"Expect company. I understand Detective Chinnici's out of town today. On his day off. T.B. hears that he's taking this case a little personally, so if you see a thick-waisted guy with an auburn mane, you may want to exit stage left."

"Thanks for the warning. And if you get news about K.T. —"

"Don't worry, Robin. I'll call you."

I gave Jill one last assignment, to check on rental

agencies where Tara Parker or Cindy Abrams could have picked up a car. The hit-and-run connection was a long shot, but I've gambled and lost before. It's the game that counts. Afterward, I grabbed my briefcase, a couple of Cape Cod maps, and aimed my wheels toward Wellfleet.

I was down to six suspects. Tzionah Stein, Tara Parker and her lover, Kathleen Fritzl, Zoogie Cocchiaro and her mother. Stein remained my best bet and I was in the mood for a face-to-face confrontation. Her hotel was located on the outskirts of town. I turned into the parking lot and hit my brakes. A stodgy, navy blue Dodge was parked across lanes right outside room fifteen. A thick-set man with wavy auburn hair and an ill-fitting gray suit stood outside. He had one hand anchored on the door frame and the other busy conducting a conversational orchestra. Tzionah Stein leaned on the wall opposite him. She looked bored.

I stuck my head outside the window for a better look. Tzionah glanced my way, frowned, and gave the man her full attention. I shifted into reverse and left skid marks on the exit ramp. There was a good chance that Detective Mario Chinnici would be visiting Kathleen Fritzl next, and I didn't want him to get there first. I got back on Route 6 and sped into Truro.

I knew the town well, knew from the address that Brian's widow lived in an exclusive bay-side enclave that housed families with names like Adams, Buchanan and Smith. I passed through the gates, amazingly unmanned, and drove uphill. The houses were massive, contemporary, with odd angles and a proliferation of windows. Kathleen Fritzl's place sat at the end of a cul-de-sac. I'd say the house was three thousand square feet, minimum, with two wings curving back from a circular, glass-enclosed structure that resembled a silo and contained not wheat but wrought-iron spiral stairs. I slammed the car door and headed for the entrance. Chad greeted me outside the house.

He wore loose mustard-yellow gym shorts, a neon-green T-shirt, Doc Martens and a Baltimore Orioles baseball cap. He kicked the spokes of his eighteen-speeder and said, "No one's here," in a tone that convinced me Kathleen was very close. She confirmed my suspicion by opening the front door and saying softly, "It's okay, Chad, honey. I'll handle this."

I got a nasty boy-man stare before he left us alone. As he slogged into the house, my gaze dropped to his wrists. Thick, raw welts scarred them. My focus shifted sharply to Kathleen Fritzl, who simply nodded and frowned. Her skin tone was pallid, the circles under her eyes marked.

"Robin Miller," she said, as if testing my name.

"Mind if I come in?"

Her smile was tired. "Excuse me. My manners seem to have been adversely affected by my grief. Of course."

I followed her inside. So much sunlight flooded the interior I could have been standing outside. We crossed the silo to a great room that would have swallowed every square foot of my brownstone, and then some. There was only one piece of art, a Jackson Pollock original that occupied a ten-foot by twelve-foot square on the far wall. Twenty-foot high windows that rose at a sharp angle marked the edge of the room, which overlooked a cascade of dunes and the full expanse of Cape Cod Bay. One thing was certain. Kathleen Fritzl was not hurting for funds.

She gestured at one of five couches and asked me to sit. I did and dragged my attention back to her face.

We both heard the footsteps at the same time. "Kathleen, have you seen Chad? He's off meds and I can't —"

I twisted around in time to see an older woman stop in her tracks and conceal her mouth with a loose-skinned hand. I'd estimate her age at fifty-five. Her silvery hair was twisted into a French knot. The dress she wore was neat, simple. She was slightly overweight, but carried herself like a woman accustomed to weighing a lot more. "I'm sorry," she sputtered and was ready to run off.

I rose and said hurriedly, "No problem. I'm Robin Miller."

Her eyes flickered from me to Kathleen. She said, hesitantly, "I'm Anna Parulski."

I cocked my head at her. She was no neighbor. She belonged here. I turned toward Kathleen, whose hands were busy stroking her throat. "Your *neighbor*?" I asked derisively.

High heels clicked toward me rapidly. Anna's face had lost color, still she tried smiling at me. "Oh yes. I live just a few houses —"

"Anna." Kathleen eyes were slits. Anna appeared to shrink as she spoke. "This is all so surreal."

"I don't have time for art theory," I blurted impatiently. "Why don't you tell me what's going on here? And while you're at it, maybe you can explain your relationship with Tara Parker."

Kathleen's head dropped as if it were a puppet's

and the puppet master had released its rope. She rubbed her temples and emitted a sound that was half laugh, half gasp. Anna scurried to her side and braced her by cupping an elbow.

A flash of color drew my eye across the room. I sought the source and found Chad Fritzl frozen in the corridor leading to the opposite wing. "You okay, Mom?" he asked. His sister soon joined him. She had lost weight this past week. Her cheeks looked sunken as she leaned in under her brother's arm. If he had moved, she would have no doubt fallen.

"This is an adults-only conversation. Please return to your rooms." Kathleen's poise had returned. When it came to motherhood, the lady was a pro.

Chad's mouth twitched. "Go to your room, Lindy."

"Chad, you know what your mother meant." Anna spoke with an odd authority.

"Chad, you know what your mother meant." Chad's mimicry of Anna was on the mark, but she wasn't impressed. She marched over and spoke to him in a quiet, commanding tone. I suspected the exchange was not atypical.

Kathleen stared out the window, clearly distancing herself. I waited until Anna had left with the kids before I spoke. "Anna's his nurse."

She didn't face me. Instead she strolled over to the glass wall, undid a latch, and stepped outside. A bay breeze snapped through the doors. After a moment I joined her on the Mexican-tiled patio.

"Have you ever considered having children, Mizz Miller?"

"Not really. I'm a lesbian."

She half-turned. "From what I understand, that

hardly rules out parenthood. What I'm asking, have you ever stopped to wonder what comes next?"

"Next?"

"Next. After us. Maybe such morbidity is reserved for artists, but I've often thought that each of us is merely a conduit for the future. I remember the first photograph I ever took. I was thirteen and the subject was my dog Pookie, a poodle with a misshapen nose and a bum leg. We had grown up together and, you may chide me for this, but that pooch was my best friend. He died a week later and all I had was that one shot of him. I slept with it for months."

I glanced back inside the house. Time was running out, but I knew better than to interrupt her sentimental and cloying reverie.

"Children provide a passage to the next world —"

My tongue wouldn't stay still. "Kathleen . . ."

"Yes. I suppose I should get to the point, though I fear your disinterest in children may limit your empathy for my situation. Chad and Lindy are, well, how do I explain this? The moment you give a child life, the air you breathe changes. You enter the fabric of time. Your own mortality becomes at once more vivid and yet less absolute. I may sound like a horrid creature, as if I'm one of those parasites who intend to extend their life by living those of their offspring. Nothing could be further from the truth. What excites me is how different Chad and Lindy are from me. And from Brian. They took the best from both of us and surprised —" Her tears were spontaneous.

I stepped forward, but she waved me off, descended slowly into a weathered Adirondack chair.

She wiped the tears with a flick of a knuckle and blurted, "I'm a sentimental fool. I lied to you to protect my children from the horrors of a police interrogation. The truth is, last Sunday I drove down to Manhattan with Chad and Belinda. It was Father's Day, remember, and I wanted the children to surprise Brian. We've had our ups and downs, all families do, the thing is, you cannot . . . absolutely cannot . . . let a family fall apart. It is, in a word, unacceptable."

The hair on my arms bristled. I thought of my mother in New York and broke eye contact.

She continued. "The last visit between Brian and Chad had been disastrous. Lurlene, of course, only made it worse."

"Hope you don't mind my asking, but what's wrong with him?"

"Wrong? Yes, I suppose that's the word people on the outside might use. My son's mildly schizophrenic . . . if you flinch, yes, I see you did, well, it's not unexpected. I should hasten to add that not all schizophrenics are Son of Sam. You may not be aware that schizophrenia is simply a chemical imbalance in the brain. In fact, in the industrialized world, approximately one in every hundred individuals will develop schizophrenia. Interesting statistic, no? My son has a tendency, hardly pernicious, to hoard high-sugar cereals, probably because Brian and I insisted he consume bran flakes his entire childhood. His thinking patterns are only slightly impaired, but I've heard the same said of great, creative minds. Van Gogh, for instance. Gaugin. The worse part was his suicide attempt."

She inhaled deeply. "Lurlene tried to use it

against him, to convince Brian that our son had to be institutionalized. Which he doesn't. Believe me, if you've ever seen one of those places, you would understand how absurd it is to believe a person could benefit from inhabiting them. My mother was locked up in one of the finer institutions in this state when I was not much older than Chad. The experience left a taste in my mouth I'd rather not share. To be perfectly frank, I'd sooner see Chad on the streets."

I rubbed my eyes to cover my shock and asked, "What precipitated the suicide attempt?"

"A silly incident. The girl he had been seeing broke up with him. He hadn't even been that fond of her . . . nevertheless, rejection hurts. I'm sure you understand that much. In any case, he's made remarkable progress in the past few weeks and I wanted Brian to see that for himself. He and our boy have always been so close. Still, it was foolish of me. I should have called first. I had never just popped in like that before. We pulled up in front and there was no place to park. I sent Chad up so he and Brian could have a chance to talk. I circled the block once, and the next time around Chad burst through the front doors as if he had seen a ghost. Of course, it was much worse than that. He had seen the whole ugly mess."

"Seen what?"

She shook herself and blinked, as if I had woken her. "The murder, what else?"

"Chad witnessed the murder?" Even to my ears, I sounded incredulous.

"Lurlene killed my husband, Ms. Miller. I thought we had established that fact back in New York."

My scalp felt blistered and a line of sweat trickled down my spine. I thought of K.T., bit my lip, then asked, "You told the police this?"

"No. My son's condition is precarious, Detective Miller. Losing Brian was bad enough. I didn't deem it necessary to subject him to the indelicate scrutiny of the New York Police Department. Besides, it sounded as if they had more than enough evidence on Lurlene without my son serving as a witness."

I shifted gears. "Who's Stephen Alsace?"

"The other half of my alibi, you mean? He's my chauffeur, gardener, chef and best friend. And a very uncomfortable liar. Anna and Step understand why it's important to protect Chad and Lindy. I don't expect many other people to."

"And the butcher?"

A wan smile. "Anna's brother."

"I see."

"Yes, I supposed you would. Will you go to the police now?" she asked.

"And tell them what?" I asked dumbly.

She harumphed. "So I'm not the only one who toys with justice to protect their loved ones. Tell me, is shielding Lurlene more important than uncovering the truth?"

I raised my eyebrows at her, declined the question, and countered with one of my own. "Why would Tara Parker have your phone number?"

A tremor ran up her neck. I watched the vein there pulse. Her facade was crumbling. She shook her head. "The name's familiar, not that I know why."

"She's a model. Your husband worked with her."

"Was she one of his lovers?"

"I doubt it."

"Well, it doesn't really matter. Now, if you don't mind, I've illuminated all the dark corners I care to." She rose and stared sharply at a spot behind me. I turned around to observe Chad's sinewy frame retreating from the patio.

Behind me Kathleen sighed. "Please go now. I think my family's suffered enough."

I paused just beyond the sliders. "One last question, what kind of car do you drive?"

She had buried her hands in the pockets of her stiff gabardine pants. "God, you're insufferable. I own a Mercedes Benz. Black. 1992 model. Automatic seat belts. Anything else?"

"Did you know Tzionah Stein inherited a pretty parcel of land over in Wellfleet?"

"So. Goody for her. And Brian. I wasn't aware of his acumen in real estate."

She walked me toward the front door, her hands laced behind her back, each pace measured. I had a sense that she was counting each step. At the entry, she glanced up, extended a hand and smiled. The zen of social pretense.

"What if I said I had a witness who could directly refute Chad's claim?"

She didn't bite. Still flashing me a smile that couldn't make the trip to her eyes, she responded, "I'd say you were lying. And foolish."

I bumped into Chad on the way out. I tried not to look at him differently but failed. All at once I noticed that he smelled funny, like sweaty socks. He sniffed at me as if I were the source. I strode past him at a good clip and just avoided colliding with Anna, who was scampering up the driveway after her charge. Meanwhile, the other Fritzl offspring stood by my car drawing circles onto the hood with her index finger. Belinda drifted away like morning mist as I approached.

I got in and turned the key in the ignition without the car exploding. I counted myself lucky and took off.

Chapter 12

Detective Chinnici had not intercepted me at Kathleen's house and he wasn't waiting for me at the Watermark. Still, he was too close for comfort. I grabbed some clothes, my files, briefcase, back pack and a box of Nabisco vanilla wafers, and returned to the car. I rammed the bike into the hatchback, made a mental note of how much I owed Beth and Dinah for this extended car loan, and drove away from the Watermark. There was only one place for me to go.

I parked the car in a lot and rode the bike toward Julie's home. Edna was outside gardening.

Her delight at seeing me seemed genuine. She slapped her dirt-encrusted gloves against her naked thighs and strode over. I extended the box of wafers, assumed my most waifish expression — a frightening prospect, but remember, I was desperate — and asked, "Would it be okay if I crashed here for a night or two?"

"Well, I don't know. The cookies are payment enough for me, but Julie's a tough negotiator." Her grin was lecherous.

I wondered briefly if sex drive could be genetically determined, then grinned back and said, "I'll take my chances. Is she around?"

She glanced at an old Timex wristwatch, its leather belt cracking like alligator skin. "Nah. She's at the Provincetown Inn, swimming. She likes to keep in shape." She gave me a Groucho Marx eyebrow-wiggle.

"Well, I can come back —"

"Hell, no. You think my daughter's cornered the market on lesbian appreciation? Come on in, I could use some company."

I waited for her in the kitchen while she washed up. She returned smelling like Ivory soap. Without bothering with small talk, she proceeded to whip up a batch of raisin bran muffins and a Waldorf salad. K.T. would have been impressed with her efficiency and talent. I remained mum during the meal. We cleared the table and Edna retrieved a chocolate cheesecake from the fridge. My eyes lit up.

She tilted the masterpiece toward me and narrowed her eyes. "I'm offering you a cake that has been written down in the annals of culinary ecstasy.

Women have swooned before me for a taste of this gem. And all I'm asking you to do is spill the beans."

The graham cracker crust was a quarter-inch thick and cradled thick chocolate chips. I dragged my focus up from the cake. "What beans?"

"For a woman who just got laid the other night by a younger and, may I add, very hot woman in a long tradition of hot women, you look mighty glum."

I pointed. "The cake first."

Edna had not exaggerated. The cheesecake melted on my tongue. A few minutes later I told her about K.T. and her connection to the murder investigation I was working on.

"I see." With the back of her fork, she made a paste out of the final bit of cheesecake and smeared it on her plate. "So Julie's a distraction?"

Instead of answering, I rose to go.

She frowned at me. "Sit down, you ass. I don't give a damn. You and Julie are adults. Knowing my daughter, she's probably thrilled you're not one of those U-Haul lesbians who propose marriage before their first orgasm has even had a chance to ripple down to their toes."

I stood up anyway, crossed to the sink, and started washing the dishes.

Edna said, "I'll be right back."

I waited for over an hour. When she hadn't returned by then, I found an empty room, dumped my possessions in a corner, made some phone calls and sorted my files. I pulled out the bundle of papers taken from Brian Fritzl's safe deposit box. In light of my conversation with Kathleen, the correspondence about Chad took on new significance. This time I unfolded the letter directed to Brian Fritzl and did more than scan the contents. On the bottom of the page, in fine print, the acronym AMI was spelled out. Alliance for the Mentally Ill.

The first page was politic nonsense: thank you for your recent correspondence, we are committed to the welfare of children like yours and to the entire American population, et cetera, et cetera. On the second page, the writer got to the point.

> *We understand the conflict you must feel as Chad's father. Your interest and devotion to your son is admirable and, unfortunately, too rare. You should know that many parents have had to make the same difficult choice and I can direct you to counselors who can assist you in coming to terms with Chad's illness. As to your specific question, involuntary hospitalization is a legal option only if your son poses a threat to others or to himself. In this case, since he has attempted suicide and consistently refuses to accept appropriate medication, the prospects for successful placement are quite good, providing that you act at once. I urge you to again discuss the matter with your wife and family psychiatrist. Please feel free to call me directly if I can be of further assistance.*

It was hard for me to reconcile Brian the rapist with Brian the committed family man. I'm inclined to classify the world in terms of black and white. Good and evil. But both Kathleen and Brian had tried to shield Chad in ways they considered best. I thought of my own family, their malevolent indifference, and felt sorrier for myself than for Chad. This case challenged my values and emotions in ways I didn't welcome.

I had to get out and move.

I changed into biking shorts and a clean T-shirt and headed for the trails. I took my time, made a bathroom stop at the Herring Cove concession stand, coasted into the dunes, pumped hard over each rise, and then allowed myself a few moments to drink in the sun. I stretched out on a bench and sighed. The nut of self-pity dissolved and I focused gratefully on the pull in my muscles. This morning the radio had broadcast a story about a storm running up the East Coast. The Cape would be spared the brunt of the squall, yet there was electricity in the air. Stinging gales alternated with periods of eerie stillness. In the pause, the sun's force became unbearable.

I swept my forearm along my brow and returned to the trail. My appointment with Tara Parker was just twenty minutes away. I hit the pedals hard, pulled up over a steep dune, then leaned into the curving slope, exhilarated by my speed, the scratch of my tires on the gravel path. At the base I braked suddenly, veered left, caught my front wheel in a puddle of sand, and fell. A family of six had spread themselves over the trail. They turned surprised faces to me, as if shocked to encounter another biker. Since no one apologized or offered to help me up, I guessed they were fellow New Yorkers.

I brushed myself off, checked my skinned knee, said, "Hey, no problem," and waited for them to move.

The father, six-three with a chest as broad as that of a race horse, sniffed at me and said, "You shouldn't be riding so fast."

One of the sons, no more than seven and with a face designed for terror, added, "She's not wearing a helmet, either, Dad."

The wife had the good sense to look embarrassed.

I didn't argue. I ignored their babble, checked my bike for damage, and got back on the saddle. The family still hadn't budged. A familiar scent hit my nose. Tuna sandwiches were being handed out. I vowed never to eat tuna fish again and tried to maneuver around their impromptu picnic. A hand slammed down on my shoulder. "Hey." It was the *Dad*. Up close he smelled like tobacco. "You could say excuse me."

The look I shot him was murderous.

A few minutes later I had lost the ill-tempered family and was struggling through the remaining dunes. The bruise on my hip, where Arnold Grau had kicked me, had begun to throb and the air had become stale, torpid. I stopped twice to catch my breath and once to fight a leg cramp. I was losing time, and the dunes seemed endless. I had obviously miscalculated the distance to the Beech Forest Trail. I bit my bottom lip and pumped harder.

An eon later I entered the cooler air of the forest. My body responded instantly. A delicious chill tickled my exposed flesh. I picked up speed and aimed for Clapp pond. I arrived almost a half-hour late. Either Tara had never showed, or she had already left. In either case, I was screwed. I parked my bike and listened. Mosquitoes buzzed around my head. A frog splashed into the pond. Birds shrieked overhead. But there was no human sound. Sweat ran down my spine and pooled on my forehead. My temples throbbed. The ride back into town would not be a romp.

I bent over and reached for my toes. My stretch came to a sudden halt. There were skid marks in the dried mud. Imprints made from two different bike tires. Overlapping footprints, one larger than the other. A trail leading into the woods, another set of prints exiting from a spot a few feet down. A vermillion stain on a patch of grass.

My knees locked. A nerve twitched above my right eye. I could feel blood rush away from my limbs. Suddenly the wind picked up and a storm-charged gust surged toward me from the ocean. I shivered, shut my eyes and concentrated on listening. What was I hearing? A footfall? A twig snapped, a crack behind me. Damn. I spun around. A squirrel stared at me from the gnarled branch of a black pine. I took a breath, stepped into the woods. A bed of pine needles absorbed the impact. My breathing was too loud, it echoed in my head, masked the natural din of the woods. I fought against slapping the flies stinging my cheeks and calves and pushed ahead. Brambles scratched my naked legs as I circled the clearing at a painstakingly slow pace.

A flash in the distance stopped me cold. Sunlight glinted off the handlebars of a bicycle lying on its side in the deep grass. The next instant the wind held its breath and I heard a moan. I damned caution and scrambled toward the sound.

Tara Parker lay crumpled on the ground, her limbs twisted unnaturally, her magnificent green eyes camouflaged by blackened eyelids that had already begun to swell. The weapon rested near her left ankle. A bike pump, bloodied and matted with hair. I knelt, felt for a pulse, sighed at the ragged beat I discovered at the base of her neck. She was alive. I dashed over to her bike, grabbed the water bottle, noting at once that her bike pump remained snapped in place, and returned to her side. Slowly I raised her head, dampened her lips with the water, urged her to speak, to tell me who had done this to her. One word made it to her lips.

"Cindy."

She fell unconscious afterward. I shoved a pillow of grass under her head, dashed back toward my bike and sprinted toward Race Point. No rangers were around. I sped to the pay phone, dialed first the police, then information, and got Edna on the phone. I told her what had happened, explained that I couldn't be there when Tara was found, but feared help wouldn't come fast enough. Before I could finish, she promised to race over with one of her friends.

I hustled into town.

The destination I had in mind made my teeth clamp together and grind. I sped down Bradford, found the alley and turned. I dropped my bike, ran to the front door, and rammed my fists against the wood. The frame rattled, but no response came from inside. I wiggled the knob and was ready to break in when a voice shouted at me from a second-floor window. "Hey! Hey, you! What are you doing?"

I stepped off the porch, stared up. Projecting from the window was the silvery head of a man in his early sixties. He wore thick glasses and reprimanded me in a diluted German accent.

"Are you the landlord?" I shouted.

"Who's asking?"

"I'm looking for Cindy Abrams. Her lover's been hurt."

"Cindy . . . her name's not Abrams. It's Wyler. And she's not here."

I noticed he hadn't asked about Tara.

"Are you sure?" I asked. "It's pretty serious."

He screwed his plastic features into an expression of disgust. "Yes, yes, I'm sure. You think because I'm elderly that I can't see or hear? Your friends had an argument. They left in a huff, maybe two hours ago, heading in opposite directions." He hesitated. "How serious? Was the girl hit by a car?"

"What did they argue about?"

"Huh? Argue? Oh, that. I don't know. I heard raised voices. I'm not a spy, miss."

Right. And he wasn't much help either.

Edna's place was silent. I shouted up the staircase. Apparently, Julie was still not home. The smell of fresh bread and tomato sauce wafted toward me from the kitchen. I walked in, found a pot of sauce bubbling over onto the stove, the oven door open, two loaf pans cooling on the inside rack and one on the counter top. The phone was off the hook. Edna had not wasted time. She rose in my estimation.

I retrieved my files and phone book and parked myself by the phone. The first call went to Kathleen Fritzl. I knew there was no way she could have attacked Tara Parker and bicycled back to Truro in such a short time. But what if she had a car and a bike rack?

She picked up after two rings. Her voice was steady, unrushed. No, she had not gone out since I had seen her. Yes, a New York detective had come by. He implied that there was another suspect besides Lurlene, but he didn't mention names. She, personally, was shocked. I asked to speak with Anna, but she was out food shopping with Chad and Belinda. Kathleen offered me her friend Stephen Alsace instead, whom I grilled for twenty minutes straight. He stuttered a bit, answered every question politely and thoroughly, and never snapped.

I hung up, bit a cuticle, then dialed my office. No one answered, so I left a detailed message on the answering machine. I wanted all the news fit to print on Cindy Wyler, a.k.a. Cindy Abrams, and I wanted it fast. I contemplated running out and buying a new laptop to replace the broken one back at the Watermark, but the prospect of tracking down an electronics shop turned me off.

The answer had to be close.

Tara Parker knew something that had made her dangerous. What if Cindy had interrupted Brian's attempt to rape Tara and killed him in a frenzy of revenge? Maybe Tara had threatened to go to the police. Or at least tell Kathleen Fritzl the truth. I recalled how angry Cindy had been when she found Tara and me talking on the porch. Maybe our scheduled meeting had precipitated the attack.

I had the nagging sensation that I was overlooking the obvious. In a frenzy I phoned, in turn, Tzionah Stein, Zoogie Cocchiaro, and my office. No answer anywhere. I almost called Kathleen Fritzl again just because I could. An hour or so later Edna found me in her den, scratching my mosquito bites and thumbing the phone book.

She looked like a marathon runner on the twenty-seventh mile. Her short locks were plastered to her head, her polo shirt stuck to her skin, the crotch of her cotton shorts appeared damp, and her socks were caked with blood and mud.

We sized each other up. She said, "She's breathing. That's all I know. No more talk before we both shower. Use the one upstairs, and if you need clean clothes, Julie has a fine collection of leftovers in her closet. And use some deodorant. The next time I see you I don't want to be forced to slip a clothes-pin on my nose."

I followed her orders, showered, and borrowed a pair of drawstring pants and a billowy white shirt that was most definitely not my style. It was the most modest outfit in Julie's closet. The funny thing was, I had jeans and a polo shirt in my back pack. But it felt good wearing someone else's clothes. They smelled like Julie and laundry detergent. I gargled and went downstairs. Edna wore a silk shirt tied at the midriff, starched white pants, and a pair of Birkenstocks. She had a beer in one hand and a spatula in the other.

"The damn sauce burned," she complained without turning around.

"I appreciate your haste."

"Not half as much as that woman's going to . . . The M.D. at Outer Cape said she was critical. They sent her down to Hyannis."

"Were you questioned?"

"Me? Hell, no. I'm legendary around this place. Everyone knows Edna Isles. I told them me and my friend Rhonda were just taking a hike. No one doubted I was telling the truth." She rested her weight on one hip, scraped burnt tomato from the bottom of the pan, bit it off the spatula and said, "You may end up with a tad of trouble, though. Just as we were leaving, this goony family showed up and started jabbering about how some demon dyke almost ran them over with her bike and how she must be the attacker. The description wasn't flattering, but I had no trouble figuring out it was you."

I should have killed them when I had the chance. "Did anyone take them seriously?"

"You tell me. Sometime tomorrow a police artist's driving down Cape just to meet them. My guess is you'll be pretty popular by Saturday afternoon."

I let my head drop to the table top.

"Meanwhile I have other news for you. Your friend K.T. is staying in one of those little waterfront shacks way out on Route Six-A, about a quarter-mile past the Watermark. That's where I ended up this afternoon, after I abandoned you so rudely. Hope you don't mind."

My hands felt numb. K.T. was less than ten minutes away.

Edna held out a spoonful of sauce. "Taste this and tell me if it can be salvaged."

I sipped it, rolled my eyes in only moderately exaggerated bliss, and asked, "How'd you find her?"

"I know practically everyone, and every inn, in P-town. I assumed you were right about them needing a month-long lease, and most places in town are booked solid through Labor Day. They needed something cheap, discrete and available. It took a couple of hours, but I finally narrowed it down to one of six places. Then I got lucky. A friend of mine mentioned she had rented her place to the Casual Cook from PBS. Said the lady's friend paid in cash and mandated absolute privacy. Well, I got it right away. Her cooking, your appetite. Must've been a match made in heaven. So K.T.'s last name is Bellflower, am I right?"

I confirmed her conjecture and took down the information. "What about —"

Edna interrupted me. "My daughter. Hey, that's for you to figure out. Me, I got a dinner party at seven. I don't care what you do, or where you do it, as long as it's not in my kitchen."

I took the hint and scrammed.

I spent a few hours trying to sniff out Cindy's trail. My efforts netted a sore throat and feet. Around nine I made contact with Jill, who had nothing to report and too much sympathy to spare.

Since the chances were good that I'd have to keep an uncomfortably low profile after tomorrow, I decided to treat myself right while I could. Lobster Pot was out. The infamous picnic family probably feasted there every night. I ended up at Risa's, a lesbian-owned restaurant the width of a bowling lane that specializes in Italian-Jewish cuisine with Japanese accents. I ate and drank until the pounding inside my brain dulled, then I stopped at the Pied Piper and had another round.

I'm not a drinker, or hadn't been until that week. The fact that I knocked back Tequila Sunrises like they were Cokes should have been a warning sign, but I was too busy running from myself to notice things were not well *chez* Robin. By eleven, I was blotto. I retrieved my car from the lot and weaved through town. If I had been going faster than five miles per, I could've been dangerous.

I veered into a spot and stared at the shack.

The curtains were sheer and the lights were on, though dim. I stepped out and leaned on the car door. At first I thought a television was on because I detected a flicker in the room. Then it hit me and I groaned out loud. I had arrived in time to witness Lurlene surprising K.T. with a birthday cake, complete with thin-tapered candles. K.T.'s jaw dropped, her head angled toward Lurlene affectionately, then she blew them out, cupped her palms over her eyes and shook her head. Lurlene kissed K.T.'s knuckles, peeled K.T.'s fingers from her face, and said something to her that made her pucker her lips pensively. The exchange culminated in a hug that was more intimate than I could stand.

I drove away, left the car in the public parking lot, and wobbled along Commercial Street. It must have been later than I thought because Julie was back. She and Edna sat outside on a hanging swing, laughing easily. I couldn't face them. I pivoted on my heels inexpertly. The next thing I knew I was surrounded. Edna braced her hand against my back and Julie said, "We were waiting for you." A little while later Julie and I retreated to the rear deck.

We had sex again that night. I don't remember it. I woke up with sand in my teeth and tender body parts. Julie said we had a great time. It would be nice if I believed her.

I showered, threw up, and went back to bed. The next time I rose to consciousness Edna was rocking the bed.

"Get the hell up!"

I set my elbows in place and hauled my torso up.

"The cops *are* looking for you." Edna's calm had a crack in it. I suddenly felt more alert.

"A Detective Chinnici called here, from New York City, and then some of the local police showed up. Lucky for me I had tossed your bike in the basement. Tom and Jim, the town dicks, kept asking me about a woman who sounds too much like you to be anyone else, but so far no one seems to know how you and I connect . . . and I like it that way. I hate to do this to you, hon, but you've got to vamoose."

Talk about rude awakenings. I rubbed my eyes and asked, "Do you know if they've been to the Watermark?"

"No, but if you want I'll call ahead and check for you. On the sly, of course."

"Of course."

I made it to the bathroom, sucked some mouthwash and freshened up. This time I put on my own clothes. I gathered the rest of my stuff and lumbered down the stairs.

Edna was waiting for me in the den. "Well, either no one knows you have a place at the Watermark, or if they do, no one cares."

For now. I felt like a deer on the first day of hunting season. All my old haunts were vulnerable. I raked my fingers through my hair and asked if I could use the phone. She waved at the receiver and said, "All yours. I'm going out now. I'll let Julie know what happened, so you don't need to leave a note."

I got the message and nodded. She wanted me to

disappear. I only wished I could. I sat down heavily and dialed the office. "Jill . . ." I coughed. Drinking was hell. "Jill, I'm a wanted woman."

"That's not what I hear. Chinnici hasn't called me in over twenty-four hours."

A strong wind rattled the windows. "The P-town police want me. For the attack on Tara Parker."

She took a sip of something. I heard the liquid slosh down her throat and felt queasy. "Yeah," she said matter-of-factly. "Guess I'm not surprised."

"Thanks for the support."

"Sorry. Look, you should know, Tony came home today. Said the Californian crunchy granola types were making him nuts. The truth is he looks like crap again. I don't thinik he should be taking these trips —"

"Jill, please. I'll talk to him when I get back. Right now I need help. There's a good chance that the person who attacked Tara is also the one who murdered Brian. If so, I bet my name's not far down on the hit list. All in all, it's a toss-up about who'll nab me first, the cops or the killer. So if —"

"Stop the harangue and I'll see what I can do."

"Have you learned anything about Cindy Wyler?"

"Yes ma'am. She's an Army brat, races cars on the weekends. Earns her living as a mechanic at a midtown garage. She's twenty-eight, banks at Crossland and doesn't use floss. Anything else you need to know?"

"Her location on the day of the murder."

"No problem. And I'll send you the smoking gun as a bonus. Sorry, boss, I'm good but Anne Bancroft's the miracle worker."

I ignored her. "Any clue about the name Abrams on Tara Parker's buzzer and mail box?"

"Tara's ex-lover. A member of the male species, by the way. Harry Abrams. A forty-year-old stock-broker. They split in November. By the way, I haven't been able to connect Tara or her lover to any of the car rental agencies here in New York. Of course, up until six o'clock yesterday I thought Cindy's last name was Abrams, so I'll have to run the entire check again." She didn't complain and she didn't offer further information on the investigation.

I hung up without even alluding to the latest news on K.T. and Lurlene. The only image vivid from last night was their cozy embrace. I cleared my throat and headed out to the parking lot. The cloud cover was dense, the wind blustery. I buttoned my jacket and picked up my pace. A few times I imagined someone following me. Murder investigations can make most anyone paranoid. Especially a guilt-ridden P.I. with a hangover. I stole a backward glance, saw no familiar faces and no posse after me, and drove straight to the Watermark.

My room had been tossed, after all. I experienced a strange satisfaction that Edna's sources weren't infallible, then I started to worry. My unannounced visitor had been a professional. I scurried to the desk. The note where I had jotted the time and place for yesterday's meeting with Parker was gone. And so was my full-size address book. Nothing else was missing, not even my damn, broken laptop.

It was already close to five o'clock. Last night's carousing had cost me a day's progress and a few thousand brain cells. I fought for clarity. If the killer was stalking me, I was proving to be mighty easy prey. On the other hand, if the intruder was a cop, by now the word "suspect" had to have been branded on my derriere in capital letters. I had to turn the table, take control again.

An explosion outside rattled me. I ran to the deck windows. A straight couple were lighting firecrackers. The woman covered her ears as her mate pitched the lit wad at the breakwater. It detonated midair. They laughed and my hands started to quake. Of course. Independence Day was less than seven hours away. The anniversary of Carol's death. A one-two punch to my glass jaw.

I suddenly craved another drink. The impulse ignited like fire in my belly. I drowned it with three straight bottles of Yoo-Hoo. This time I intended to preserve my wits.

The phone rang. I hesitated only a half-second before picking up. It could be Jill with more news. But it wasn't. The connection was bad, the voice worse. "Lurlene, is that you?"

"I did it, Robin. Oh God, I did it." My skin went cold.

"Did what Lurlene?" I tried to distinguish the sounds in the background. A motor revved.

"Killed Brian. I did it. The ghost is on my back." Her voice sounded odd, strangled. The timbre was too deep and her words slurred.

"Are you drunk?"

Her laugh was biting, frantic. "You have to come. Meet us after sunset." She gave me the name of a beach. "Come alone."

The background noises finally gelled. I heard a loudspeaker, something about the Center for Coastal

Studies, right whales. Lurlene had to be at MacMillan Pier.

I rammed the phone down and dashed to the front entrance. My hand faltered at the door knob. Something was wrong. I urged myself to slow down, stepped toward the window and edged the curtain aside. A police car had just pulled into one of the inn's parking spots. I ran toward the deck, stepped over the rail, and reminded myself that I had no choice. I rolled my eyes toward heaven and jumped. One ankle turned, but the sand largely absorbed the impact of my fall. I limped toward the house next door, then walked through the alley, up through the parking lot at the Surfside Inn. When I finally got to Bradford I ran.

Chapter 13

So now I was a fugitive. I had car keys, but no car, and a sore ankle. My wallet bulged in the back pocket of my jeans, but I couldn't use my credit cards or ATM card. I had less than eighty dollars in cash and three New York City subway tokens. And Lurlene Hayes had confessed.

I had to find her fast. Her voice had had a strangely tremulous quality, as if it were on the verge of collapse. I didn't like the thought of K.T. trapped with a killer decompensating rapidly. Worse, knowing K.T., she wouldn't abandon Lurlene until the bitter end. And I didn't want to speculate about what that end might be.

I bought myself a cheap baseball cap and a whale sweatshirt at one of the tackiest gift shops in town. I emerged twenty-four dollars lighter and fused instantly with the flood of tourists on Commercial Street. I had one factor in my favor: it was the start of the July Fourth weekend, one of the busiest times in P-town. Lurlene must have been thinking the same thing when she called me from the pier. I headed there now, not really expecting to find her, but hope springs eternal, fools rush in, et cetera, et cetera. There was a line forming for the next whale watch. I examined their faces carefully.

Familiar eyes stared back into mine. Shit! The family from the bike trail. What had I been thinking? The father and I made the connection at the same time. I spun around, damned the pain in my leg, and sprinted back toward Commercial. Behind me, the bastard was screaming for the police and breathing hard and loud, like a Doberman out for a romp.

Okay, asshole, I thought. Two can play this game, especially in this town. I caught the attention of two formidable dykes with can-do attitudes and yelled, "This fuckin' breeder's gonna kill me," without slowing my pace. The next thing I knew, a veritable softball team of young, virile lesbians raced past me. I never stopped.

In a narrow residential alley I paused to catch my breath, grit my teeth, and curse. The ankle was far worse now. The throbbing resonated to my kneecap. How the hell was I going to get out of town? My car was back at the Watermark and my rental bike was in Edna's basement. I didn't have enough cash for a bribe and hitchhiking was out of the question.

I had no choice.

I ambled back out onto Commercial, tucked myself into the thickest pack of pedestrians, and let their movement carry me back to the East End. When the crowd thinned out, I shifted to the narrow bay-side beach and hobbled back to the Watermark. The police weren't hanging out on my deck. I took that as a good sign. I slipped through an alley, checked to see that Commercial Street was clear, then edged myself closer. The car keys were in my hands, and transportation less than ten yards away. My breath caught in my throat and my heart pumped wildly. Darting across the final stretch of sidewalk, I actually prayed. For once, someone up there heard. The car turned over easily and I backed out without guns being drawn or bullhorns blaring.

I had half a tank of gas and at least an hour and a half to kill. I drove by the place Tara and Cindy had rented. With the car idling, I scrambled toward the front door. My suspects were suddenly all potential victims. If Lurlene had cracked, anyone with incriminating information posed a threat to her and could be in serious danger. Including Tara's partner. She wasn't around and neither was the landlord. I left her a warning note and got back on the road. I paused by a pay phone, tried to contact Kathleen Fritzl and Tzionah Stein. One wasn't home and the other one's line beeped steadily.

I hung up, frustrated, and aimed the car toward Route 6A. The sky was magnificent, torn between heavy, roiling storm clouds and a sliver of brilliant orange where the sun drifted toward the horizon. I cranked down the car window and let the wind slap through.

The windows of the shack were dark. I pulled into a spot, massaged my ankle for a few seconds, and just watched. Eventually I got out, checked for observers, then pressed my ear to the door. Silence. I tried the doorknob and froze. It was unlocked. I didn't move. Something was seriously wrong here.

I don't believe in carrying a weapon, a predilection my partner Tony has disparaged on more than one occasion. Right then, he would have won the argument hands down. I stepped toward the window cautiously, attempting to peer inside, but the glare the setting sun cast on the glass panes masked the interior. I took a deep breath, glanced both ways, then kicked the door open and rolled inside. In the next instant, I was in a defensive squat, the edge of my palms ready to strike out.

No one attacked me. The reason was apparent. Lurlene and K.T. had cleared out. I straightened up and resumed breathing. The closet doors and dresser drawers hung open, the bed — a single queen-sized bed — was unmade. Dishes caked with scrambled egg remained on the small kitchen table. I searched the premises, even tossed the garbage cans. Nothing indicated where they had gone, or explained the haste with which they had departed.

Outside I checked the angle of the sun. Why had Lurlene insisted on meeting me after sunset? The beach would be deserted by then, of course. But was her motive privacy or something else?

My suspects weren't the only ones at risk.

I could've contacted the police, and in retrospect I

probably should have, but knowing how the wheels of justice turn I guessed I'd end up in a holding cell and Lurlene would book again, taking K.T. with her. My back was against a brick wall, and the sun was dropping fast. I slid into the Toyota and, despite the chilled air, broke into a sweat. Long Nook Beach was in Truro, I knew that much, but I had never been there before. There was no time for me to get lost, and too much risk involved in asking for directions.

I accelerated to five above the speed limit and struggled to calculate the best route. The beach had to be on the less populated oceanfront. I made two wrong turns, skidded near the outskirts of Truro, reversed direction, and finally found a pay phone and called Edna, whose directions to Long Nook Road were right on the money. By then, it was already dusk. The sky above was midnight blue; toward the horizon, it faded to violet. No cars were parked by the dunes.

I picked up the steering wheel Club and stepped outside. My breathing tightened, my knees threatened to vaporize. I squatted by the car, squeezed my eyes shut so they'd adjust faster to the encroaching darkness, then slowly edged around the fender. Lurlene must be here already, I thought. I didn't care that my car was the only one around. I was late and Lurlene was sharp. She had to be watching me. I stared hard at the shadowy shrubs jutting up from the dunes, branches whipping madly as damp gales buffeted them. In the tumult, there was no way to discern human motion. I had to take the same advantage.

I scurried onto the nearest rise. Almost instantly, sand whipped into my mouth and eyes. I shielded my face with my arm and labored up the dune. As I climbed, the force of the wind and the gritty assault intensified. There was no way I could withstand the blizzard of sand for long. I crouched down, cupped my palms around my eyes, stared back down at the car, and confirmed what I already knew. Even after the car lights had gone out, my movements would have been clearly visible in the empty parking lot.

Thorns pierced my jeans as I scrambled down the slope. A piece of gravel smashed into my cheek. I licked my lip and tasted blood. At the base, I hunched over and secreted myself in the recesses of a bush. The scent of bayberry rose around me. I had to wait her out. Sooner or later, she'd make a move. I took a deep breath, unworried about the sound. In the howling wind, even a shout would have disintegrated into chaos.

I hunkered there so long my feet went numb. I put down the Club, stretched my legs. I was ready to give up and stand when I finally detected a vertical shadow moving cagily across the far end of the road. The shadow headed toward me. I went prostrate, spit out a bug, and crawled uphill on my elbows and knees. For a split second, the clouds parted and spilled a silvery illumination over the landscape. The wind stung my eyes, made them tear profusely, but nevertheless I distinguished her figure against the sky. She stood less than fifteen feet dead ahead, her back toward me, her hood and jacket billowing in the ocean's gust. I made an end run toward her. The plan would have worked, too, if my ankle hadn't twisted in the shifting sand. I went down hard, the air knocked out of my lungs, a sharp wheeze escaping from my mouth.

She pivoted at once, moved to tackle me before I could stand. I slid past her arms, spun on my knees, made visual contact and gasped. It wasn't Lurlene after all.

I lunged for the Club that had slipped from my grip, but my attacker got there first. I scrambled in the opposite direction, my mind reeling. I had been dead wrong. Dead wrong. The mental calculations wouldn't stop. Focus on moving, I warned myself. My ankle burned as I slogged over the dune. I had to get to pavement. I let myself skid down the slope, felt the heft of the Club swing within a hair of my scalp. I ducked, cursed as my sweatshirt caught on some bramble, tugged hard, heard the fabric tear, and continued my mad dash toward the road.

The ligaments in my ankle burned. I was doing permanent damage and I didn't give a damn. If I slowed even for an instant, that damn Club would make contact and I'd be out cold. There was a brief lull, the wind paused and I heard the panting way too close. I veered left, lost my balance, and dove rather than fell, landing on solid ground. The impact stunned me. I stood up, wobbly, my sense of direction scrambled. All I knew was that I had to keep running.

I charged forward, the wind hard on my chest, spray splashing against my face, my mind a step ahead of my legs. I felt sand again, then nothing. I had run past the edge of a steep, ocean-carved embankment. I forced myself to go limp as I plunged to the shoreline in horrifying slow motion.

When I hit bottom, there was an instant when I thought I had a choice about losing consciousness. I was wrong.

* * * * *

I don't think I was out long, but then again how do you measure time when a homicidal maniac has carte blanche to bind your wrists and legs? Cognizance resurfaced as hands clamped down on my ankles and lugged me to within a few feet of the water's edge. Within minutes I was soaked to the skin.

Sand caked my lips. I cleared them with spit, choked at the effort, and retched. Bile burned up through my throat. My captor just laughed.

"Just tell me why," I finally managed to utter.

He laughed. "They do that in the movies, don't they? Explain the murder so the victim can die in peace. Yeah, I can do that for you. No problem. Do you eat cereal? My favorite's Cocoa Puffs. Do you know the commercial?"

Chad jumped on my calves and I howled. Pain shot up into my hip. He dropped down suddenly and began digging feverishly with his bare hands. The sounds he made were closer to growls than words. Clearly the boy had lost his battle with madness. For a moment I pitied him. And then I remembered who was about to be killed.

"Chad . . ."

He stopped, startled by my voice. "Want to know, want to know, everyone wants to know." He almost sang the words.

"What happened to your dad?"

"Did you hear about the storm? Lindy's so afraid of lightning, she wets her bed."

I exhaled heavily, fought the panic pressing down on my chest. There was no way to communicate with him. I averted my eyes, watched a wave crash nearby, the closest yet. The tide was rushing in, propelled by the force of the wind. Sand swirled around my head, stung my ears. Chad's plan for me was diabolical. Already I was buried in sand up to my kneecaps. An uncontrollable tremble took over my limbs.

"Pop used to do this," he said unexpectedly. "Bury me and Lindy. We'd wiggle out and then we'd bury him. Fun, huh? Stay still, son, my little mummy man. If Lindy wins, it's gruel tonight."

His voice had transformed in mid-sentence. It had become a duplicate of Brian's. I dropped my head back and groaned. Goddamn it. How did I miss it? The boy was a perfect mimic. I said, "Do Lurlene, Chad."

His impersonation of her was imperfect, but close enough to fool me. "I can do you, too," he said happily, "Though it needs more work."

I was sobbing by the end of his demonstration. All the clues had been there from the start. I had just been too dense to notice.

Chad chattered on. "You've got a bad ear. I noticed it right away when you tried to imitate our upstairs neighbor. You gotta watch people use their lips. I do. I could teach you how . . ." He giggled. "But you're not going to be here much longer. Oh, wow." It was as if the thought had just struck him. His face suddenly became more serious and alert.

I tried again. "Why'd you kill your father?" If I could delay the burial long enough, the incoming tide might erode the part of the tomb he had already built.

He stuck out his bottom lip in an exaggerated

pout. “I killed a man, but he wasn’t my father. He let the witch Lurlene convince him to put me away in a dark house. Did you know? But I wouldn’t have killed my father.” A break in the cloud cover suddenly spilled moonlight over him. A twitch contorted his features and he shook his head as if a bug had flown into his ear. “It was an accident, I went up to show him I was okay, but when I got there someone was shouting help. Horrible, horrible sound. Do you like turtles?”

He rambled on and I tried in vain to draw him back. Eventually he said, “The darkroom. The danger was inside. I grabbed the gun, Dad told me to do it, be a man, son, gotta defend yourself. I do. We killed a deer once. Ate it, too. I’m a man, like him, so I kicked the door open and boom.” He winced, began digging again, but with less conviction.

I tried to move my legs, but they were completely immobile. A wave surged over my head. I swallowed too much, struggled to raise my head as a spastic cough ripped through me.

“It was like they were dancing, but she was screaming and crying and it was just wrong,” Chad was saying, oblivious to my struggle. “He was hurting her, a real pretty black girl. Green eyes. I noticed that right off. Green eyes, like a cat. I had a cat once. Kodak. Pop named her.”

I didn’t have much time, the muscle in my neck was tugging my head down and my lungs hurt. I strained to ignore his babble and free my hands.

“The woman ran out, like a cat, on her hands and knees. The man called her name out. Tara. Wasn’t that a house? Tara? He was bleeding, you know, but he didn’t collapse. In the movies, the body always jerks back and falls. But his just kind of twitched. Mom showed up, with Lindy. They almost knocked each other over. Tara and mom. Weird, huh? I don't know what happened after I left. She gave me the car keys, ordered me to get out. She was angry, not with me, with him. He was whispering ugly things . . . about me. Spit was on his mouth. I heard him, get help, lock the fucking kid in a nuthouse." His nostrils flared. "You should've seen her."

The rope around my wrists started to give.

Chad gaped at my hands. "You're trying to escape." He sounded shocked. "Okay. I get it. You want to play the game. Okay." He hunched down and frantically scooped sand over my hands. He was working against the waves now. Either way, I didn't see a way out.

In the distance, toward Provincetown, fireworks flared into the sky. He noticed them at the same time I did.

"Cool," he said, sounding like a teenager again. "Spaghetti strands." He turned toward me. "I can drive your car, you know. I don't have to use the bike. I drove Anna's in New York. She wasn't even angry about the dent in the hood. We got home fast."

The hit-and-run. Of course. Chad must've been at the wheel. What was one pedestrian after you'd already shot your own father for raping a stranger?

He chuckled proudly. "I'm going there, now. You can't come."

I had no idea what he was referring to. I was so cold and tired and in so much pain, focusing had become impossible. I choked on a surge of salt water, tasted fish, knew my lungs were giving out. Was he sitting on my head? The pressure was unbearable. I strained to open my eyes. Chad was gone. By then the water was up to my chin. Intermittently, the waves rushed over my mouth. Just a matter of time. My time. I no longer coughed. My eyes closed. Still I saw lights.

A bright beam, widening as I approached. I wanted to smile, but water rushed into my throat.

Maybe others really have seen a flash of white light at the end of life's tunnel. In my case, the light belonged to a high-beam flashlight. Edna Isles and Julie were my angels of mercy. After my phone call, Edna worried about why I had rushed off to Long Nook at such a late hour. She picked up Julie and the two of them tracked me down and rescued me from the water's onslaught. Edna even practiced a little CPR on me for good measure. I usually don't like getting intimate with the mother of a woman I slept with, but in this case I made an exception.

By the time they arrived, Chad had disappeared. I wanted to search for him, but Edna snorted and ordered Julie to fold me into the back seat, informing me that the police could pick up Chad later, first things first. She drove me to the Outer Cape Medical Center. I slumped down, shivering uncontrollably. At the center, Edna gave me permission to call the police, but by then I was more interested in dry clothes, painkillers and hot cocoa. I offered her the task, which she accepted with an expression that was half scowl, half smile.

A few hours later I was escorted to the police station. In honor of my splitting headache, the cop at the wheel decided to forgo the siren. Small favors like that can mean a lot to a gal who's just swallowed a few gallons of the Atlantic.

The place was compact, neat, with a few institutional desks, a holding cell or two, and an overly bright interview room. Considering it was late Friday night and the start of the holiday weekend, the place was bustling. I had a feeling there hadn't been this much action in a fortnight. A few minutes later, an officer informed me that Chad Fritzl's body had been discovered spiraling in the tide crashing onto the shoreline of Long Nook Beach. I was surprised at the kick of grief I felt when I heard the news. Kathleen Fritzl was already in the interview room, an hysterical, grieving woman whose howls vibrated through the thin, plasterboard walls.

Police Officer Tom Mateo sat me down at his desk, poured us both mugs of black, muddy coffee, and exchanged glances of disbelief with Edna, who refused to leave my side. Julie, however, had decided to go on with her midnight show. A real trooper, that girl. Tom and Edna quickly established my innocence and overall impudence. We progressed to a phone conference with a disgruntled Detective Chinnici of the NYPD, in which the two men agreed to exonerate Lurlene and further castigate me. Unfortunately, my throat burned too much for me to argue with them. Not that they were wrong, I just hated to forfeit the fight.

According to Chinnici, Lurlene and K.T. were still on the lam, though not for much longer. Yesterday afternoon they had finally resorted to pulling cash out of an ATM. The police had tracked them down to the shack on Route 6A, but the manager of the place must have warned them because they fled before the local authorities arrived. He felt confident they'd be picked up within twenty-four hours. He promised to subject them to a torturous interrogation and procure at least a quart or two of good, repentant sweat before turning them loose. I thanked him. He grunted, warned me to watch my ass and my license, reminded me to lick my partner's retired NYPD shield, and ordered Tom to send him a formal transcript of my report ASAP. Tom smiled the smile of a man who hates New York, mouthed "fuck him" and politely hung up.

A minute later Tom's partner Jim interrupted us. "You've got to hear this." He pointed down the hall. "The observation suite."

Tom patted my arm. "What about her?"

Jim shrugged. "Your call."

He gave me a nod. I leaned on Edna's arm and hobbled after them.

Kathleen Fritzl slumped on the far side of what looked like someone's discarded dining room table. It was six feet wide and wobbled as she leaned her elbows on it. She said, "Those minutes just disappeared . . . I didn't remember them at all. At all. I do recall ordering Chad to leave. Brian was so . . . he kept grabbing at me. He wanted me to help him, but he wouldn't shut up. The blood wasn't as bad as the venom he was spewing. That's the last thing I remember thinking. He's venomous. This man's venomous. For years I made excuses for him, his affairs, his small, persistent cruelties. Then he turns out to be a rapist and has the gall to order me to lock up Chad, as if he didn't know what institutionalization had done to my mother. The next thing I remember is wiping the gun clean and exiting." She looked up at the woman who sat opposite her. Kathleen's eyes were wide, wild, her lips trembling. "I swear, I didn't remember pouring the bleach fix until you just mentioned it. Oh God! The image." She pressed her palms over her eyes. "Dear God. Chad didn't do that, I did! Christ. *I killed my husband.* And now my son's dead."

I lurched out of my seat. Edna understood immediately and helped me to the bathroom. She even wiped my mouth off when I was done throwing up. For a moment I wanted to marry her. When we returned to the observation room, Kathleen's affect had gone flat. She explained the events of the past two weeks in painstaking, monotonous detail. After all the lies, she must have been relieved to divulge the truth.

Any sympathy I might have felt for her evaporated when I heard she was the one who had choked me in Brian's darkroom. Her goal, she revealed, had been not to kill me, but simply to protect her son. Kathleen was an upstanding citizen, really, not to mention a phenomenally loving mother — as long as one ignored the fact that she had watched her husband staggering from a gunshot wound and then, in some supposed fugue state, poisoned him with the bleach fix. It wasn't just the rape, or the affairs, or the years of heartbreak he had caused her. No. The straw that broke this aristocrat's back was Brian's audacity to contact a psychiatrist with the intention of having their son institutionalized. An outlandish scheme, indeed.

According to Kathleen, the root of all evil—including hers and her son's I suppose—was Lurlene. She was the one who had convinced Brian that Chad was, well, sick. If it hadn't been for her, Kathleen would never have sent Chad up to the apartment first to make amends with his father. *She* would have interrupted the rape instead of Chad. Father and son would still be alive.

Instead, after she emerged from her fugue to discover Brian writhing on the floor, Kathleen's maternal instinct kicked in—her words, not mine. She knew how the police would treat her son if they arrested him. A schizophrenic in the New York court system would be chewed up and destroyed. Kathleen was a quick thinker, and resourceful to boot. She wiped the gun, dropped it, and dashed outside. The kids were gone by then. She caught a cab and met them at home. According to her, the hit-and-run was incidental, a blip on a day marked by tragedy. Her only concern was sheltering her son. I wanted to crack through the two-way glass and remind her that she was more culpable than Chad.

She took a delicate sip of water, swallowed, then went on to explain how she and Chad rapidly devised a scheme to pin the murder on Lurlene. With staggering nonchalance, she related how Chad had dialed Lurlene's house until the phone rang ten times and the answering machine picked up. He hung up the first time, a pang of conscience stopping him. Later, he tried again and left a scathing, incriminating message in Brian's voice.

And I had bought it. Every stinking syllable.

Meanwhile, Kathleen had concentrated on identifying the model whom Brian had attacked in his darkroom. She returned to the studio, tore out the appointment page for Sunday, poured through his files and, except for the unexpected encounter with yours truly, her search had proceeded at a grand pace. The next day Kathleen contacted Tara Parker, who was in anguish about the attempted rape. Cindy grabbed the phone from her partner and instigated a series of wily negotiations with the rapist's murderer and widow. In the end, they made an uneasy peace. Silence for silence, sweetened with an exchange of greenbacks.

The scheme might have worked had my appointment with Tara not tipped Chad's scale. The model called Kathleen a few hours before our scheduled meeting and told her she couldn't abide by the agreement. She had to come forward. She apologized, advised Kathleen to turn herself in before "that detective" — namely me — had a chance. Unbeknownst to both of them, Chad had picked up the extension. He bicycled to Clapp pond and tried to talk Tara out of meeting me. Something went wrong and he attacked her viciously.

He had called his mother, frantic and confused, then disappeared. Fear prevented Kathleen from doing much more than organizing a small, inefficient search party consisting of herself, her daughter, Anna Parulski and Stephen Alsace. When they returned home earlier tonight, a police officer had been there to greet them.

Kathleen's interrogation was hardly over, but my tolerance and energy had been depleted long ago. It was after 2 a.m. I asked permission to go, received a nod from the men in blue, and allowed Edna to carry me back to the Watermark. She left me alone reluctantly and, amazingly, I slept.

In the morning the pain set in with a vengeance. A ligament in my ankle had torn, my throat felt stripped raw, my stomach rejected even plain toast, and the rest of my body appeared pretty evenly divided between bruised and battered. I made the required follow-up phone calls to the Provincetown and New York police authorities and discovered that K.T. and Lurlene had in fact been picked up and dragged in. I left the phone off the hook and indulged in a long, hot bath.

Later I found out that the Watermark had had another cancellation on my room. I booked it for as long as I could, then called Tony and suggested he hire Luce Lorelli for the next few weeks. In a rare impulse to play good girl, I touched base with my therapist and even dialed my brother Ronald in Staten Island. He informed me, rather brusquely, that my mother was too ill to come to the phone, which was just as well. Reality isn't plastic and it's not wise to carve stone with your bare hands.

That night I watched the fireworks erupt over Cape Cod Bay from a chaise lounge, alone on my private deck. For the first time since I could remember, the anniversary of Carol's death passed without trauma. I didn't bawl, tremble, have a flash-back or consume more than a pound of pasta or a six-pack of Yoo-Hoo. I raised a hot cocoa toward the Pilgrim Tower and remembered my sister with a nod of my head.

Edna visited me a few times over the next few days, entertained me, replenished my stock of Yoo-

Hoos and Twinkies, and kept me up to date on Tara Parker's progress and Kathleen's deterioration. The model was expected to go home by week's end. Lucky for me, Edna was able to convince the infuriated Cindy Wyler that I had never meant to put Tara in danger. I sent the two women flowers and a check to cover Tara's hospital bills; neither one acknowledged the gesture. I wasn't surprised. Kathleen, meanwhile, had taken up residence at a sanitarium for the mentally disturbed, pending trial of course.

An unexpected package from my partner Tony arrived midweek. Inside I found a pound of Kenya AA coffee and the August issue of a new magazine, *Out,* that featured Arnold Grau and Cardinal O'Connor on its cover. Apparently, Brian Fritzl had made good use of his photographs.

Over a week elapsed and K.T. and I had still not talked, unless you count my letter to her and the message she sent me via my friend Beth. I doubted there was much left for us. She couldn't forgive me for sleeping with Julie, and I felt similarly about her escapade with Lurlene. We didn't call it quits so much as cease and desist.

Julie wanted to continue our physical relationship, but I wanted to keep my distance.

The suite became my sanctuary. I hobbled from bed to deck and back again. The only problem was that I kept hearing Kathleen Fritzl's voice in my head, speculating about what comes next. After us. I wished I knew because what existed today seemed hardly enough.

I wobbled my way out of the chaise lounge, crossed the deck and rested my elbows on the railing, a cup of steaming Kenya AA nestled in my hands. It was early morning in one of the most exquisite places on earth. The buoys clanged gently in the distance. I took a deep breath, closed my eyes. A stiff, salty breeze fought with the intense sun for dominance over my skin.

After a while I opened my eyes. Two young girls, no older than five, each sporting long, sand-tangled hair, romped along the shore, an Irish Setter darting between them. Peels of laughter drifted back toward me. I watched them lock hands and smiled. Almost.

A few of the publications of

THE NAIAD PRESS, INC.
P.O. Box 10543 • Tallahassee, Florida 32302
Phone (904) 539-5965
Toll-Free Order Number: 1-800-533-1973
Mail orders welcome. Please include 15% postage.

SOMEONE TO WATCH by Jaye Maiman. 272 pp. A Robin Miller mystery. 4th in a series.	ISBN 1-56280-095-7	$10.95
GREENER THAN GRASS by Jennifer Fulton. 208 pp. A young woman — a stranger in her bed.	ISBN 1-56280-092-2	10.95
TRAVELS WITH DIANA HUNTER by Regine Sands. Erotic lesbian romp. Audio Book (2 cassettes)	ISBN 1-56280-107-4	16.95
CABIN FEVER by Carol Schmidt. 256 pp. Sizzling suspense and passion.	ISBN 1-56280-089-1	10.95
THERE WILL BE NO GOODBYES by Laura DeHart Young. 192 pp. Romantic love, strength, and friendship.	ISBN 1-56280-103-1	10.95
FAULTLINE by Sheila Ortiz Taylor. 144 pp. Joyous comic lesbian novel.	ISBN 1-56280-108-2	9.95
OPEN HOUSE by Pat Welch. 176 pp. P.I. Helen Black's fourth case.	ISBN 1-56280-102-3	10.95
ONCE MORE WITH FEELING by Peggy J. Herring. 240 pp. Lighthearted, loving romantic adventure.	ISBN 1-56280-089-2	10.95
FOREVER by Evelyn Kennedy. 224 pp. Passionate romance — love overcoming all obstacles.	ISBN 1-56280-094-9	10.95
WHISPERS by Kris Bruyer. 176 pp. Romantic ghost story	ISBN 1-56280-082-5	10.95
NIGHT SONGS by Penny Mickelbury. 224 pp. A Gianna Maglione Mystery. Second in a series.	ISBN 1-56280-097-3	10.95
GETTING TO THE POINT by Teresa Stores. 256 pp. Classic southern Lesbian novel.	ISBN 1-56280-100-7	10.95
PAINTED MOON by Karin Kallmaker. 224 pp. Delicious Kallmaker romance.	ISBN 1-56280-075-2	9.95
THE MYSTERIOUS NAIAD edited by Katherine V. Forrest & Barbara Grier. 320 pp. Love stories by Naiad Press authors.	ISBN 1-56280-074-4	14.95
DAUGHTERS OF A CORAL DAWN by Katherine V. Forrest. 240 pp. Tenth Anniversay Edition.	ISBN 1-56280-104-X	10.95

BODY GUARD by Claire McNab. 208 pp. A Carol Ashton Mystery. 6th in a series. ISBN 1-56280-073-6 10.95

CACTUS LOVE by Lee Lynch. 192 pp. Stories by the beloved storyteller. ISBN 1-56280-071-X 9.95

SECOND GUESS by Rose Beecham. 216 pp. An Amanda Valentine Mystery. 2nd in a series. ISBN 1-56280-069-8 9.95

THE SURE THING by Melissa Hartman. 208 pp. L.A. earthquake romance. ISBN 1-56280-078-7 9.95

A RAGE OF MAIDENS by Lauren Wright Douglas. 240 pp. A Caitlin Reece Mystery. 6th in a series. ISBN 1-56280-068-X 9.95

TRIPLE EXPOSURE by Jackie Calhoun. 224 pp. Romantic drama involving many characters. ISBN 1-56280-067-1 9.95

UP, UP AND AWAY by Catherine Ennis. 192 pp. Delightful romance. ISBN 1-56280-065-5 9.95

PERSONAL ADS by Robbi Sommers. 176 pp. Sizzling short stories. ISBN 1-56280-059-0 9.95

FLASHPOINT by Katherine V. Forrest. 256 pp. Lesbian blockbuster! ISBN 1-56280-043-4 22.95

CROSSWORDS by Penny Sumner. 256 pp. 2nd Victoria Cross Mystery. ISBN 1-56280-064-7 9.95

SWEET CHERRY WINE by Carol Schmidt. 224 pp. A novel of suspense. ISBN 1-56280-063-9 9.95

CERTAIN SMILES by Dorothy Tell. 160 pp. Erotic short stories. ISBN 1-56280-066-3 9.95

EDITED OUT by Lisa Haddock. 224 pp. 1st Carmen Ramirez Mystery. ISBN 1-56280-077-9 9.95

WEDNESDAY NIGHTS by Camarin Grae. 288 pp. Sexy adventure. ISBN 1-56280-060-4 10.95

SMOKEY O by Celia Cohen. 176 pp. Relationships on the playing field. ISBN 1-56280-057-4 9.95

KATHLEEN O'DONALD by Penny Hayes. 256 pp. Rose and Kathleen find each other and employment in 1909 NYC. ISBN 1-56280-070-1 9.95

STAYING HOME by Elisabeth Nonas. 256 pp. Molly and Alix want a baby . . . or do they? ISBN 1-56280-076-0 10.95

TRUE LOVE by Jennifer Fulton. 240 pp. Six lesbians searching for love in all the "right" places. ISBN 1-56280-035-3 9.95

GARDENIAS WHERE THERE ARE NONE by Molleen Zanger. 176 pp. Why is Melanie inextricably drawn to the old house? ISBN 1-56280-056-6 9.95

KEEPING SECRETS by Penny Mickelbury. 208 pp. A Gianna Maglione Mystery. First in a series. ISBN 1-56280-052-3 9.95

THE ROMANTIC NAIAD edited by Katherine V. Forrest & Barbara Grier. 336 pp. Love stories by Naiad Press authors. ISBN 1-56280-054-X 14.95

UNDER MY SKIN by Jaye Maiman. 336 pp. A Robin Miller mystery. 3rd in a series. ISBN 1-56280-049-3. 10.95

STAY TOONED by Rhonda Dicksion. 144 pp. Cartoons — 1st collection since *Lesbian Survival Manual.* ISBN 1-56280-045-0 9.95

CAR POOL by Karin Kallmaker. 272pp. Lesbians on wheels and then some! ISBN 1-56280-048-5 9.95

NOT TELLING MOTHER: STORIES FROM A LIFE by Diane Salvatore. 176 pp. Her 3rd novel. ISBN 1-56280-044-2 9.95

GOBLIN MARKET by Lauren Wright Douglas. 240pp. A Caitlin Reece Mystery. 5th in a series. ISBN 1-56280-047-7 10.95

LONG GOODBYES by Nikki Baker. 256 pp. A Virginia Kelly mystery. 3rd in a series. ISBN 1-56280-042-6 9.95

FRIENDS AND LOVERS by Jackie Calhoun. 224 pp. Mid-western Lesbian lives and loves. ISBN 1-56280-041-8 10.95

THE CAT CAME BACK by Hilary Mullins. 208 pp. Highly praised Lesbian novel. ISBN 1-56280-040-X 9.95

BEHIND CLOSED DOORS by Robbi Sommers. 192 pp. Hot, erotic short stories. ISBN 1-56280-039-6 9.95

CLAIRE OF THE MOON by Nicole Conn. 192 pp. See the movie — read the book! ISBN 1-56280-038-8 10.95

SILENT HEART by Claire McNab. 192 pp. Exotic Lesbian romance. ISBN 1-56280-036-1 10.95

HAPPY ENDINGS by Kate Brandt. 272 pp. Intimate conversations with Lesbian authors. ISBN 1-56280-050-7 10.95

THE SPY IN QUESTION by Amanda Kyle Williams. 256 pp. 4th Madison McGuire. ISBN 1-56280-037-X 9.95

SAVING GRACE by Jennifer Fulton. 240 pp. Adventure and romantic entanglement. ISBN 1-56280-051-5 9.95

THE YEAR SEVEN by Molleen Zanger. 208 pp. Women surviving in a new world. ISBN 1-56280-034-5 9.95

CURIOUS WINE by Katherine V. Forrest. 176 pp. Tenth Anniversary Edition. The most popular contemporary Lesbian love story. ISBN 1-56280-053-1 10.95

Audio Book (2 cassettes) ISBN 1-56280-105-8 16.95

CHAUTAUQUA by Catherine Ennis. 192 pp. Exciting, romantic adventure. ISBN 1-56280-032-9 9.95

A PROPER BURIAL by Pat Welch. 192 pp. A Helen Black mystery. 3rd in a series. ISBN 1-56280-033-7 9.95

SILVERLAKE HEAT: A Novel of Suspense by Carol Schmidt. 240 pp. Rhonda is as hot as Laney's dreams. ISBN 1-56280-031-0 9.95

LOVE, ZENA BETH by Diane Salvatore. 224 pp. The most talked about lesbian novel of the nineties! ISBN 1-56280-030-2 10.95

A DOORYARD FULL OF FLOWERS by Isabel Miller. 160 pp. Stories incl. 2 sequels to *Patience and Sarah.* ISBN 1-56280-029-9 9.95

MURDER BY TRADITION by Katherine V. Forrest. 288 pp. A Kate Delafield Mystery. 4th in a series. ISBN 1-56280-002-7 9.95

THE EROTIC NAIAD edited by Katherine V. Forrest & Barbara Grier. 224 pp. Love stories by Naiad Press authors. ISBN 1-56280-026-4 13.95

DEAD CERTAIN by Claire McNab. 224 pp. A Carol Ashton mystery. 5th in a series. ISBN 1-56280-027-2 9.95

CRAZY FOR LOVING by Jaye Maiman. 320 pp. A Robin Miller mystery. 2nd in a series. ISBN 1-56280-025-6 9.95

STONEHURST by Barbara Johnson. 176 pp. Passionate regency romance. ISBN 1-56280-024-8 9.95

INTRODUCING AMANDA VALENTINE by Rose Beecham. 256 pp. An Amanda Valentine Mystery. First in a series. ISBN 1-56280-021-3 9.95

UNCERTAIN COMPANIONS by Robbi Sommers. 204 pp. Steamy, erotic novel. ISBN 1-56280-017-5 9.95

A TIGER'S HEART by Lauren W. Douglas. 240 pp. A Caitlin Reece mystery. 4th in a series. ISBN 1-56280-018-3 9.95

PAPERBACK ROMANCE by Karin Kallmaker. 256 pp. A delicious romance. ISBN 1-56280-019-1 9.95

MORTON RIVER VALLEY by Lee Lynch. 304 pp. Lee Lynch at her best! ISBN 1-56280-016-7 9.95

THE LAVENDER HOUSE MURDER by Nikki Baker. 224 pp. A Virginia Kelly Mystery. 2nd in a series. ISBN 1-56280-012-4 9.95

PASSION BAY by Jennifer Fulton. 224 pp. Passionate romance, virgin beaches, tropical skies. ISBN 1-56280-028-0 10.95

STICKS AND STONES by Jackie Calhoun. 208 pp. Contemporary lesbian lives and loves. ISBN 1-56280-020-5 9.95
Audio Book (2 cassettes) ISBN 1-56280-106-6 16.95

DELIA IRONFOOT by Jeane Harris. 192 pp. Adventure for Delia and Beth in the Utah mountains. ISBN 1-56280-014-0 9.95

UNDER THE SOUTHERN CROSS by Claire McNab. 192 pp. Romantic nights Down Under. ISBN 1-56280-011-6 9.95

GRASSY FLATS by Penny Hayes. 256 pp. Lesbian romance in the '30s. ISBN 1-56280-010-8 9.95

A SINGULAR SPY by Amanda K. Williams. 192 pp. 3rd Madison McGuire. ISBN 1-56280-008-6 8.95

THE END OF APRIL by Penny Sumner. 240 pp. A Victoria Cross mystery. First in a series. ISBN 1-56280-007-8 8.95

HOUSTON TOWN by Deborah Powell. 208 pp. A Hollis Carpenter mystery. ISBN 1-56280-006-X 8.95

KISS AND TELL by Robbi Sommers. 192 pp. Scorching stories by the author of *Pleasures.* ISBN 1-56280-005-1 10.95

STILL WATERS by Pat Welch. 208 pp. A Helen Black mystery. 2nd in a series. ISBN 0-941483-97-5 9.95

TO LOVE AGAIN by Evelyn Kennedy. 208 pp. Wildly romantic love story. ISBN 0-941483-85-1 9.95

IN THE GAME by Nikki Baker. 192 pp. A Virginia Kelly mystery. First in a series. ISBN 1-56280-004-3 9.95

AVALON by Mary Jane Jones. 256 pp. A Lesbian Arthurian romance. ISBN 0-941483-96-7 9.95

STRANDED by Camarin Grae. 320 pp. Entertaining, riveting adventure. ISBN 0-941483-99-1 9.95

THE DAUGHTERS OF ARTEMIS by Lauren Wright Douglas. 240 pp. A Caitlin Reece mystery. 3rd in a series. ISBN 0-941483-95-9 9.95

CLEARWATER by Catherine Ennis. 176 pp. Romantic secrets of a small Louisiana town. ISBN 0-941483-65-7 8.95

THE HALLELUJAH MURDERS by Dorothy Tell. 176 pp. A Poppy Dillworth mystery. 2nd in a series. ISBN 0-941483-88-6 8.95

SECOND CHANCE by Jackie Calhoun. 256 pp. Contemporary Lesbian lives and loves. ISBN 0-941483-93-2 9.95

BENEDICTION by Diane Salvatore. 272 pp. Striking, contemporary romantic novel. ISBN 0-941483-90-8 9.95

BLACK IRIS by Jeane Harris. 192 pp. Caroline's hidden past . . . ISBN 0-941483-68-1 8.95

TOUCHWOOD by Karin Kallmaker. 240 pp. Loving, May/December romance. ISBN 0-941483-76-2 9.95

COP OUT by Claire McNab. 208 pp. A Carol Ashton mystery. 4th in a series. ISBN 0-941483-84-3 9.95

These are just a few of the many Naiad Press titles — we are the oldest and largest lesbian/feminist publishing company in the world. Please request a complete catalog. We offer personal service; we encourage and welcome direct mail orders from individuals who have limited access to bookstores carrying our publications.